christmas
with
you

"Another wonderful story to add to Tari Faris's lovely Heritage series. A great Christmas story that made me want to decorate my house and wait for the snow to arrive. Just so happens Christmas is my favorite time of year so this sweet romance was right up my alley."

—KATE, GOODREADS

"This is a heartwarming story about trust and forgiveness, it's extra special since it takes place during the Christmas season. I couldn't put it down and finished it in one sitting."

—LISA, GOODREADS

christmas with you

TARI FARIS

To Susie,

Thank you for believing in me all those years ago when I met you and I had no idea how to write. You have been my teacher, my mentor, my inspiration, and my friend.

Thank you for helping me make these books shine.

The Lord will fight for you;
you need only to be still.

EXODUS 14:14

one

FALLON JAMES'S ENTIRE LIFE HAD BEEN RE-
duced to a small storage unit back in Detroit and whatever
would fit in the back seat of her new-to-her-but-very-old Chevy
Impala. She eyed the cardboard boxes and bags in her rearview mirror
as she exited US 31 and drove east toward her childhood hometown
of Heritage, Michigan. Soon she would be snuggled up in her pink
comforter in her bed next to the poster of Justin Bieber and she could
pretend like the past three years hadn't happened.

She might not be a fan of the Bieber anymore, but no matter
how many years went by, her parents' home always seemed as if
she had been gone only a few hours. It was both why she had been
excited to leave and why it felt so wonderful coming home. This
place had always been her safe haven, her constant, and her parents
a steadfast source of strength.

She bypassed the turn that would lead to the heart of the small
town and a hot cup of Donny's amazing coffee. She actually could
use a coffee after the three-and-a-half-hour drive from Detroit, and
the warmth of the diner would sure be nice. They might only be

ten days into November, but the chill of northern Michigan had arrived even if the snow hadn't. But there was no such thing as a quick stop in Heritage. The same people would be there talking about the same old things, and Fallon's return would be noticed by all of them. It would be an hour visit minimum and right now, all Fallon wanted to do was be home—for a peaceful Sunday evening.

The houses of the town slowly gave way to the larger properties and driveways that disappeared into tall pine forests. The phone rang through her car and the face of Sadie Hoover, her childhood friend, popped up on the screen. Fallon tapped to accept. "Are you ready for the big day?"

"Not even close." Sadie released a deep sigh as if she'd just flopped on her bed. "Was your wedding this stressful?"

There was that all too familiar ache in Fallon's chest.

"I'm sorry." Sadie's voice dropped lower. "I shouldn't have—"

"It's fine." Fallon was tired of the apologies.

I'm sorry you lost your husband.

I'm sorry Robert kept so much from you.

And the big doozy she'd gotten last week. *I'm sorry but you're no longer welcome here.*

She shook her mind away from the memory and back to her friend. "Weddings are probably less stressful if you don't try and plan them in four weeks."

"Eight weeks." Sadie's voice carried a touch of attitude. "I only have seven left."

"Because eight weeks is so much longer. Are you sure you're ready for this?"

"When you know, you know. And face it, David and I have been waiting ten years for this. We weren't waiting for another year."

"Not a year but maybe a few months. And it isn't the ten years that you have been in love that has me concerned. It is the nine years and eight months that you weren't speaking." She was happy for her friend. But marriage had been the hardest thing she'd ever done, and she hoped Sadie knew what she was getting into. Fallon released a sigh—then again, David wasn't the heir to Winterbourne Enterprises who refused to grow up and cut the apron strings. "Sorry, I'm happy for you. It's just—"

"Fast? I know. But we are ready, trust me. Besides, we want to start the new year as Mr. and Mrs. Williams. When are you getting to town?"

"I'm here. Well, sort of. I just passed Dearing Road."

"I thought you weren't coming until next weekend."

Right. But that was when she still had a job, a house, her Tesla, and a bank account. "Plans changed. I'm here through the wedding. Figured it would be good to be home with my parents for the holidays."

And who knew how long after that?

"Yay, then you can go cake tasting with us tomorrow." The lightness in Sadie's tone lifted something in Fallon. At least the whole world hadn't turned against her. "But if you're going to be here for the next few weeks, I should probably warn you . . . "

"Warn me? That's ominous. I've already seen the glow-up in the middle of town on my last visit. Isn't that about as much change that Heritage can handle for a decade or two?"

"It's just . . . "

"Say it."

"Cole's back."

Fallon's breathing slowed.

So many emotions swirled through her with the name that she couldn't even land on one. "Cole Scott?"

"Do you know another Cole?"

"What is he doing back?" And why hadn't her mom mentioned it? She gave a hard blink and kept her focus on the road. "Last I heard he was living out in California, married to the wicked witch of Heritage High."

"Tiffany's not with him. I'm not sure why. He's bagging groceries at JJ's of all things. But I don't know more than that." Sadie's voice muffled a moment before she was back. "Hold on a second, David needs something."

Fallon released a wry laugh. A hot, successful Cole Scott, to whom she'd lost the valedictorian spot by a tenth of a GPA point, might be intimidating. But she could handle an old, fat, and—with any luck—balding Cole Scott who stocked shelves and bagged canned goods at the local grocery store. So much for Mr. Most Likely to Succeed. Maybe some people *did* peak in high school.

At least she'd been the lead designer for Winterbourne Industries for eight years—eight long years that should have earned her some loyalty.

Fallon flipped on her blinker and began to slow as she neared her parents' property. The twenty-foot white pines lining both sides of the road were like a channel leading her home. She opened the vent and let the woodsy scent fill the car. It smelled like safety, comfort, and a happy childhood all rolled into one. Her constant. A constant that was just over forty degrees. She shut the vent and slowed as she neared the drive.

Why was there an obnoxious yellow sign rudely planted right in front of the James Tree Farm welcome sign? Taylor Realty? No. No. No. It had to be a mistake.

Fallon turned in the drive and stopped just off the road. A small part of her mind told her the obvious truth—the sign *wasn't* a mistake. But the rest of her thoughts raced through even more far-fetched scenarios like a local teen prank. Anything other than the one that simply couldn't be true.

Her parents were selling the Christmas tree farm. The thought pressed in on her like a crushing weight.

Her childhood home. This place was all she had left.

"Fallon, are you still there?" Sadie's voice came through the speaker again.

"Are my parents really selling the tree farm?"

"Oh, Fallon. You didn't know?"

"Why didn't they tell me?" She put the car back in gear and wound down the long dirt drive.

"The sign appeared last week. Maybe they planned on telling you when you got here. I can't believe there will be no more tree farm. It's been a staple in the community for my entire life."

"Since my grandfather opened it back in the sixties." Fallon navigated around a large rut in the dirt path. "In its heyday people would drive up to four hours to get their Christmas trees here." The car jerked as it hit another pothole. "Why would they close it?"

"I know you weren't here, but the past few years it's been different."

"Different how?" Fallon eyed the broken fence as she made her way toward the house.

"It's not like when we were kids and it had a live nativity, cookies with Mrs. Santa, sleigh rides, and remember when we could get photos with Santa himself? Last I heard it was more of a stop by and cut down your own tree and leave money in a box."

Fallon parked in front of the white two-story farmhouse with a wraparound porch and took in the place with critical eyes. The arch over the entrance of the tree lot had fallen over. The windows of the Sugar Shack were so dirty she doubted any light was getting in. And the wooden letters that hung by the old barn spelled *Jam s T ee Fa m*. Maybe it had seen better days, but her dad loved this place. It wouldn't take much for him to fix it up. "They still should have told me."

"You're right. But hear them out. I'm sure this is hard on them too. I'm sorry, but I've got to go. It's going to be okay. We can talk more tomorrow. I'll text you the time of the cake tasting."

Fallon ended the call and climbed out, the chill of the approaching winter running down her neck. Her boots crunching in the gravel was the only sound on the farm as she approached the house.

Her hand paused on the new white railing. If her dad had fixed this, why hadn't he bothered with the rest of the place? Maybe that was in the plan.

She gave two quick knocks and reached for the knob. After all, this was home and her parents were probably stretched out in their recliners as they watched their evening round of *Jeopardy!*

She pushed through the door and stepped into the mudroom, securing the door behind her. Her father's tan Carhartt coat hung on his usual peg, her mom's fall hat up on the shelf, and the same green-and-brown carpet that she'd stained with mud as a kid were all there to welcome her.

But instead of the voices of game show contestants, "Dance to the Music" blared from the stereo at a volume level she would have never been allowed in her teen years. She hung her coat on a hook then stepped out of the mudroom into the wide family room.

She stopped behind the teal couch straight from the nineties. It was the same couch, facing the same two gray recliners, all sitting a few feet from the same dining room table she'd sat at to do her homework. She even recognized her mother's prized collection of Hummel figurines on the wooden shelf her father had made.

What she didn't recognize was the little girl with blonde curls, who was maybe seven, spinning in circles or the teenage boy with dark hair lounging on one of those gray overstuffed recliners with his nose in his phone. The little girl bumped into the five-tiered shelf full of figurines. Fallon winced as they rattled, but none fell.

"Careful!" the teenage boy yelled at the girl, his gaze never leaving his phone.

If it weren't for the row of her school photos on the far wall showing Fallon's annual progression from kindergarten to gradua-tion—including those special middle school years—Fallon would have believed her parents had already sold the house, furniture and all.

She opened her mouth to ask the kids who they were, but stopped as her mother walked through the swinging door that led to the kitchen. She wore an apron that was dusted in flour and her hair pulled up into a messy gray bun, most of which had escaped. Her face was a little flushed. Maybe the doctor needed to up her blood pressure medication yet again.

Her mom paused by the dining room table and leaned down to pick up a pink backpack that lay open on the floor, then grabbed a child's stray sock. "Your dad just texted. He should be here soon. Let's get you ready."

Fallon blinked from her mom to the children then back to her mom. "My dad or their dad?"

Her mom stood up with a jerk. "Fallon! You startled me. I didn't hear you arrive."

"I wonder why." Fallon stepped over to the stereo and lowered the music, earning her a mid-twirl "aww" from the girl, then wrapped her mom in a hug. Did she feel more frail than the last time she was here? "Who are these kids? And why are they here?"

The little girl stopped dancing and waved with a big smile that stretched from ear to ear, revealing two front teeth that were only half-grown in. "I'm Susie. Are you the daughter who painted that?"

Susie pointed to the wall, but Fallon didn't have to look to know what she was talking about. It was the first of her Tiny Angels series with two fat cherubs looking up in awe at the star of Bethlehem. The abstract watercolor technique had given the quaint scene an unearthly quality. As if looking into a dream.

"That's me." She didn't clarify that she was the only child so she had to be "the daughter."

"Can you paint me one?"

Legally? Nope. Because the Winterbourne family not only owned her house, her car, and all her accounts, they also owned her rights to the entire series. None of it was hers anymore.

She couldn't have imagined how different her world would become when she took her brush to paper that day to create her mom a Christmas gift. Those fat cherubs quickly became a series that was bought up by Winterbourne Enterprises. And just like that she'd become an overnight success in the world of wall-art and ornaments. The next Thomas Kinkade, that's what they had called her. What would they call her now?

"Maybe she'll paint you something else." Her mom's hand landed on her arm. Her mom understood the legal ramifications, but what she didn't know was that Fallon hadn't been able to paint anything even halfway decent since Robert's death. The inspired part of her seemed to have died with him.

"That's Zane." Her mom motioned to the boy in the recliner. "Zane, say hi to my daughter, Fallon."

Zane offered a grunt with a slight nod. His dark mop was in need of a haircut, but the long gangly arms and legs, plus the attitude, probably meant he was in junior high.

She focused back on her mom. "So why are they here?"

"They've been here for the weekend. Their dad was supposed to pick them up this afternoon but he was delayed."

Delayed. Great. Some deadbeat dad had somehow convinced her mom to watch his kids. No doubt playing into the fact she didn't have her own grandkids. Not that that had been Fallon's choice.

Wasn't that just wonderful.

"Where's Dad?" Fallon took the tie from her wrist, pulled her long blonde hair up in a loose bun, then bent over and started picking up strewn clothes and toys.

"He's in bed. Threw out his back again last week trying to move some boxes in the Sugar Shack."

Fallon dropped the bundle into an open duffel and stood upright. "You didn't think to tell me?"

"He's fine. This isn't our first rodeo with his bad back. Just needs a little rest."

"So you've been playing nursemaid *and* watching some guy's

kids. No wonder you look exhausted. Maybe I should check on Dad."

Her mom dismissed the idea with a wave. "He's asleep. Those pain meds knocked him out."

"Then at least sit down. Let me do this."

"I'm fine." But she still sank into a chair with a sigh and checked the time. "I'm not as young as I used to be, that's for sure. But I agreed to this before your dad hurt himself."

"Let me guess, you didn't mention to their father that Dad had gotten hurt either." When her mom didn't respond, Fallon sat on the edge of the recliner and rubbed her forehead against the building headache. First the house, then her dad's back, and now these kids. What else hadn't her mother told her? "Is this about money? How much is he paying you?"

She blinked at Fallon a moment then reached for another sock. "Nothing. I offered for free."

"Free?" She stood and motioned for her mom to follow then walked into the kitchen. She could calm down easier away from the mess and the noise. Or maybe not. The remains of a cookie-making endeavor were everywhere. There was even batter on the cupboard.

She shook her head at her mom. "You're too nice. You're giving the guy free childcare and he can't even show up on time. He's taking advantage of your kindness. You should've called me to come help."

Her mother grabbed a rag from the sink and wiped a splatter off the cupboard. "I have it under control."

"Are you sure? Because this"—Fallon motioned to the mess surrounding them—"doesn't look like it's under control."

"Relax, Fallon. Do you think you didn't get the house this messy when you were young? It's what kids do. We'll just clean it up." With that, her mom pushed back open the kitchen door. "Susie, put away the dolls, please."

Fallon followed her mom back out as Susie wandered over to

the pile of dolls and dresses and started dropping them in their box. Fallon did a double take. Those were *her* dolls. Dolls that she'd been meticulously careful with. Dolls that now had messy hair and mismatched clothes and were being tossed in a box. They were dolls she'd saved for her future daughter.

The familiar pain squeezed her chest.

She was about to give her mother a few words about the value of those dolls when the doorbell rang. Susie jumped up and ran over to the door. "I bet that's my daddy. I have so much to tell him."

Her daddy? Fallon had a few things she wanted to tell him too. Like he would no longer be taking advantage of her mother's kindness. Couldn't he see that she was in no shape to do this? All so he could go have a weekend away kid free.

Susie flung open the door, and Fallon took a step forward and froze.

Cole Scott?

What? Cole Scott was a *dad*. Of a little girl. And a teenage boy. And oh, she should have seen the resemblance in the kid's surly expression and arrogance. It was so obvious now that she was looking. He had Cole's chestnut brown hair and those cold blue eyes. And Susie was the spitting image of Tiffany at that age. Back when Tiffany's hair had been blonde and she'd been Fallon's best friend.

Any hope that Cole had gone fat was dispelled by the way the tactical gear molded to his upper body, highlighting an impressive set of shoulders. Drat. He bent down to pick up his daughter with a smile that highlighted that memorable set of dimples. But his boy-next-door baby face that she'd last seen those dimples on had been replaced with a strong jaw covered with a full day's scruff. And when his daughter yanked off the black beanie, underneath revealed a full head of thick dark hair with just a hint of wave to it.

Shoot. He wasn't just not fat. He was handsome too.

Could nothing go her way?

His gaze met hers, his piercing blue eyes creasing at the corners as he seemed to shift from surprise to confusion to recognition all within a matter of seconds. "Well, if it isn't Feisty Fallon James—or is it Winterbourne now?"

"It's James." Her lips pressed together a moment as she drew a calming breath. "And look at you, if it isn't Can't Keep—"

"Why don't you two continue this reunion outside while I get the kids ready." Her mom rushed forward and grabbed Susie's hand.

Cole lifted his brows but Fallon just grabbed her coat and marched past him out the door and waited to see if he'd follow. But by the sound of footsteps on the porch behind her, he had.

Fallon spun toward him but the move put him just inches away. She took a hasty step back, and for some reason it bugged her when he did the same. "Why are your kids here?"

Cole crossed his arms over his chest, annoyance settling into his gaze. "Nice to see you too, Fallon."

"She's busy enough with taking care of my injured dad. She doesn't need to take care of your irresponsible life." Okay, that didn't make sense now that she was face-to-face with him. One look at what he was wearing and anyone could guess that he'd been working. But she'd already been rehearsing the speech before she had that bit of information. "Why can't Tiffany watch the kids?"

"Tiffany's gone."

"Well, maybe you two need to figure out your work schedule better."

Something dark passed over his features. "I'm sorry I'm late. It was out of my control. But I didn't even know your dad wasn't well. What's wrong with him?"

She didn't buy the concerned look. "He threw out his back. And you don't know because you didn't ask. You never think through things. You do what you want regardless of how it affects others. Then again, why should this surprise me? Same ole Cole."

His face reddened slightly as his jaw twitched. He opened his mouth but the door opened and he instantly transformed his expression into something soft and sweet as he took in his kids. "You guys ready?"

"Yup." Susie slipped her hand in his, but Zane just grunted and walked toward an old blue Chevy Blazer that was idling behind her Impala.

Cole glanced back at her but seemed to change his mind about what he was going to say. He just nodded. "I'll make other arrangements next time."

The door opened again and his dark stare instantly transformed into something soft once more as her mother walked out. "Thank you again, Mrs. James."

"I told you, call me Deb. You aren't seventeen anymore."

"Bye, Deb." Susie waved with her free hand as she hopped down the first step.

Cole tapped her gently on the head. "Mrs. James to you."

Susie giggled and waved at Fallon's mom again, then looked at Fallon. "Thanks for letting me play with your dolls. Sorry I got that hair tie stuck in the one doll's hair."

Fallon flinched at the words but smiled.

Cole walked off the porch as her mom waved. "Bye. Come again soon."

Her mom slipped her arm into Fallon's. "He's like fine wine, he has really improved with age."

She looked at her mom, who was sending her a pointed look. "No, Mom."

"No?"

"No. I had my chance at love with Robert. Besides, the last person I'd want in my life is Cole Scott. Trust me."

"I think if you knew everything about Cole, he might surprise you."

"Surprise me? Like when we were best friends and then—surprise, he chose my nemesis over me?"

"That was a long time ago. You really should let it go. Cole's grown up and so have you."

Maybe she had grown up, but somehow, she'd landed exactly back where she started. "Cole is a part of my past. Not my future."

"You can't keep a mom from praying." Her mother patted her arm, let go, and then moved toward the door.

Fallon watched the Blazer make its way down the driveway, kicking up late season dust.

She wanted to argue, but what did it matter? She'd long stopped believing in the power of prayer. Her mom could pray all she wanted. If God had wanted to answer prayers, He'd have kept the man she loved alive.

She turned away from the cloud of dust but her mom stood at the door. "Now, want to tell me why that car is packed to the ceiling? And where is your Tesla?"

"The Tesla wasn't in my name either." Fallon cast a quick glance at the 2004 Impala. "I was hoping to move in here until I can get back on my feet."

A touch of weariness pulled at her mother's eyes. "There's nothing I would love more, but we are—"

"Moving. I saw the sign. When?" *Please say January.*

"Someone is coming to look at the place tomorrow."

"Tomorrow?" Her voice hit an all-time high.

"It's all happening much faster than we planned." Her mom motioned her back in the house, the weight of the world on her shoulders. "But they want to break ground by spring and need to start working on permits."

"Break ground?"

"It's some developers. But they're offering decent money, so maybe it's better this way."

Better? For who?

Her mom kissed her cheek then angled toward the hallway. What was happening? This place was supposed to be her constant, her anchor. She stared into the tree line. Soon it would be gone. Not just owned by someone else but gone. Bulldozed. All replaced by cookie-cutter houses.

She really had nothing left.

You do what you want regardless of how it affects others. Fallon's words from the night before still rang through Cole's head as he slathered peanut butter on a piece of white bread. Do what he wanted? Because making sandwiches and hurrying his kids out the door to the bus, all the while trying not to be late for his pathetic job at JJ's Food Mart where a kid half his age took perverse pleasure in bossing him around, that was what he *really* wanted. Forget being one of the top technical surveillance specialists in the SEALs a year ago, he'd thrown all that away because he *wanted* to make sandwiches.

Cole grabbed the jelly from the fridge and added it to both sandwiches, then finished them off by cutting one into triangles, leaving the other whole. He slipped them each into a Ziploc bag then added one to Susie's pink My Little Pony lunchbox and the other to the brown paper sack for Zane. Because evidently a lunchbox at age thirteen was embarrassing.

He had no doubt that he'd had just as much attitude once upon a time, but sometimes it was hard to imagine.

Cole walked to the bottom of the stairs of the small two-story rental house and looked up. "Bus will be here in fifteen minutes. And breakfast is getting cold. I made waffles."

He pulled up his work scheduling app on the phone and grimaced. He stared at his watch and then back at his schedule. No. How could he be opening this morning? Cameron must have adjusted the schedule this weekend while he was gone. He should have double-checked last night, but he'd been so exhausted. As soon as he got the kids down, he'd showered and climbed into bed. Not that he'd been able to sleep with Fallon's words running through his head on a loop. She had no idea what his life was like.

Irresponsible? What about her? She'd tossed their friendship away like it had meant nothing when he'd needed her the most. Maybe he had been irresponsible for a moment, but he'd been taking responsibility for that moment ever since.

He pulled the Christmas lists that the kids had presented him last night from his pocket and unfolded them. Their top items were so out of his budget that it was laughable. Zane had starred, circled, then highlighted the latest Xbox that was supposed to drop this week. And Susie had drawn all sorts of pink and red hearts around the word "puppy." Like he had the money to feed one more mouth. Or the time to clean up after the other end.

He'd figure it out. Not the puppy, but something just as good. Maybe he could pick up double shifts stocking shelves at JJ's.

He'd already canceled his NFL+ this fall so he could afford new coats for the kids. But that was him, being irresponsible. He dropped the lists back on the table.

Okay, so maybe it wasn't just her words, but also Fallon herself that had occupied his mind. He hadn't seen her in what, thirteen—maybe fourteen—years? Time had been good to her. Before recognition had settled in, he'd taken full notice of her curves and intense blue eyes and quickly wondered how long he had to wait until he started dating again. That was until she opened her mouth.

Still as sharp and quick to judge as she'd always been.

Susie was the first down the stairs but Zane was only a few steps behind. His hair was not combed, but the kid didn't seem to care. He wore a black hoodie and a scowl on his face. He stood in the entry to the kitchen and stared at the waffles stacked up on the table. "*You* made waffles?"

"Yup. Me and Mr. Eggo." Cole pointed to the box next to the toaster.

A slight smile twitched at Zane's mouth as he sat and pulled a few to his plate. Then he seemed to notice what his face was doing and the scowl returned. It wasn't much of a reaction, but Cole would take it.

"I love waffles." Susie pulled one onto her plate then got to her knees and reached for the syrup. She had convinced Cole to do two braids in her hair this morning. He'd learned that skill last month via YouTube. He still wasn't great at it, but it had gotten to the point the casual observer could at least tell it was supposed to be a braid. But it was clear as she poured way too much syrup over the single waffle on her plate that one side was definitely higher than the other.

She smiled up at him, her blue eyes bright. "We're like one of those TV families."

"Yeah, just like it." There was a fair amount of sarcasm in Zane's tone but he smiled at his sister.

The sweet exchange was both a gift and a punch to the gut. The kids were close because they *weren't* like a TV family. They had spent much of their lives depending on each other rather than a parent. But he was determined to do right by them now, no matter the cost.

His phone rang on the counter and he snatched it up. Walker. His old teammate had started working in the private sector in security a few years back and now designed security systems for the rich, famous, and sometimes sketchy power brokers of the world. Walker had gotten him the gig this past weekend. It had felt good to get back in the field, but it was a one-off thing. He couldn't justify that much time away from the kids, but he'd agreed to consult for Walker when he could. It paid a *lot* better than JJ's.

Cole walked over to where he'd left his laptop and opened it as he accepted the call. "Cole."

"Did you get the file?"

Hello to you too. Cole didn't expect anything different. Walker had served with him for over ten years and when he had a task at hand, the guy had always been straight to business.

Which felt right, since he spent most of his life compartmentalizing. Work. Family. Cover job.

"I looked it over briefly." Cole opened the file and scanned through it. It had appeared in his inbox more than an hour ago, but he'd been going non-stop since. "I think your problem is in the southwest quadrant. I'm marking three spots I see as potential weak points. Probably big gaps in camera coverage." He sent the file back. "I can't be sure without getting eyes on it, but you definitely want to double-check those."

"This would be a lot easier if you'd come work for me instead of consulting on the side. I got more accomplished this weekend with you on-site than what we could have accomplished in a month of back and forth. Not to mention good pay and seeing the world."

"I've seen the world." He glanced back at where his kids were finishing up. He wet a cloth in the sink and carried it over to Susie. "I have to be here."

Susie took it and wiped at her face and hands as Zane stood, carried both plates to the sink, and then disappeared back up the stairs.

"Doing what? Bagging groceries and being a part-time rent-a-cop?" The disdain dripped from Walker's tone. He should have never told his friend about his current jobs. "Those are jobs for a high school kid, not one of the top surveillance guys in the country."

Maybe his jobs weren't every former Navy SEAL's dream, but he needed to keep his kids in Heritage for now. They had both been through enough and he wanted to offer them some stability, even if it meant stocking bananas.

But Walker wasn't done. "I have the perfect job for you this weekend. Fly out on Friday, back by Sunday."

"I have kids. You forget that part?" He glanced back at Susie but she was just disappearing up the stairs. He claimed the rag from the table, walked back to the steps again, and covered the phone. "Five minutes before the bus gets here!"

"Find a babysitter. With the kind of money I'm talking about, hire two."

"Do you have kids? Didn't think so. Finding a babysitter isn't that easy. I can't just leave them with anyone, especially overnight." Even though he'd been back for almost six months, he hadn't connected with anyone yet. He hadn't had the time with working two jobs.

He'd been thankful that Deb had taken him under her wing. He wasn't sure if it had been because of her friendship with his former mother-in-law or because of his long-ago friendship with her daughter. Either way, he'd been thankful. That was until Fallon ended that connection with her little tirade last night.

His gaze lingered on the Christmas lists still lying face up on the counter, but shook away the idea. If his ex-in-laws weren't in Florida, it would be a no-brainer. But they were, and besides, it was *his* job and his alone to protect and provide for the kids. He'd learned long ago not to depend on anyone else. "You know I'd have your back if I could, but I don't think—"

"Don't say no. I can give you twenty-four hours to figure out your complications. But you're the best—maybe the only man for this job. I'll be waiting to hear from you." Walker ended the call.

Cole pocketed his phone. "Two minutes!" Though he itched to get back to that type of work, he didn't see changing his mind. Because his kids weren't complications.

They were his life.

Zane hurried down the stairs, his backpack on one shoulder. Cole did a subtle sniff test as Zane walked by and came up with only a heavy dose of Axe body spray and morning breath. So either he'd showered recently or just slathered on enough deodorant to cover it up.

Cole pointed back up the stairs. "Go brush your hair and brush your teeth. It smells like something died in your mouth."

Zane offered a hefty eye roll but did as he was instructed as Susie ran down the stairs with one shoe on. "I can't find my other shoe."

"Then wear the brown ones I bought you. They're by the door."

"Today's gym day!" Her hands flew into the air. "I have to wear my tennis shoes. Maybe I left it at Mrs. James's house yesterday."

"Didn't you wear them home from their house yesterday?" He wouldn't classify himself as the world's best parent, but he would have noticed if she didn't have any shoes on. Wouldn't he?

"I wore my boots." She slapped her head. "I got mud on one shoe, so I left it in their mudroom to dry. We have to go get it. It's kickball day."

Cole checked his watch and ran his fingers roughly through his hair. He needed to head to JJ's as soon as they were on the bus if he was going to be on time for work. But his kids came first. He needed them to see that. "I'll figure it out."

Cole hurried up the steps to change. He grabbed a pair of jeans that were mostly clean and his work shirt from the closet. At least he'd showered last night, but his hair didn't look that much better than Zane's had a few minutes ago. He hung his head over the sink and splashed some water on it. He brushed his teeth, grabbed his sweatshirt, and hurried back down just as the front door shut behind Zane, who hurried off the porch toward the bus. So much for "have a good day."

Susie sat on the couch, her feet swinging back and forth. Her one foot wore the pink glittery tennis shoe, the other empty. "Zane went to the bus."

"We'll run to the James's before I take you to school. Grab your backpack and put your boots on for now."

They hurried out the door toward the Blazer, but Susie halted on the sidewalk. "Otis moved across the street. Can I go see him?"

"What?" Cole glanced at the brass six-foot-long and two-foot-high hippo that sat across the street. Its back gleamed in the morning sun testifying to the years it had been used as a climbing structure for kids. Every one of them was convinced they'd figure the secret of how it mysteriously moved about town. "Not right now. We don't have time."

"But Jane at school said she's going to figure out how he moves and I don't want her to figure out before I do." Susie's eyes rounded in despair.

Cole scooped her up and set her in the back seat of his Blazer. "Well, since generations of kids have been trying to solve that mystery with no luck, I think you can wait until after school."

She nodded, but the moment her eyes began to tear up, Cole was undone. "I'll tell you what. After school you and I will go together and try to look for clues. But right now we have to go. Now buckle up."

She blinked at him with a watery smile and did as he said. Cole circled the Blazer, hopped in, and hurried toward the James's farm. With any luck, Fallon would still be asleep or have gone back to wherever she had driven in from last night. She didn't know him anymore and he didn't like the fact she acted like she did.

But that small hope he wouldn't see her died ten minutes later as the bane of his sleepless night opened the door of the James's home. She was not as put together as she'd been last night. She wore a thick gray robe with turquoise polka dots. Her hair testified to a rough night's sleep of her own, and her face was scrubbed free of makeup. Was it bad that he preferred this Fallon?

She pulled the thick robe tighter around her middle. "What do you want?"

Right, because again, she was sure she knew him.

"Good morning to you too." Cole motioned to Susie, who still sat in the car, waving through the window. "She said she left her shoe here in the mudroom. Can I get it? Or do you need to lecture me on being irresponsible again?"

Fallon stepped back, allowing him entrance, then pointed at a small shoe in the corner of the mudroom by the door. "That one, I'm assuming."

He bent down and grabbed it but paused in the doorway. "I know you said my kids were too much for your mom. But I have this opportunity this weekend—"

"No."

"Can I talk to her?"

"She's still in bed. I told you, the kids wore her out."

He winced. He hadn't meant to be too much, but he needed this job and he didn't have other options. Maybe Deb could at least give him another suggestion. "If you'd hear me out. It is a job where I could—"

"What about the word *no* do you not understand? Besides, shouldn't the great Tiffany be returning soon?"

"She *lives* in Vegas."

"Oh." That seemed to blow away some of that attitude. She cleared her throat and crossed her arms. "Well, did you know my mom has high blood pressure and the doctor told her to take it easy?"

"I didn't know that." Cole pressed his lips together to keep from saying anything else. He gave her a curt nod and turned away. "Me and my irresponsible self have to get this girl to school."

"See, we finally agree on something."

"See you around, Fallon." Cole hurried out the door, letting it shut behind him, but not before he heard the mumbled word "Typical."

If he hurried, he might be able to make it to his shift on time. Cole navigated to the elementary school just as kids were climbing off the bus. At least Susie wouldn't be late. He got out and led her across the parking lot and headed her to the kids in her class who were starting to line up.

Her teacher, Mrs. Miller, stepped toward them and his heart

sank. The woman was kind as could be, but she had been his second-grade teacher as well and Cole had not always been the model student that year.

"Good morning, Susie. What did you bring for special snack today?"

Susie's eyes rounded, and she looked up at him. Oops. She seemed to be holding her breath as her eyes filled with tears.

"Don't worry. Your dad can drop it off."

Drop it off? He didn't have time for that. Then Mrs. Miller shot him the look, the one-eyebrow up frown, and, yup, he was back in second grade. He'd faced terrorists and drug lords, but one stern look from a five-foot gray-haired woman had him nodding. "I'll figure it out."

Her face morphed into a wide smile. "It needs to be here by eleven."

Eleven? Which meant the first thing he'd have to do after arriving to work late was ask for a long break. He'd be lucky if they didn't fire him, and then where would he be? He needed this money, even if it was only minimum wage.

This single parenting thing was tougher than a lot of the ops he'd run. If Fallon thought he was irresponsible, maybe she should give it a try.

two

AFTER THAT LITTLE INTERACTION WITH COLE, she definitely needed a second cup of coffee. Maybe a third too. Fallon pushed through the swinging oak door that led to the kitchen. She pulled a K-Cup from the drawer, dropped it in the machine, and set it to brew. Extra strong. After all, she had bigger problems in her life than Cole Scott. She needed to figure out how to save this place. She'd spent half the night tossing and turning over what she would do next, but the answer always came back to the same thing. She needed to figure out a way for her parents to stay. She'd seen the sadness in her mom's eyes when she admitted they were selling. This couldn't be what they wanted and she needed to help them.

Her mom stepped into the kitchen in her light blue terrycloth bathrobe tucked close around her and fatigue still in her eyes. "Did I hear the door?"

"Susie had forgotten a tennis shoe." She tried to push away the image of Cole's clean-shaven jaw or how adorable the small pink shoe was in his hand. "How's Dad this morning?"

"Didn't sleep well, but he's resting now." Her mom settled onto a stool. "I shouldn't have missed the shoe. I told her to leave it there to dry. Poor man. He's got so much on his plate these days."

"Poor man?" Fallon slid her freshly brewed cup to her mother and started a new one. Her mother needed it more than she did if she was calling Cole Scott a *poor man*. "I'm sure Cole doesn't have anything on his plate that he didn't bring on himself."

Her mother sipped at the cup and eyed Fallon over the rim. She looked ready to argue, but thankfully let it drop.

Fallon's eyes landed on some paperwork on the counter from Taylor Realty. "I thought you never wanted to leave."

"We didn't." Her mom rubbed at her temple a moment before taking another long sip. "We both took early retirement because we always planned on having the extra income from the farm. But we haven't made money on this place since 2019, and even for years before that, it wasn't much. We just can't keep going. I had hoped to have one last strong year, but with your dad's back out, I don't even think that's possible. So when the investors reached out, it seemed like the only option. We keep praying for a way to keep it, but so far there has been no answer."

No answer from God? Shocker.

Fallon tapped her hands on the table. "I'm here now. Maybe we can figure this out together. I have plans with Sadie this afternoon, but until then let's brainstorm." Fallon pulled a legal pad from the desk drawer and grabbed a pen just as the doorbell chimed. Her mom started to rise, but Fallon held up her hand. "I'll get it. You need to relax."

And if Cole was back, there was no way she would let him talk her mom into anything else. Fallon pulled open the door, bracing herself.

Sadie stood there, grinning with two to-go cups from Donny's. She wore a tan coat with a navy scarf and her light brown hair fell over her shoulders. "Surprise."

Fallon took one of the cups and offered her friend a hug. Well, as much of a hug as they could manage with their coffees still in hand. She ushered her inside and shut the cold air out. "I thought we were cake tasting this afternoon."

"We are." Sadie set her cup on the table and unwound the scarf from her neck. "But when I told David, he suggested I take the whole day off and work on wedding plans. I guess my stress is showing. So, what do you say? Want to help?"

She glanced at the legal pad in her hand then back at her mom. Her mom nodded. "Your dad and I haven't found a solution in the past few months . . . another morning won't matter."

It would matter because if they didn't figure this out, she would truly be homeless soon.

The desperation must have shown because Sadie slid into a spot at the kitchen table. "I'm in no rush." She angled her head at the papers. "I saw the For Sale sign. Do you have any offers?"

"A couple of developers were supposed to come today but they had to reschedule. Which I'm actually glad about, as we would prefer not to go that route." Her mom took another sip of her coffee.

Her mom's words hit her just as hard in the chest as they had the night before. Fallon dropped back into her seat at the table. "Can you believe that? A developer in Heritage?"

"Actually, yes." Sadie leaned back in the chair and sipped at her coffee. "Vacation homes, I'm guessing. Being fifteen minutes from Lake Michigan is a selling point. And Heritage is growing again. Heritage Fruits is expanding, and young families are moving back. There's even talk of a tech company buying that old field off McCain, but that could just be a rumor."

"I can't believe you would sell it off to a developer." Fallon couldn't disguise the hurt in her tone. She might be thirty-three, but this was still home and all she had left.

"It will break your father's heart—all of our hearts—if it were turned into a subdivision."

Fallon stared out the window at the distant woods. How many

times had she walked those woods? How many times had she ridden her horse through those woods as a teenager? Her gaze flicked to the empty barn. It had broken her heart to sell her horse, Pepper. But when she'd moved to Detroit to work for Winterbourne Enterprises, she'd given up a lot. She didn't realize how much she had been giving up until now. Right before it was all gone.

A month ago, she would have offered to buy it, but that was before she discovered she had nothing to her name. She couldn't believe Robert had meant for this to happen to her, but he'd apparently set it up this way. Now his father and brother Bryce were determined to make sure she walked away with nothing, and they had deep pockets for powerful lawyers. It didn't skip her notice that they waited until the press lost interest in her husband's high-profile death before they let her know she had nothing. Wouldn't want the world to know that the King of Christmas was really Scrooge himself. "Maybe if we had one really good season, someone besides a developer might be interested."

"One really good season and we could avoid selling. At least put it off another year or two." Her mom closed her eyes a moment, her brow pinching. "But with your dad's back out, there's no way I can pull off a successful season. Even if you did help, there's a fair amount of labor-intensive work needed. Skilled work too. Speaking of which, I need to call Hannah Taylor and tell her that we can't provide the tree for the Hanging of the Greens this coming weekend. And we can probably cancel the table I signed up for to promote the tree farm."

"Only Heritage would have the Hanging of the Greens two weeks before Thanksgiving." Fallon took another swig of her coffee. She definitely would need another cup—or two.

Her mom shrugged. "Ever since the big Thanksgiving snowstorm a few years ago that canceled it, they moved it earlier. That year we never got the town tree up and the council determined not to let it happen again. But now it looks like, it just might happen again."

Fallon drummed her fingers on the table a moment then turned to Sadie. "Know anywhere we can get free labor?"

"I'm sure we could get several of the men from town to come cut down a tree, but as far as regular help? I've got nothing. Most of the high schoolers already got their volunteer hours in." She shrugged and sipped her coffee again. "David was my free labor. Got any ex-fiancés lying around?"

"Sorry, all out."

"We do have an ex-Navy SEAL." Her mom sent a conspiratorial look over her cup.

"No way." Fallon shook her head as if the words themselves weren't enough. "Besides, he would never agree. Cole is all about Cole and Cole only."

"Not true. He is all about those kids. And working his tail off to provide for them. Who do you think fixed the porch railing, or kitchen sink last week, or cleaned up the leaves in the yard?"

Fallon lifted a brow. That didn't sound like Cole. "And he did it out of his generous heart?"

"I watched his kids and he worked for me."

"Of course."

"Don't give me that look. It was a win-win for both of us."

She hadn't realized he was helping. "Is Tiffany really living in Vegas?"

"If you got that much out of him, it's more than any of the rest of us. The kids say she went on a trip, but he hasn't talked about her once." One of her mom's eyebrows rose. "Interesting that he'd share that information with you."

"I asked." More like accused, but close enough. "It doesn't matter. We don't need him, and he doesn't need us."

Her mother pinned her with a look that made her feel nine

again. "Are you going to pretend he didn't ask for help with his kids when he was here?"

"You heard that?"

"My bedroom window is right by the front door." She motioned toward the porch. "I'm sure he would help you here as some sort of exchange. He is very generous with his time."

Generous? Not likely.

"I don't think I can work with Cole. Maybe you're right, we can't solve this today." Fallon stood and walked toward the hall. "I'm going to get dressed. I'll have to wait to see Dad at dinner."

Ten minutes later, they were headed out the front door, but instead of walking toward Sadie's car, her friend angled toward the old Sugar Shack. When Fallon hesitated, Sadie motioned for her to follow. "Come on. For old times' sake."

Might as well.

From the outside, it didn't look too bad, other than the dirty windows. It still bore the red-and-green wooden sign that read *Mrs. Santa's Sugar Shack.* She turned the knob and pushed it. The door stuck briefly then gave. The dust testified that it had been a few years since they'd used the space. The whole place was less than fifteen hundred square feet, but it had been enough for them to create a slice of the North Pole for visitors.

Sadie walked over to the wingback chair covered by a sheet located on the far end. She lifted a corner and ran her fingers over the red velvet and golden tassels. "This place was so magical to me as a kid. Even though I knew it was your dad dressed as Santa and your mom handing out cookies as Mrs. Santa, it was like stepping into a storybook. You guys made tree buying an adventure. I wish Lottie could experience that."

"I still can't believe you're a mom of a nine-year-old."

"The adoption was final this fall."

Fallon stepped toward the counter where a few of the shelves were broken. There were boxes strewn everywhere. "It's a nice idea, but my mom is right. It's already late in the season. People start shopping for Christmas trees as soon as Thanksgiving, and that's just two weeks away."

"The hardware store seemed like an impossible task at one point, but look at it now. David and I are back together and finally operating in the black."

"But look at this place." Fallon gestured to the chaos.

"Need I remind you that a month ago there was a car sitting in the wall of the hardware store? If you can't do everything this year, just focus on selling trees."

Fallon walked back out, waited for Sadie to follow, then secured the door behind her. She took in the farm in the morning light. "The main parking lot has a lot of branches from the summer storms. And my dad is in no position to cut and move trees right now. And I'm not strong enough to do that."

"I've seen the muscles on Cole. I bet he could fix those shelves and move a tree or two. Goodness, he could probably move half the forest, the guy is so ripped."

"I hadn't noticed." Fallon turned away so her face wouldn't telegraph the lie. Yes, she'd noticed. Noticed, mulled over, and thought about way too much. "Besides, I told you. I can't—"

"Work with him. I know. He chose Tiffany. So what? Get over it. You chose Robert."

She glanced back at Sadie. "But he and Tiffany—"

Sadie held up her gloved hand. "I know. And you know how things ended with David and me when he walked away ten years ago—and we were nearly engaged. You and Cole weren't even dating. So if I could work with David, you can handle a couple of weeks with Cole."

"You do realize that your situation ended with you two getting back together, right?"

"True, but I had to be in the same space as David. You have

forty acres. You could literally never be in the same space at the same time."

Staying out of each other's way would be a must. Because it wasn't just Cole's good looks that had plagued her mind since last night. Seeing Cole with his kids had been like a sucker punch. Cole was a *dad*. And as much as she wanted to think of him as irresponsible, by the look of it, he was a good dad.

It was all a constant reminder of what she'd never have—a family of her own.

But maybe Sadie and her mom were right in that if she wanted to help the tree farm last another season, she needed to fix up this place. And to do that, asking Cole for free help seemed to be her only option. She glanced around again, so many emotions swelling inside her.

If she still had her art—if she still had her life—maybe she could let it go, but she'd lost everything. She couldn't lose this too. This was her home, her heritage, her childhood. And maybe, if she could get Cole to agree to help, her future too. At least until her parents could sell on their own terms. By then she'd be back on her feet again. Until then, she had to save this place.

She turned back to Sadie. "I don't even have a way to contact him."

A look of satisfaction filled Sadie's face as if she'd won. She slipped her arm in Fallon's and pulled her toward her car. "Don't worry, I know where to find him. I'll get you two together—to talk, I mean."

Sadie's smile left no doubt Sadie was hinting at something else, but that wasn't going to happen. She refused to ever open that door again, no matter how much a small piece of her wanted it. Besides, once she was back on her feet, there wasn't really anything for her in Heritage.

No matter how much he tried, Cole couldn't get Walker's job offer out of his head. He grabbed the bag of long-grain rice sliding toward him on the conveyor belt and added it to the bottom of the paper sack, then reached for the box of cereal.

As it was, it looked like he was going to need to find a new emergency babysitter. Extra weekends away were simply not going to happen. Maybe after Tiffany's parents came home from Florida in the spring, he could take some jobs. If Walker was still offering by then.

What he needed was a nanny. Then again if he could afford a nanny, he wouldn't be bagging groceries. He lifted the paper sack and added it to the cart. "Morning, Mrs. Jamison. Would you like help out to your car?"

The elderly woman smiled and reached up as far as she could to pat his chin with her wrinkled hand. "I'm fine, thank you, boy."

Boy? He was pretty sure he hadn't been a boy for more than ten years. But that was okay—the woman was sweet, and he was happy to offer a smile back.

Cameron walked up, tapping on a clipboard with his skinny index finger. The guy had to at least be ten years his junior but he relished every chance to remind Cole that he was the assistant manager and Cole was not. "Why don't you go continue to restock aisle five?"

Maybe he had insecurity issues, but that wasn't Cole's problem. All he had to do was work hard, keep his head down, and collect that paycheck.

Except—aw, he'd forgotten. "I need to take a long break. I have to run my daughter something at school."

Cameron looked at him over the black rims of his glasses. "Then you'll have to stay late."

"I have to be home by four to get my son to basketball practice." Cole motioned to the nearly empty store. "There's no one here. I won't be gone more than fifteen minutes."

"Your job is here. That is, if you want to keep it." Cameron marched away.

Cole tightened his jaw and strode toward the back room. He'd love to tell Cameron where he could stick that clipboard. But Cole had to keep the roof over their heads, not to mention pay off the mountain of debt his ex-wife had left him. Which was why the job from Walker would be really handy about now.

Cole collected the pallet marked for aisle five and navigated it that way. At least it was just shelving tea and coffee. Much better than when he got stuck removing old produce.

"Hey, Cole." Seth Warner pushed a cartful of Gatorade toward him. Seth wasn't tall but Cole was pretty sure Seth could beat him in an arm-wrestling contest. And that was saying something. The guy wore a gray T-shirt and dark athletic shorts. Not quite winter wear but he was probably headed to work. If only the gym was hiring. But the business was just getting off the ground. Seth stopped his cart next to Cole. "How's Zane? Haven't seen him at The Arena in a while."

"He's been keeping busy with basketball, but that wraps up Wednesday night. I'm sure he'll be back."

Thunder Arena—The Arena to locals—was the newest addition to the town. Half the building was a full court that could be set up for a variety of sports while the other half of the building was split into a ninja gym and weight room. Seth owned the place and Zane had been a regular attendee this summer. The gym had been an escape for Zane and pulled a regular smile out of the kid, which was more than Cole could do.

"You should join him. I'm sure it's nothing compared to what you used to do with the SEALs, but we have fun with it. And we've built up quite a weight room."

"I'd love to if I had the time." And he would, but he could barely keep up with all he had on his plate as it was. "Besides, I think Zane goes there to get away from me."

"Don't let him fool you. He thrives on time with you."

Someone cleared their throat nearby, and Cole turned to find Cameron tapping the clipboard with his pen. He nodded at Seth. "See you around."

He made quick work of the tea section and had only broken into the second box of coffee when a voice stopped him. "Just the man we're looking for."

Cole looked up as Sadie Hoover walked toward him with determination in her gaze.

Behind her, way behind, Fallon paused midway down the aisle. She stared at him a moment, as if holding her breath. Then shook her head. "I think I've changed my mind."

Changed her mind? About what? Coffee? He lifted a box of coffee pods in the air. "Looking for some Seattle's Best?"

When neither of them reached for it, he added it to the correct spot on the shelf. Sadie just stared at Fallon, waiting.

No movement from Miss Judgmental.

Whatever. He shrugged and reached for another box. "Sorry if I'm in your way. I decided to take a break from being irresponsible and stock some shelves."

"I thought you were a Navy SEAL," Fallon finally blurted out. "Why are you doing this?"

But by the way her eyes closed, as if in a pain, clearly that wasn't what she'd come to say. It was still hard to hear, though. The damage to his pride was unbearable sometimes.

He tried to keep the bitterness from his voice. "And here I didn't think you gave me another thought after high school. I guess you've been following my career. Nice of you. I *was* in the Navy SEALs until last year. And now I'm doing this"—he saluted her with a box of Starbucks K-Cups—"because a kid not old enough to shave but was granted the clipboard of power says I have to."

"But isn't this a bit below your skill level?"

"Thank you for pointing that out, Fallon, I hadn't thought of that." He shoved the box onto the shelf with a little more force than necessary. "I'm limited to what's here in Heritage. Not all of us married into a multi-million-dollar family. Speaking of which, why aren't you off spending all your money?"

She seemed to blink through his words. "But last night you were—"

"In tactical gear? I had a job with a buddy not far from here and I was still wearing it because, as you pointed out, I was late getting my kids." It didn't escape his attention that she'd bypassed the question of what she was doing in Heritage.

Something he couldn't quite read washed over Fallon's face for a moment but then was gone. "Do you work only here?"

"I also pick up security shifts when I can at the factory. But I hate doing that because I don't like leaving the kids all evening." He moved on to the box of Caribou K-Cups. "And yes, that is below my skill level as well."

"And the job you were offered this morning? What was that? More like last night?"

He stared at her a moment, then flicked his gaze to Sadie, but she was no help. She seemed to be actually shopping for coffee. "Sort of. But it would be analyzing a security system for a high-profile client. That is what I was trained to do." He stared at her a moment then shelved another box. "Is there a reason we're having a *This Is Your Life* moment?"

She ignored the question as her pink lips pinched together in a slight pucker as if solving a problem. Maybe he should stop staring at her mouth.

Her arms crossed in front of her as she shifted her weight to one leg. "What about the pay for that job?"

Was she seriously asking him how much he would earn? This conversation had turned all shades of crazy. "More than I can make here. A lot more. In fact, enough that I could quit this job and the security job and still be way ahead of where I am."

"And you would need someone to watch the kids to do this."

"Right, but don't worry, I won't ask your—"

"When would you be back?"

He leaned on the handle of the pallet jack. "You have a lot of questions for somebody who doesn't seem to like to talk to me."

"I'm just . . . well . . . if you took that job and you quit working here and the security, would you have more time in Heritage?"

"I would be gone for stretches of two or three days at a time, three or four times a month. But other than those times, yeah, I suppose I would. Why, do you want to run me out of town?"

"No. It's just . . . " She glanced at Sadie but her friend just nodded, waiting. She focused back on him, teeth pinching her bottom lip. "Would you consider . . . maybe . . . working at the James Tree Farm?"

Ahh. That was what this was about. She needed something. He didn't relish the idea of working with Fallon, but he owed Deb big time. He shelved another box of coffee. "Doing what?"

"Prepping trees, clearing debris, and fixing fences. Cutting down a big tree for the square."

"That's a little below my skill set, don't you think?" He meant to keep a straight face, but he couldn't.

Her lips pressed together but she waited.

"How much?"

She shifted her weight to the other leg. "We couldn't pay you, but I could watch your kids while you travel for that job."

"*You* want to watch my kids?"

"I'm just saying it might benefit us both. I want to help my parents. They need a successful season at James Tree Farm or they have to sell. But I can't do that on my own. I need help."

"How much time have you spent with kids?"

"How hard can it be?"

Sadie covered a laugh and Cole lifted an eyebrow. "I don't think this is a good idea."

Doubt flickered across her face, but she straightened her shoulders. "I can watch them at my parents'. My mom is used to them and they're comfortable with her, but I'll be there to help with all the things so she doesn't get too tired."

When he didn't immediately answer, she took a step forward. "Come on. It's a win-win."

His phone buzzed in his pocket and he pulled it out. A text from Walker with an offer of payment. The amount nearly made his jaw drop. He glanced back at Fallon. "I don't want to work evenings."

"No problem."

More time with Zane and Susie would be a positive too. Seth's comment came back to him. *He thrives on time with you.* "I'll do it but only if you agree to watch them at your mom's house."

"You have such little faith in me?"

"I just think your life is a little too orderly for kids."

"You don't know me."

He couldn't hold back the smirk. "Oh yeah? How late did you stay up putting your toy dolls back the way they were before Susie played with them?"

Her eyes narrowed as she extended her hand. "Do we have a deal?"

"Deal." He took her hand but paused. He shook his team members' hands all the time, but he didn't often shake a hand this soft, this frail. For as strong as she liked to come across, there was a vulnerability in her eyes. She was going through something. And for just a moment she wasn't the girl who hated him. She was that seventeen-year-old girl that he'd sat with in the attic of the Sugar Shack as they discussed what they each planned to do after high school. Plans that had blown up with one night of poor choices.

He dropped his hand and reached for more coffee. They weren't those idealistic teenagers anymore and he needed to remember that.

He started to add the box onto the shelf only to realize there wasn't room for it. He glanced back at Fallon, but she had already marched back up the aisle. He found Sadie studying him. She gave a little smile and a wave and then hurried to follow her friend. He wasn't sure what that look was about, but it didn't matter. He was going to be able to take the security job.

Which meant he could go tell his manager he was done shelving coffee. That felt way better than it should.

He walked to the end of the aisle, grabbed two packages of Oreos—not even the generic brand—and hurried to the checkout. As soon as he told Cameron he was done, he had a snack to deliver.

On the way out to his car, he pulled out his phone and texted Walker back.

COLE

I'm in.

three

SOMEHOW COLE HAD IMAGINED THAT HELPING the Jameses with the tree farm would be glorified yardwork, but the list Fallon had presented him with Tuesday morning had him working from sunup to sundown for the third day in a row. Cole crossed "clearing the parking lot" off the list, set the clipboard on the seat of the tractor, and coughed against the icy breeze. A cold front had moved in, and windchill had dropped into the single digits the past couple of days, but still no snow. Not unheard of for this time of year but not the norm. San Diego would be nice about now.

Over the past few days, he'd developed a new level of respect for Fallon. She was a hard worker, had a good mind for business, and cared for her parents. Who else poured this much into a business that wasn't theirs?

He probably needed to find a way to bury the hatchet between them, but the girl was determined to hate him.

His phone chimed and he pulled it from his pocket. It was a notification from the Amazon app. He'd set an alert to show up when the Xbox dropped. He tapped on the link, but an error message appeared. He tried again. Error. At the third attempt, a message appeared: Due to a high volume of sales, this page is unavailable at this time.

Perfect. Zane seemed to have asked for the product everyone was fighting for this season, which meant the price would go up. Not that it mattered. With the bills he had, it would take more than one job with Walker to have the cushion to buy that.

He shut the app and slid the phone into his pocket just as the front door to the house opened and Mr. James stepped out. Wasn't he supposed to stay in bed?

He wore a tan Carhartt coat and a blue stocking cap over his gray hair. He carried an extra twenty pounds around the middle, but overall, the guy was in decent shape for his age. It had to be killing him to stay in bed. The man was moving slowly and a little stiff, but at least he was moving. "How are you feeling, Mr. James?"

"Call me Tim. And I feel like I'm getting old." He glanced around then back at Cole. "How's it going?"

"Almost done with the list."

"I'm pretty sure Fallon is already working on a second list." Tim offered a slight laugh, his words puffing in the cold air. "Did you find a tree for the town?"

Cole walked to the corner of the barn and pointed to where he'd parked the flatbed trailer. "What do you think?"

Tim walked up and dug his hand into the branches, checking for who knew what. Cole had just found one that looked nice and was about the twenty feet Fallon had asked for. But it must have passed whatever test Mr. James had because the guy nodded and stepped back. "That's a good one."

"Do I need to get it to the square?"

"No, Luke Taylor and a few of the guys from the fire department will pick it up and secure it in the square for us." Tim shifted his weight and seemed to wince at the movement. "Fallon has high hopes for a lot of tree orders at the Hanging of the Greens this Sunday."

"And you don't?"

Tim shrugged. "Times are changing." He motioned to the Sugar Shack a few yards away. "Were you able to fix the shelf in the outbuilding?"

"When I checked earlier it was locked. You have a key for that?"

"It's not locked, it just sticks. You have to give it a wiggle and a push." Tim motioned for him to follow, his steps uneven. "I'll warn you, it's a mess. I was moving a crate from the little storage attic in there when I threw my back out. It took out a shelf or two on the way down."

"You're lucky that's all you did."

"Tell me about it." Tim wiggled the knob, leaned firmly against it with a slight wince, and it popped open. He walked in and Cole followed.

Dim light greeted them as it fought to penetrate the dirty windows. There was a heavy layer of dust everywhere, a large number of crates scattered haphazardly around the room, and the broken shelves took up a good share of one wall. They looked easy enough to fix.

"The nice thing about this place is that it's heated." Tim disappeared into the back room and a moment later the hum of a heater started up.

Fallon opened the door and walked in. She wore a jean jacket over an old Heritage High sweatshirt, jeans, boots, and a stocking cap, her blonde hair tumbling down around her shoulders in big curls. Her pretty if not distant blue eyes found him first. She held two coffee thermoses. "There you are, Dad. Mom isn't happy."

"I don't imagine she is." He walked toward the door. "Just needed some fresh air."

Fallon motioned to the dust particles shining in the sunbeam that peeked in the door. "Fresh air?"

"Anything is better than another minute in bed."

"Timothy Allan James," Deb's voice called in the distance.

He sighed and hurried out the door, leaving them alone.

She watched her father go, then marched up to Cole and held one of the thermoses out to him, without even a hint of a smile. "Here. It's hot coffee."

"Why, Fallon, are you worried about me?"

Her eyes narrowed a bit more. "It's from my mom."

Clearly.

Cole uncapped the thermos and took a long sip of the hot liquid.

Maybe burying the hatchet started with an apology. He wasn't the only one who was in the wrong, but he'd learned that the best way to move forward was extreme ownership. Whether ten percent wrong or ninety percent. He needed to own up to his part and let go of the rest.

He opened his mouth to do so, but Fallon lifted the clipboard and scanned down the list. She dropped her finger on the paper. "Did you clear all the paths of any fallen debris?"

Apologies were easier when she wasn't always talking down to him. He took a step closer and pulled the clipboard from her hands. "If it's crossed off, it's done. If the government could trust me to carry out sensitive covert missions, I think you can trust me to pick up a few sticks."

He put the lid back on his thermos and checked his watch. He still had over an hour before he needed to pick up the kids.

Fallon checked her phone and sighed. "My mom said you and the kids are welcome again for dinner."

"Wow, what a welcome invitation. Is hospitality your gift?"

When she only stared at him with one brow lifted, he added, "Not having to cook tonight sounds great. And don't worry, I recognize the invitation is also from your mom."

As had been the invitations for the past three nights. Deb and he had hoped that them all eating together would give Fallon and the kids time to connect. Except the kids were not on board with that. For some reason they ignored Fallon no matter how hard she tried. He needed to fix that before he left this weekend.

Fallon slipped her phone back in her pocket and then sent him a fake smile if he'd ever seen one. "I'll let you get to it then."

He'd run out of time. If he was going to apologize, it was now or never. She started to walk past him, but he stepped in her way. "I'm sorry."

"For what?"

Apologizing had seemed simpler and easier in his head. "For everything that went down with Tiffany. You were right, I shouldn't have gone to the party and I should never have trusted her." He rubbed his hand over his head and back, swallowed, then met her eyes again. "Think we can call a truce—at least while I work here?"

She stared off to the side a moment. Drew a slow breath, then looked back at him. "Why is Tiffany living in Vegas?"

"Living with her boyfriend last I knew. We've been divorced for over a year."

The harsh lines faded from her face as she nodded. "I'm sorry too. I could have handled . . . everything better. I do appreciate all your work here. I think I'm getting the better end of the bargain. Thank you."

He stepped back and offered her a look that would hopefully lighten the mood. "That's because you haven't spent the weekend with my kids yet."

She gave a small laugh and hurried out the door.

That was new. He could get used to the sound of her laughter.

Cole lifted a piece of the broken shelf, then another. There were several other boards still connected to the wall but at an odd angle as if the brackets had been bent. He'd probably need to replace most of them, but he'd save what he could. Maybe Fallon could pick up some stuff from Hoover's Hardware for him.

The distinct scent of burning dust filled the air. Must have been a while since that furnace had fired up, but by the heat pumping from the vent, it was working just fine. Cole slipped off his coat and hat then grabbed the electric drill and began the tedious process of backing out all the screws. He'd never considered it hard work, but twenty minutes later he'd worked up a sweat. Cole held his hand in front of the vent. The thing was still pumping out air straight from the Sahara.

He unbuttoned his red-and-black flannel and shucked it off leaving just his white T-shirt. He tossed it aside and walked into the closet where Mr. James had turned it on. He scanned the room that wasn't much more than a glorified closet. Where was the thermostat?

"Cole?" Fallon's voice filled the main room.

He stepped out and then motioned to the vent. "How do you turn that off? Feels like we're going to hit triple digits in here."

Her gaze flickered over him a moment before she drew a deep breath and blinked at him. "What?"

"The furnace. Do you know how to turn it off?" He bit back a smile. He hadn't had time for the gym in a while, but he was suddenly thankful that he'd kept up with his chin-ups, pushups, and sit-ups, because she'd clearly been checking him out. That helped his damaged ego a bit.

But the last thing he needed was to revive the old crush he'd had on her once upon a time. He had wasted half of high school pining after her only to have it blow up in his face. He wouldn't make that mistake again. He couldn't. Because now he had kids to consider.

"Right. My dad said to tell you the thermostat is broken. You have to turn it on and off by hand." She stepped past him, grabbed an Allen wrench, and slipped into the room just before the hum of the furnace cut off.

She stood, the movement putting her face inches from his chest in the small space.

They blinked at each other a moment before he took a quick step back. "Do you think you could pick up a board for me from Hoover's?" He lifted his keys from his pocket and held them out. "You'll need to take my Blazer."

She'd again been looking at his chest, but now her gaze shot to his. She grabbed his keys and walked toward the door. "Board. Got it."

With that, she practically sprinted out of there. He debated running after her to tell her what size board he needed, but he'd let her put that together on her own.

But as he watched her start up his Blazer and kick up dust, he had the terrible sense that he might have misjudged the enemy.

And, in fact, could be heading straight for danger.

Nothing highlighted the fact that Fallon had made a fool out of herself quite like Sadie's face as she tried to explain that yes, she needed a board and no, she didn't know the size because she hadn't hung around long enough to find out. Fallon stared at her friend across the counter at Hoover's and stretched out her arms in front of her then tried to estimate the other two directions with her hand. "About that size."

Sadie laid her pencil down and raised one eyebrow as if waiting for Fallon to recognize the ridiculousness of her request.

Ugh. Fallon bent over and leaned her elbows on the counter and dropped her head in her hands. "I got a little distracted."

"With what?"

"His shoulders." When Sadie only laughed, Fallon stood and crossed her arms. "I had to tell him the thermostat didn't work in the Sugar Shack, which he'd obviously figured out, because when

I showed up it was about a hundred degrees in there and he had stripped down to his white T-shirt. And that man wears a T-shirt too well. And smells . . . amazing. He'd been working all morning. He shouldn't smell amazing."

"But you're still mad at him." It was said as a statement but there was definitely a question in Sadie's gaze.

"Yes. But no. I don't know. He apologized."

"Wow. For everything with Tiffany?"

"We didn't get into the nitty gritty of it, but yeah."

"So are they . . ."

"Divorced. He said that too."

"Interesting." Sadie smirked as she picked up her cup of coffee.

Fallon stood a little taller. "No, that is not interesting. Not even a little interesting. It is the most uninteresting thing I have heard today."

Sadie seemed to be trying to bite back a smile but failing. "Because he is a terrible human being. Who looks awful in a T-shirt and smells terrible. And—"

"Stop."

Fallon lifted her phone and sent a quick text to Cole.

FALLON

What size board do you need?

"It's not fair." Fallon smacked the counter. "I've been doing good all week keeping my emotional distance and not finding him attractive one bit. Not the way he walks around with confidence. Not his dark intense looks. Not even the way his heavy scruff accents his jaw and makes his blue eyes pop. And definitely not that way he is such a good dad. You should see the way he throws Susie in the air, making her laugh before catching her."

"Sounds like you haven't noticed at all." Sadie drew a long sip of coffee and seemed to be holding back yet another laugh.

"My point is that I have kept my distance. Then he's in a white

T-shirt and I turn into a schoolgirl. I was one of the top design executives at Winterbourne, for goodness' sake."

"I know I don't mind when David walks around in a white T-shirt."

"Talking about me again?" David stepped out of the back room, boxes in hand. He stepped around the counter and set one of the boxes on the floor then stood.

"Only good stuff." Sadie patted his arm.

"I've heard that before." David dropped a kiss on Sadie's forehead and then carried the other box toward one of the aisles.

Fallon looked at Sadie. "What am I going to do?"

"So you're attracted to him. You have been since high school. Why was this a new revelation?"

"Because that is *not* the guy I went to high school with. I went to school with a boy. That"—she pointed in the rough direction of the farm—"is a man. A man shaped by the Navy. God bless America."

"You have obviously revived your old crush on him, but unless you're staying in Heritage, this is a temporary situation. You just have to make it through."

"I wasn't staying either." David's voice lifted from the aisle.

Sadie looked at Fallon and shrugged. "He has a point."

"Well, unless you know of a high-paying art job in this little town, staying isn't an option." Fallon's phone vibrated in her hand and she glanced at it and swiped the screen.

COLE

Wondered if you were going to
ask or just **guess**.

You ran away pretty **fast**.

FALLON

I did not run **away**. I simply
wanted to get to Hoover's before
it closed.

COLE

It closes at 5.

It's 3.

FALLON

What size board did you need?

COLE

3/4" x 12" x 8'

1.5 in wood screws

6 wall brackets

She liked the message and turned the phone to Sadie.

Sadie picked up her pencil again and made a note on a Post-it. "I'll grab these things for you and be right back."

Fallon was about to slide her phone back into her purse when it vibrated again.

COLE

Any chance you can pick up
Susie and Zane? They should get
off the bus soon at my house.

FALLON

Which is?

COLE

About 50 yards from the
hardware store.

247 Richard Street

The one next to Ms. Margret.

She sent back a thumbs-up emoji. Everyone knew where Margret Bunting lived. The woman was as old as Otis.

Pick up the kids. She had yet to spend time with them alone, but if she was going to have them all weekend, might as well start now.

As if Cole had the bus schedule memorized, the squeal of the air brakes sounded outside moments before Sadie's daughter, Lottie, burst through the door. "Mom?" She stopped in front of Fallon. "Who are you?"

David stepped out of the aisle and pointed to Fallon. "This is your mom's childhood friend, Fallon. Your mom's in the back. She'll be right out."

"Thanks, Dad." Then she leaned toward Fallon and said in a very loud whisper, "He's not my dad yet but he will be in six weeks and five days."

"It is good to officially meet you, Lottie." Fallon leaned her hip against the counter. "I have heard a lot about you."

"And I heard a lot about you." She set her backpack behind the counter. "You two are like me and my friend Annabelle. We are still going to be friends at your age too."

Sadie reappeared with the brackets and the wood screws in hand. "David, can you grab this board for her?" Then she seemed to spot Lottie. "Hey, sweetheart. I see you met Fallon."

"Yup." The girl climbed up on a stool at the end of the counter. "Are you here for the wedding?"

"Sort of." After all, that was one of the reasons she came to town.

Sadie rang up the items, rattled off the total, and Fallon passed her a credit card.

"Do you know Susie and Zane Scott? They live down the street." Fallon took her credit card and slid it back into her wallet.

"Yup, they ride my bus. Susie's younger than I am, but she's really nice. Zane is quiet but seems nice too."

Zane, nice? She swore the kid had it in for her but maybe that was her imagination. "I have to go pick them up for their dad. It was nice meeting you."

"David will have the board for you around the side of the building." Sadie handed Fallon the bag. And sent her a meaningful look. "Don't be a stranger. Now I'm invested."

"There is nothing to invest in. Nothing is going on. Nothing *will* go on." Fallon hurried out the door as she kept repeating that to herself and as she loaded the supplies into his Blazer.

She drove the fifty yards to his house with the board sticking out the rear window. Cole had always talked about wanting to live where there was a lot of land and away from the crowds. But here he was, living across the street from the heart of the town.

Otis stared at her from across the street by the playground. The old hippo statue would probably only move one more time before snow came. Then he'd be stuck for the winter.

She hopped out of the car and hurried up the wooden steps in much need of a repainting. She knocked but there was no answer. She knocked again.

"You have to answer the door. I'm too young." Susie's muffled yell came through the door.

"It's Heritage, not San Diego," Zane's voice came back, but it seemed as if it were getting closer. He pulled open the door and stared at her then at Cole's Blazer behind her then back at her. "What do you want?"

Oh. Clearly, he was still not a fan. "Your dad sent me to pick you up and bring you back to the farm."

"I don't want to go." Zane walked back to the couch. But he hadn't slammed the door, so that was good.

Fallon stepped into the house and secured the door to keep the heat in. "I understand, but that's where dinner is tonight, so why don't you grab your backpacks or anything you need for this evening and we can head out."

Susie stared at her for a moment with crossed arms. She was no doubt going for tough, but with her blonde ringlets and pink tutu she wasn't pulling it off. "Are you trying to date my dad?"

Fallon choked on—air maybe—what else could it be? "No. Why would you say that?"

Susie shrugged, sat on the floor, and reached for one of her shoes. "You have his keys and you're driving his car."

Fallon dropped them on the entryway table and walked over to Susie's matching shoe a few feet away. She grabbed it and held it out to Susie. "He needed me to pick up a board from the hardware store and didn't think it would fit in my small car."

"Ladies try to date him wherever he goes." There was an innocence mixed with a threat to her tone. She wiggled her foot into the tennis shoe without untying it. "But he won't do it because he still loves my mom."

The idea sent an uncomfortable twinge through her chest but she ignored it.

Fallon held out the matching shoe. "Your dad and I are old . . . friends." Old enemies didn't sound quite right, and they had been friends once upon a time. "That's all. He's helping me at my parents' farm. And I'm helping him by watching you guys this weekend."

Susie nodded as she took the shoe and even Zane's shoulders seemed to have relaxed a bit. Maybe that was all it was. Maybe she didn't have to be public enemy number one. They just weren't ready for someone to replace their mom.

"Now grab your stuff. We need to go."

Zane stood and stared at her for a moment. Then shrugged, picked up his coat from the floor, and pulled it on before marching out to the porch. Susie picked up her backpack and hurried after him. Fallon flipped off the lights and pulled the door closed.

She turned toward the Blazer. "Susie, where is your coat?"

Nothing like highlighting how capable she was of taking care of them. She reached for the keys in her pocket, but they weren't there. She tried the door. Locked. She rested her head against the door and ran the past few minutes through her mind. Then looked at Zane. "I locked the keys in your house. Is there any special secret way in by chance?"

Zane just shrugged, and Susie shivered. "It's cold out here."

Zane slipped off his coat and wrapped it around his sister as Fallon picked up her phone and called Cole. He answered on the second ring. "Everything okay?"

"I'm sorry to have to bother you but I think I've locked the house keys and your Blazer keys in the house."

"Didn't Zane tell you where the hide-a-key is?"

Her gaze flicked to Zane, who was watching her with a smirk. The little pill. "Looks like he's getting it right now. We should be there soon."

Without a word, Zane retrieved a key from a hidden spot by the ledge and unlocked the door.

This weekend with them was going to be *so much* fun.

four

HALF THE TOWN HAD SHOWN UP TO THE TOWN square for the Hanging of the Greens tonight. And if even half of them placed a tree order, then the tree farm would be fully on its way to making the season a success. Fallon pulled another silver tray from under the vendor table and filled it with the Christmas-tree sugar cookies her mom had made and then passed it to Susie.

The little girl took it with a grin on her face. She wore an over-sized apron tied tightly around her waist and her fuzzy pink coat zipped up to her chin.

"Now make sure when you hand them a cookie you encourage them to order a tree as well."

"Got it." Susie gave her a thumbs-up and lifted a cookie from the tray and popped it in her mouth.

"You ate plenty yesterday when we were making them." Fallon bopped her on the nose. "Those are for the townspeople."

"I'm a townspeople." The words came out around the cookie in Susie's mouth, but she grinned at her, something warm in it. The weekend, so far, hadn't been a total disaster. It turned out she had worried for no reason because with Cole gone, the kids had been complete angels. Okay, maybe not angels, but at least not outright villains.

Fallon wasn't exactly sure why. Maybe it was a conversation she'd seen Cole have with them Thursday night when she returned to the farmhouse. He'd pulled them aside, and Zane had returned less surly. She wouldn't call him warm and friendly, but at least neutral.

And ever since Cole dropped them off on Friday night, they'd seemed different.

Maybe it was her mother's cooking. Fallon agreed that her mom's homemade cinnamon rolls, and now amazing sugar cookies, could charm a smile out of anyone.

About an hour later, Fallon's phone buzzed. She pulled it out.

COLE

Plane landed early. Should be there within the hour. Don't tell the kids. I want to surprise them.

She sent back a thumbs-up and slid the phone into her pocket but found Zane staring at her. "Who is that?"

She dismissed it with a wave.

"Did you see Otis moved next to the gazebo?" Susie pointed with one hand, nearly dropping the tray, but she caught it. "My dad said that he'd stay there till spring. He's hiberg-natein like a bear. But I'm not sure how he does that with his eyes open. I just think he's too cold to move. What do you think? That is a really big Christmas tree. Is it from your house?"

Fallon wasn't sure which question to answer first. Ever since Susie had warmed up to her, the chatter was nonstop. And she loved it.

Fallon eyed the twenty-foot tree that had been erected on the south side of the square between the playground and the new clock. "Yes. Your dad cut it down last week."

"Why is it only half decorated?" Susie reached for another cookie, but pulled back when Fallon raised an eyebrow.

"They're letting people decorate ornaments with their names on them and add them to the bottom." She pointed to the table where kids were bent over making all sorts of glitter creations.

"Green ornaments?"

"You can make them whatever color you want. Do you want to make a green ornament?"

"No. I don't think that would look good. But I was figuring they had to be green because it's called the Hanging of the Greens."

"The tree is the green, you goofball." Zane ruffled her curls.

She shot her brother the stink eye. "You can't hang a tree."

Fallon glanced at the stack of freshly printed order forms and then at the empty clipboard in front of her. Not one sale? That couldn't be right. Tonight might not make or break the season's success, but it had always been a good projection for that year's tree sales. The night was still early, but zero sales weren't a great sign.

She turned toward Zane and Susie, who had been handing out the cookies all evening. "Have you been making sure to hand them an order form every time?"

"Every time." Zane gave her the token eye roll, but it seemed a half effort. "People keep telling me they're going to get an artificial one because it's better for the environment." He lifted a shoulder. "They're not wrong."

Fallon's shoulders tensed as a familiar fire built inside her. "But they *are* wrong. Artificial trees are so much worse for the environment. The carbon footprint that comes from making and shipping them, the space in the landfill after they're discarded, not to mention that well-kept tree farms are great for conservation and provide a lot of natural benefits."

"O-kay." Zane's brows were about at his hairline as he stared at her.

"Sorry, I'm a little passionate about it."

"Obviously." He lifted an order form and scanned it over. "You should've handed that information out rather than these."

She took the paper from him and read it over. Maybe he was right. They were on the drab side.

A gust of wind came up and knocked over one of the display signs. Her mom said buying these lightweight, retractable marketing signs had been a waste. They were the kind she always used when she had gone to conferences for Winterbourne Enterprises, but then again, this wasn't a fancy conference at a fancy hotel. This was simply the Hanging of the Greens in Heritage Square.

Clearly, she needed to rethink her approach.

Fallon collapsed the sign and tucked it under the table. "We're slow here. Why don't you two go make an ornament? You could make one for your dad and me as well. I doubt I'll have time to get over there. Just come straight back when you're done."

Susie handed her the tray and tugged her apron off before grabbing her brother's hand and pulling him in that direction.

Bo Mackers walked up to her table and lifted a cookie from the tray. With his well-worn farm coat and stocking cap, no one would guess he owned the local bank. But then again, Heritage had always been a salt of the earth place. She glanced back at her signs that had fallen over again. Yes, she'd really missed the mark.

He reached for yet another cookie—was that his fourth? But the Mackers family had always been faithful tree customers, so maybe at least she would make one order today. She pulled out an order form and held it out. "Are you ready to order your regular tree?"

He shook his head as he finished off rest of the cookie. A few crumbs clung to his thick mustache. "Wife is thinking of getting one of those artificial ones, doing our part for the environment and all. They make them pretty big."

Fallon gripped the clipboard a little tighter and forced her smile to stay in place. "Actually—"

"I was hoping you'd have some of your Tiny Angels ornaments

for sale." Marie Mackers appeared next to her husband and slipped her arm into his. "They're *pricey* but every year I get a new one for the tree. I thought if you had them here at a discount, I might be able to afford two. I still need the one that has the two angels looking over the shepherds."

"Sorry. They're available online, though." What could she say other than that? If she wanted to sell them, she had to buy them first. Not to mention she didn't set the price.

Mrs. Mackers leaned forward with a conspiratorial twinkle in her eye. "Can you at least tell me what the new design is for the year?"

A lump formed in her throat. "We aren't releasing one this year."

The woman's brow pinched in confusion, but Fallon had nothing else. There wouldn't be any Tiny Angels again—ever. She couldn't even form the words. It was like losing a piece of her. And she couldn't tell people how she'd failed. Failed them. Failed her art. Failed God.

An arm settled around her shoulders as her mom's jasmine scent filled the air. "Thank you for stopping by."

A moment after the couple wandered away, her mom turned her toward her. "How is it going? You look terrible."

"If I hear one more person say they switched to an artificial tree, I might go insane." Fallon gave in and took a large bite out of one of the cookies. "It's either that or wanting me to give them discounted Tiny Angels ornaments."

"I was afraid of that." Her mom reached for one of the cookies, broke it in half, and ate one of the pieces. "If you were more transparent about the Tiny Angels series then—"

"No. It's all too embarrassing." She reached under the table and started refilling the cookie tray. "If we were selling these cookies instead of giving them away, then maybe we could turn a profit. People talk about these cookies all year long, you know."

"I know. Lucy often tried to get me to sell my cookies at Donny's year-round, but that was back when I was teaching and too busy." She ate the other half of the cookie. "Maybe the days of the tree farm have gone by the wayside. This is such a shame because James Tree Farm was quite the Christmas spectacular once upon a time. Do you remember when we offered sleigh rides? And don't forget your father as Santa."

"I remember. But things change."

"But maybe that's what we need." Her mom held out another cookie to her. "Heritage loves events. If we are going to bring people back, we need to make buying a tree an event again—a Christmas spectacular."

"With Dad still flat on his back, I don't see that happening."

"You could do it. And I bet Cole would help. You two made quite the team over the past week."

"I think Cole has served his time."

"Where are the kids, anyway?"

Fallon glanced to the ornament table and then around the square. "They were right there."

Her mom must have heard the rising panic because she took the tray from her hand and set it on the table. "They're fine, I'm sure. You walk that way and I'll go this way. We'll meet on the far side by the playground. The square isn't that big."

"Who'll watch the table?"

"What's going to happen?" Her mother gave her a wry shake of her head. "People take cookies without ordering. Sorry to tell you, but that's happening now."

Fallon passed by the gazebo and searched the faces of the children who were playing on the steps, but no Susie. The library was closed for the evening and the old schoolhouse sat with dark windows. By the time she met her mom on the far side by the playground, her mother had Zane. But only Zane.

She stopped right in front of him. "Where's Susie?"

Zane shrugged but she could see the tension in his eyes. "We got in a fight at the craft table and she said she was going to find you."

"What did you argue about?"

He pulled out his phone and tapped the screen. "It says she's . . ." He extended his arm, pointing and turning, then stopped. "There. It says she's at your table."

"You can track her?" Fallon leaned over and glanced at his screen.

"Dad set it up this summer when we couldn't find her at the fair." He began walking in the direction he'd pointed. "He said with only one set of eyes watching her, he needed help."

Smart. They walked toward the table and then looked to Zane for more direction. But his brow creased as he glanced around. "It says she's right here."

His gaze darted around then froze on a spot on the ground. His face paled. Fallon followed his line of sight to a small pink watch under the table.

She reached down and lifted it. "The tracker?"

He nodded. "It couldn't have fallen off. She either took it off or—"

"Deep breath, Zane." Fallon gripped the sides of his arms, taking care to look him right in the face. "We'll find her. Heritage is a safe place."

At least it had always been.

Please, God, she hoped it still was.

"There you are." Cole's deep voice approached her from behind and she spun to face him. He wore a few days' worth of scruff on his face and exhaustion laced his features. She had called him irresponsible more times than she could count, but she'd lost his kid. Everything must have shown on her face because without her saying anything, his smile faded. His gaze shot from Fallon to Zane then back to Fallon. "Where's Susie?"

He'd seen more in his life than anyone should have to see, but nothing had ever made his blood run cold like the expression on Fallon's face when he asked where Susie was.

He'd panic later. Now, Cole did a quick sweep of the area for points of threat.

She normally wouldn't cross the street on her own, but with the roads surrounding the square shut down, it extended her range. "Who saw her last?"

Zane hesitantly raised his hand. "We had a fight."

"About what?"

Zane's gaze flicked to Fallon and then back to him. "Does it matter?"

Cole nodded and forced calmness he didn't feel into his words. "If we know what she was mad about, we might be able to figure out where she went."

"She was making an ornament for Fallon."

"And?"

"And I said something that made her mad."

"And that was . . ."

"I said . . . I said she shouldn't get attached." The boy's gaze again flicked to Fallon then back to Cole. "Because Fallon would eventually leave too."

Cole glanced at Fallon. Her eyes were closed tight. Part of him longed to reassure her that he didn't blame her but that had to wait. He nodded at Zane and scanned the square then the surrounding area again. He had just made the second pass of the street when his gaze landed on their house.

A small light flickered in Susie's window like a flashlight moving around the room.

Of course. Retreat to safety.

He focused on Zane. There was definite panic in his son's eyes.

For as much as Zane liked to play the too-cool-to-care part, his sun rose and set on his sister. He rested his hand on Zane's shoulder and gave him a reassuring squeeze. "This isn't your fault, Zane. It's going to be okay. Continue to search the square. I'm going to check the house."

He hurried across the street and up his porch. The door was locked and deadbolted, which they usually only did from the inside. He pulled out his keys and unlocked the door. Then without turning on the lights, he made his way up to Susie's room. There was a hint of a light peeking out from under the bed.

He released a deep breath as he shot off a text to Zane and Fallon that he'd found her. Tension released from his shoulders for the first time since he'd stepped into the square and saw Fallon's face.

Cole sat on her floor then knocked on the frame of the bed. "Anyone home?"

"No." The voice was angry but also held a hint of lostness that broke his heart.

Cole lay down on his stomach on the floor and lifted the ruffle that hid the space under the bed. Susie was on her back in an oversized fluffy pink robe. The flashlight in her hand that pointed at the underside of the bed didn't produce a lot of light, but it was enough to highlight the tears that had traveled from the corners of her eyes into her hairline.

"Fallon and Zane were worried about you."

"Sorry."

"Want to talk about it?"

She was quiet for so long that he'd nearly given up hope that she'd speak. "Why did Mommy leave? Did she not love us anymore?"

He'd give his right arm to keep his kids from experiencing this type of pain, but there was nothing he could do. "Of course she loves you. It was me she left."

She turned her face toward him. "Don't lie to me. I'm not a baby anymore, Dad. I'm seven."

Not a baby? The idea was laughable and heartbreaking. "No lies."

She sighed, swallowed, her eyes glistening. "You were gone on a mission when she left. So she left us, not you. Right?"

"No, sweetie." He tucked the ruffle between the mattress and the frame so he didn't have to hold it up. "She knew if I were there, I would try to talk her into staying."

"Because you still love her?" When he hesitated, her eyes narrowed. "No lies, remember."

"Your mom and I have a complicated relationship." How did a dad truthfully explain to his seven-year-old that her mom had left him because she wanted to recapture the carefree days of her teenage years that he'd stolen when she got pregnant at eighteen? Never mind that somehow Tiffany liked to conveniently forget that she'd been the one pursuing him that night. Giving him drink after drink until he didn't know wrong from right. He didn't claim to be innocent in the whole situation, but neither was she.

"Do you still love her?" Susie must have thought he'd missed the question.

He stretched an arm under the bed and wiped away one of her tearstains. "I love that she gave me you."

She swallowed again, nodded. Then, "Is Fallon really leaving after Christmas?"

"Where did you hear that?" And why did the suggestion put a burr into him?

"Zane said he heard her talking to Mrs. James about it this weekend."

"I don't know what her plans are. We haven't talked about it." But maybe they should, because if his kids were getting attached, he needed to be careful. Who was he trying to fool? He was getting attached. There was something about Fallon that had always drawn him to her. And the way her cheeks had pinked up when she'd walked in on him fixing the furnace . . . He'd been thinking about that all weekend as they searched for the glitch in the security system.

Yeah, he needed to be careful. "Did you have fun with Fallon this weekend?"

Susie smiled then, her eyes lighting up. "So much fun. We made cookies and she showed us pictures of when she had a horse. I want a horse. I'm going to add that to my Christmas list. I know you said I couldn't have a dog, but a horse can stay outside."

Perfect. A horse. He schooled his voice. "Where would you keep it?"

"In the backyard." Her brow wrinkled as if it were obvious. "You could fit at least six horses back there and I only want *one*."

"I don't think Santa brings farm animals. They would be too heavy for the reindeer."

She frowned. "Maybe you're right. Do you think she's pretty?"

"Mrs. Santa?" Navigating a conversation with his daughter sometimes felt like acrobatics.

"Fallon."

Oh. "I think . . . "

"Tru—uth."

Fine. "I think Fallon is very pretty."

Susie smiled again. "Me too."

Downstairs, the front door opened and shut. "I bet that's Zane. Why don't you come out of there and we'll make some hot cocoa?"

"Okay." Susie wiggled out from under the bed and stood.

"Where did you get that bathrobe?" The thing was huge on her.

"It was Mom's." She blinked up at him, a touch of uncertainty on her face. "Are you mad?"

He ran a gentle hand over her hair, brushing away a few dust bunnies, then lifted her into his arms. "Of course not. I'm glad you have it. It's like she's here hugging you."

Her face lit up as she leaned back a little and wrapped her arms around herself and squeezed. "I know. It even smells like her."

She shoved the sleeve into his face. The mix of perfume and expensive shampoo filled his nose. "That's your mom, all right."

Only that scent didn't bring him warm feelings. It reminded him of betrayal and abandonment. He headed back down the stairs, setting Susie down when they got to the bottom.

Zane stood there, scowling.

"You had me worried." Zane knelt in front of her and then wrapped her in a hug. "Don't do that again. You and me to the end. Right?"

"Right." She leaned back and then held up her pinky and Zane grabbed it with his.

You and me to the end.

He'd been absent a good share of their younger years and Tiffany was absent now. He might have missed a lot, but he was determined to give them the relationship with their dad and the childhood they deserved moving forward.

His phone buzzed with an incoming text and he pulled it from his pocket.

WALKER

Another job came up for this weekend. More than triple of what we made last week. But it is a bit of travel so I would need you Th-Mo. You in?

He glanced at his kids. Cole hated leaving them again so soon, but with the debt Tiffany had left him, this weekend's job had only put a dent in it. Not to mention he still had the Christmas lists to contend with. He might not be able to get Susie that horse or dog, but he'd seen the coolest robot dog this weekend. He did a quick search for the Xbox again, but the price had doubled. Got to love profiteering. The only hope he had was to take whatever work Walker could throw at him.

But to do that he'd need Fallon, and after this scare, she might never agree to watch his kids again.

He pulled up their texting thread. He must have missed one from her while he was talking to Susie.

FALLON
Let me know if everything is okay.
I am so sorry about all this.

COLE
Everything is great. She's all smiles now. I'm making cocoa as we speak.

The three little dots popped up almost immediately. He set it on the counter facing up as he pulled the mugs from the cupboard and filled them with milk then put them in the microwave. When he grabbed his phone, the message was there.

FALLON
I am so glad. I was so worried.

He took a breath. Here went nothing.

COLE
Any chance you could watch them again Thursday-Monday?

When she didn't immediately respond he added another text.

COLE
I will work for free at the farm until Christmas.

Her reply came back almost immediately.

FALLON
You honestly think that is a good idea?

Good idea as in, did he trust her? Absolutely. Good idea as in leaving the kids again so soon? Probably not. Good idea as in the kids—and let's face it, him too—were getting more attached? Definitely not.

FALLON

Besides. With the lack of tree sales the farm might be a bust.

He pulled the mugs from the microwave and added a pack of cocoa to each, then picked up the phone and tapped her number. She answered on the first ring. "Hello?" Her voice was hesitant.

"What happened with the presales?" He dipped the spoon in each cup and stirred.

Fallon hesitated a second as if debating if they were going to do this. She must have decided it was all right because she sighed. "We had one."

"One what?"

"One tree presale."

"Ouch."

"Tell me about it. So I'm not sure there is any point to you working at the farm."

Was this a no about watching the kids?

"What kind of attitude is that? Where is the nothing-gets-in-my-way Fallon from high school?" He handed Susie her hot cocoa with a wink.

"I'm not her anymore."

"Yes, you are. I saw the way you took charge of the farm this week. That booth you had set up on the square looked great—the little I saw of it." He handed Zane his hot cocoa.

"It didn't matter. It didn't help get people to the farm."

He walked to the front window, spotted the square still lit up, and imagined her sitting in her booth, shivering. Hated that thought, suddenly. "Maybe you could do something at the farm."

Another sigh. "That's what my mom said. She suggested trying to do the whole spectacular. A Christmas kickoff. We could offer photos with Santa and cookies with Mrs. Santa."

"Your mom's a smart lady. People would love that. Once they're there in person, they'll remember why they want a real tree this Christmas."

A beat. Then, "Maybe you're right."

"What was that? I didn't hear you."

"Fine. You're right. Cole Scott is right. Better?"

"Much." He walked back to the kitchen, where Susie wore a chocolate mustache. Picked up his cocoa. "Now what are you going to do?"

"Make a Christmas Extravaganza for the town to remember. A Christmas Kickoff Extravaganza."

"That's my Fallon." The words were out before he could think better of them. And by the silence that stretched across the line, she hadn't missed them. "I mean, that's the Fallon I remember. So about this weekend. Can you watch the kids?"

"Can you help me get ready for the Christmas spectacular? It will be a lot of work. The shop. The lights. Santa."

"I'm not dressing as Santa."

"Fine. My dad should still be able to do that. He is feeling a lot better. But we'll need help getting the whole Sugar Shack ready including the half that is Santaland—the spot he sits, the chair, and the stage."

"As long as I'm not Santa himself, I'm in. And you'll watch the kids from Thursday night to Monday?"

Silence.

"I trust you, Fallon."

Another beat. "Okay. Sure."

"Could you do it here?" He knew he was pushing it, but it would be easier for the kids to get ready for school here both Friday and Monday.

"You sure you really trust me?" There was a hesitancy to her voice that nearly broke him. And he got it. His lack of trust had destroyed their friendship. He wouldn't make that mistake again.

"Yes. I really trust you." He ended the call.

Zane stood in the doorway, eyes hard. "You're leaving again?"

"Just for a few days. I hate being away, but we need money to live."

Zane shook his head and left the kitchen.

He didn't blame the kid for being mad. He hated that he had to leave too, but he did what he had to do.

He opened the Amazon app again, found the game console still at double the price, and added it to his cart. Then he typed in *robot dog* at the top and started searching the listings. They might be angry now, but come Christmas morning they would appreciate all he did for the family.

He hoped.

H OW HAD SHE THOUGHT GROCERY SHOPPING with Cole and the kids on this Wednesday night would go smoothly? Fallon lifted a crown of broccoli in one hand and a bunch of asparagus in the other, waiting for the kids to choose. They stared back at her with their noses wrinkled in disgust. Seriously? So far all they had in the cart was cereal, peanut butter, and jelly.

When neither seemed to budge, she opted for another approach. She motioned to Cole, who was rounding the aisle in JJ's Food Mart, coming toward them carrying a gallon of milk. "Zane, you lift weights. Do you think your dad got his big muscles by living off Pop-Tarts and cookies?"

Cole's brows raised as he stepped closer. "She has a point. My grandma's asparagus was actually pretty good. She always loaded it up with garlic butter and Parmesan cheese."

The kids exchanged looks as if trying to decide, then turned toward each other to confer. Cole leaned close to her ear, amusement in his tone. "Glad to know you like my big muscles, though."

"I didn't say I liked them, I said they were there," she whispered back. "I was just observing."

"Oh, well. That's good. I would hate to think you were objectifying me."

"You wish." She'd meant it to come off light, but the way Cole's eyes flashed—something a little dangerous for a half second—it was clear they needed to get back into safer waters.

"We decided broccoli, as long as we can have it with cheese," Zane finally spoke, pulling their attention to him. *Thank you, Zane.*

"I'll tell you what." Cole set the gallon of milk in the cart. "Why don't you two pick half the meals and Fallon picks the other half. But you have to eat hers without complaining. Sound fair?"

Cole sent her a look questioning if she was on board with the plan, and she nodded. After all, she could do pizza with cauliflower crust and they'd never know.

"Sounds good to you because you don't have to eat"—Zane picked up the list lying in the cart—"sweet potato and kale stir-fry."

Cole stared at her with a look that pretty much said, *I've got nothing because that does sound gross.* It was much better than it sounded, but maybe she didn't really know how to feed kids.

Cole took the list from Zane and studied it. "How about regular stir-fry and"—his finger trailed down the page—"tacos, and, Zane, you can make French bread pizza tomorrow night. His specialty." The last bit was directed toward Fallon.

So much for the cauliflower crust, but cooking with the kids might be fun.

"What about me? I want to make her goop." Susie jumped up and down.

Goop?

Then again, maybe cooking with kids was overrated.

"I'm only gone four meals, and Mrs. James already planned Sunday. But . . ." Cole faced Fallon. "How do you feel about tuna melts—aka goop—for dinner tonight?"

Shopping for the weekend was one thing, but dinner with Cole and the kids together like a happy little family hadn't been the plan. She was helping him and he was helping her, but she wouldn't call them friends.

But one look at Susie's hopeful eyes and she couldn't say no. Fine, a quick dinner and she'd leave. It might help her to get a lay of the kitchen too just in case she needed to bring any other kitchen supplies. The Cole she'd known hadn't been much of a cook. And if their favorite meals were French bread pizza and goop, she didn't expect that had changed.

An hour later, as Susie, Cole, and Fallon moved around a kitchen much too small for three people, Fallon debated whether agreeing to this little domestic moment had been a mistake. The groceries were put away and Susie was walking her through the process of making tuna melts—which the little girl affectionately called goop. If only Cole didn't take up a good share of the room.

"Can you take us to church Sunday?" Susie pulled two cans of tuna from the cupboard and set them on the counter.

"Church?" Fallon had grown up going to church, but it had been a while since she'd been. She had dropped the habit even before she'd felt as if God abandoned her. Robert wasn't into church.

"We go every Sunday." Susie lined up the can opener and squeezed. When she didn't have enough pressure, Cole reached over and helped her close it.

Fallon studied Cole. "You go to church?"

"Am I really so bad you can't imagine me in a church?" He didn't seem offended. His words and the look on his face appeared more teasing than anything.

"Practically a hoodlum." She bit back a smile. Maybe they *could* be friends. "I just remember always having to drag you to youth group with me. You were not a fan, if I remember."

"Well, you've heard the saying there are no atheists in foxholes.

It was true for me in the military. And my buddy Chap was a Christian. He had a pretty big impact on me."

"Was?"

"He died." He cast a quick glance at Susie as if to suggest not to ask more about that, then reached over to help Susie finish up the opening of the can. "Tiffany refused to take them to church, but now we go as a family. I like Pastor Nate. I think you would too."

"My parents like him." Fallon nodded.

Cole trying to get her to go to church. Well, hadn't things come full circle.

Susie scraped the tuna into the bowl, added a spoonful of mayo, and did her best to stir it. "Can you get the relish out?"

Fallon sidestepped Cole without looking at him and ducked into the fridge. It was better stocked than she expected. The whole place was, actually. Yet it felt impersonal. Furniture but no pictures, almost like an Airbnb rather than a home.

"You went to youth group with my dad? Did you like it? Zane goes to youth group. I'm too young but someday I'll go too. Is that where you two met?"

Fallon held out the relish. That was a lot of questions in only a few seconds.

Cole stepped up, took the relish, and added it in. "We met in the seventh grade spelling bee. We were the final two."

"Who won? Did you get a trophy? I've never gotten a trophy. Do you still have it?" Susie grabbed the pack of buns and began working on the twist tie but gave up and tore a hole in the bag, sending them across the counter.

"I did." Fallon gathered the stray buns and arranged them on the cookie sheet like Susie had done. "I don't remember a trophy."

Cole, who had taken over the mixing, glanced at Susie over his shoulder. "She won because her last word was a softball."

"And you're a sore loser." Fallon rolled her eyes at the argument they'd always had.

Yes, okay, they were friends again. And the idea settled something in her. A calm feeling she hadn't known in a long time.

"You guys are the same age?" Susie's head tilted to the side.

Cole leaned back, the familiar smirk peeking through his grin. "She's way older."

"By three months."

He gave a small shrug. "Still older."

"Then why don't you have kids?" Susie's curious eyes were locked on her now.

Cole's head jerked toward his daughter. "Sweetie, you can't ask that."

"It's okay." Fallon laid a gentle hand on Susie's shoulder. "My husband and I wanted kids, but we waited and then . . . he died before we had any."

"Why did you wait? My mom and dad had Zane just a few months after they married."

Fallon cast a glance at Cole, but he seemed quite focused on mixing the tuna. She turned back to Susie. "We waited because he loved racing cars and he didn't think it was fair to a child to constantly be putting himself into danger. And his hobby was more important to him than what I wanted."

She winced at her own words. She hadn't meant to say that last bit out loud.

"Is that how he died?" Zane stood in the doorway. She'd hadn't even realized he was still hanging around. She thought he'd retreated to his room.

"No. Not directly anyway." She waited for the usual piercing pain to come, but it didn't. Just a dull sadness of the waste of it all. "He died on a road trip to one of his races. Just a mugging gone bad. They took his wallet and they—" She glanced at Susie. She'd never had to give a PG version of the story before. Most people just knew. "And he died."

She glanced to Cole with an apology, but his gaze froze her in place. It wasn't a look telling her to watch her words around the kids, it was a look of deep pain and sadness. As if he were reaching in and seeing everything she normally kept neatly packed away. The grief. The scars. And even the hint that her marriage had been far from perfect.

"Are you going to get married again?" Zane's words broke the silence and she blinked away from Cole.

"I . . . I don't know." Nothing like the third degree from kids. Was the kitchen getting smaller?

"You should. I like you." Susie climbed up on a stool and scooped out a sloppy mix of tuna. She dropped it on one of the buns then put the top on. "When my mom comes back, can we still be friends even if you don't need to babysit anymore?"

"Hey, why don't you two go watch TV." Cole grabbed Susie and lifted her down from the stool and steered her toward the living room. Evening TV time must be a treat because both lit up and ran for the couch.

Cole leaned his hip against the counter. "Sorry about all that. Are you okay?"

"It's been three years. I'm okay talking about it." She took over Susie's job of scooping the tuna mix onto the buns but didn't lift her eyes. "Why does Susie talk like Tiffany is coming back?"

"Because when she left, their grandparents told them she went on a little trip, and I have never corrected them. I think Zane suspects, but I don't want to talk bad about her in front of them. I don't know if you remember, but my parents' divorce was ugly. I don't want to do that to them. I don't want to make them choose between believing me or being faithful to the good memories that they had of their mom."

"It would be okay to share some of it." Fallon completed the last tuna burgers then set the bowl in the sink. "So she just left them with her parents?"

He pushed away from the counter, walked over to the fridge,

and pulled something out. He opened a plastic package of sliced cheese. "About a year and a half ago she took up with some weasel in Vegas. I did receive the divorce papers, but she managed to open two credit cards in my name and then max them out before it was final." He gave a dismissive shrug as he dropped a piece of cheese on top of each bun. "The courts issued me full custody and that's what is most important."

"You guys haven't heard from her?"

His hand paused for a fraction of a second. "She resurfaces every once in a while, to ask for money, but she has had no contact with the kids."

Resurfaced? What did that mean? But when he didn't offer more, she let it go. After all, maybe their new friendship had its limits.

"So why did you move back here?" She ran some water in the bowl then dried her hands. "Your parents aren't even here anymore."

"I was an active-duty SEAL at the time. I was on a mission when I got the message that she was done. With me. With being a mom. She left the kids with her parents and took off."

"What did you do?"

"Wasn't a lot I could do. When I got home from the op, I took an emergency leave to come here to make sure the kids were okay. Her parents are awesome even if they did raise a spoiled, entitled daughter. They agreed to keep the kids while I finished my service term, which was another nine months. As soon as I had the opportunity to get out, I did."

"Not a lot of opportunity for work for a former Navy SEAL around here."

"With everything the kids have been through, I don't really want to uproot them one more time. They don't need to suffer any more than they already have for their parents' poor choices."

"What about your parents?"

"Mom still blames me for her and Dad's divorce and she lives down near my sister in South Carolina."

"Wait, what? I thought your dad left because she was cheating."

"Yes, but he didn't know she was cheating. I was watching my sister and she fell out of the tree house. It was just a broken leg, but I didn't know that and I panicked and called 911. They couldn't get hold of my mom, so they called my dad. Which led to him finding out that she left us alone a lot and why. I was trying to do the right thing and still ended up the bad guy."

"But weren't you close to your dad?"

"Up till then, yeah. But he was so mad when I told him I got Tiffany pregnant. He said I was a disappointment like my mom."

"Oh, Cole. I'm sure he didn't mean it. Have you reached out to—"

"I always wanted to prove to him I turned out okay. Come back with some military honor." He ducked his head. "He died of a heart attack a few years ago. I came for the funeral but the kids had never even met him."

"I'm sorry."

"I want to say that if I could I'd go back and make all different choices that I would." Cole stared back toward where the kids were watching the TV. "But part of me would do it all again—with all the pain—just to have those two kids. They are the best piece of me and I can't imagine my life without them."

"Are you glad you joined the Navy? I hadn't even known you thought about that."

"I ended up there because even with a scholarship, I couldn't afford to support a family and go to school. But with my scores they fast tracked me into the SEAL program. BUD/s was the hardest thing I ever did, but I loved being an operator. For the first time in my life, I had a family—a brotherhood. Guys who had my back no matter what. I was good at my job. It was like God had made me for it."

"And now you're here."

"And now I'm here. Because my family needs me. But leaving my team was the hardest thing I ever had to do."

Why did that surprise her? He'd always been the total package. Kind. Thoughtful. And if she really was honest with herself, responsible. Which was why everything with him and Tiffany had burned so much. He'd claimed that he'd been drunk. That he didn't even remember much beyond arriving at the party. But that wasn't the Cole she knew. Cole was the designated driver. The measure-twice-cut-once kind of guy. He wasn't irresponsible.

So she'd drawn the only conclusion that made sense back then. That either things had been going on between him and Tiffany for a while or Fallon had been completely wrong about his character. And being wrong about his character hurt much less than being betrayed. He'd crushed her back then when he'd told her what had happened at the party and she couldn't give him the power to do that again.

She needed to keep her emotional distance and avoid little moments like this that travelled down memory lane. Or when he looked at her like he was right now. As if he was trying to see into her. But she couldn't—wouldn't let him in there again.

"Is dinner ready?" Susie yelled from the couch.

"Almost." Cole glanced at the tuna on the buns still waiting to be put in the oven. He slid them in and set the timer. "Just ten minutes."

Fallon stepped over to her purse and pulled out her phone and stared at the blank screen. "Oh, I need to go. But I'll be here tomorrow. Six o'clock sharp."

"But you haven't had a goop." Susie appeared in the door.

Fallon glanced at Cole then hurried to the door and pulled on her coat. "Save one for me, I'll reheat it."

Susie followed her to the door. "Can you bring your paints tomorrow? I want you to teach me to paint."

"Sure thing." She slipped on her shoes and was out the door without even one more glance at Cole.

The door rattled as she slammed it shut in her wake and she released a deep sigh. If she had been wrong about Cole—which it was looking like she had been—then what else was she wrong about?

He'd said or done something wrong but for the life of him he wasn't sure what. Cole stared at the front door, the white lacy curtains that blocked the window still swaying. Man, those were ugly curtains. But they came with the rental and he wasn't much of a decorator. He had brought in the secondhand furniture, but the rest of the decor was what he referred to as mess-de-kids.

He'd cringed when they'd walked in, but Fallon hadn't seemed to take notice of the disaster. She seemed to accept them for who they were until . . . until her face had morphed from friendly to panic before his eyes. She had glanced at her phone, but he was pretty sure that was an excuse. He'd said or done something. He just didn't know what. And everything in him wanted to figure it out and fix it.

Despite hashing out some of the ugly past, he'd been enjoying their little trip down memory lane. It wasn't a place he let himself go often. He'd only even kept a few things from before he left for the Navy. So few that they all fit in a shoebox. A box that he hadn't opened since the day after graduation when he sealed it shut. Maybe it was time.

"Zane, pull the goop out when the timer goes off. I'll be right back." He hurried up the stairs. His bedroom was the first one on the right and the smallest of the three. The walls were muted pale green with hardwood floors that looked as though they hadn't been polished since the eighties. Like the curtains, he hadn't updated the place. There was something in him that refused to make this place home.

The room was barely big enough for a dresser, side table, and the queen-size bed—his one investment had been the mattress. A good night's sleep made all the difference.

It was also the only room that came with two closets. One for his clothes, which he kept military neat—he had to have some order in this house. And the other was full of boxes. His stuff that he never unpacked. Why bother, since the rental was temporary.

He walked over to the one full of boxes in the far corner and pulled it open. He tugged the string to light the small space and scanned the wall of boxes of all shapes and sizes for the recognizable orange Nike shoebox. He pulled down two possibilities along with another plain brown one that was on top of them and tossed them all on the bed.

"Can I go to Jimmy's?" Zane appeared in the doorway.

"You're supposed to be watching dinner. Besides, it's a school night."

Zane looked ready to argue but he seemed distracted by one of the boxes. He sat on the edge of the bed and lifted it. "What's this?"

Cole took it from his hands and spun it for a clue, then froze. The name Stan Scott was written in bold Sharpie on the side. A chill ran through him. He carried it back to the closet and tossed it on top. "It's nothing."

"Is that Grandpa's name?" Zane watched him for any trace of untruth.

"He was your grandfather. He was never a grandpa to you. You didn't even know him."

"Have you ever opened it?"

"No."

"Can I—" Zane started to walk past him, but Cole blocked his way.

"No." He didn't know why he was being like this. But ever since he'd been given that box at his father's funeral, it had remained sealed. Locked away. He'd been a disappointment to his father and he didn't need a box of his old junk to remind him of that.

Zane stormed out and Cole dropped onto the edge of the bed. He reached for one of the shoeboxes, but it contained photos from when the kids were small. He reached for the second and ran his fingernail along the aged tape, breaking the seal, and lifted the top. Bingo. He hadn't kept much from high school but what he did keep was all in here. His tassel from graduation lay on top, displaying the blue and yellow colors of Heritage High. He pulled it out. Next was his letter in football. He lifted the blue H and froze as his heart picked up speed. This was why he'd never opened it.

He set the letter aside and lifted out a photo of him and Fallon at Lake Michigan taken just before their senior year. That summer everything had been fun, easy, simple. That was the night he told her of his plans to go to U of M and she hinted she might too. He almost asked her out that night but chickened out at the last minute.

"It's Fallon's horse." Susie was on the bed, peeking in the box. When had she come in?

He glanced at her then her pink glittery shoes. "Shoes off the rack."

She lifted her feet in the air and looked under her. "What rack?"

"Sorry—bed."

Susie kicked her shoes to the floor then reached in and pulled out a photo of Fallon with her horse. Her long blonde hair was lifting in the breeze as she looked at the camera. He'd been taking photography that semester and she'd agreed to let him take pictures of her horse for an assignment. He'd snuck in a few of her as well.

Susie leaned over and took the other photo from his hand and giggled. "You were skinny. You look like Zane."

He could definitely see the resemblance. Man, they were

young—too young for making adult decisions that would affect the rest of their lives.

"Were you two best friends?"

"We were."

"Are you going to be best friends again?" The question was said with such innocence he couldn't keep in the chuckle.

"Probably not." Because he'd never really seen her as just a friend. And if he were honest with himself, he definitely wasn't as aware of his friends as he was of Fallon. Every smile, every innocent touch, even as she'd navigated around the kitchen earlier. It was as if he was tuned into her at all times. And if his honed military senses hadn't failed him, she was tuned into him too.

"Too bad. I like her. And I think she likes us."

Too bad? That was one way to put it. Part of him wanted to change that. Move things forward with her. He glanced back at the photo. They had been good together once and they could be good together again.

He sighed and ran his hand roughly across his jaw. But none of it mattered if she was really leaving after Christmas like Susie suggested. His life was here. His family was here.

"Is this me?" Susie shoved a photo from the other box in his face.

He held it back and studied it. It was from a few Christmases ago. "Yup, and that's me, and that is Zane."

"I'm going to put it on the fridge." She hopped off the bed and thundered back down the stairs.

A moment later a faint clang came from downstairs followed by an exclamation by Zane. He didn't sound hurt, just mad. Cole hurried down the stairs. Zane sat on the couch holding his foot and Susie stood a few feet away with wide eyes.

Cole focused on Zane. "What happened?"

When Zane didn't answer, Susie jumped in. "He yelled at his game, then kicked that footrest thingy. It made a weird noise and so did Zane."

Cole stepped around the couch. The footrest of the recliner sat at an odd angle. He knelt in front of his son and held out his hand. Zane only hesitated a second before extending the foot toward him. Cole poked at the bones, but everything seemed stable. Would probably be a nice bruise. He walked over to the recliner. And pushed on it. It didn't move for a moment, then gave with another loud pop and clicked shut. He tested the lever, but it didn't pop back out. Great, one more thing to fix.

He turned back to Zane. "Is this how we handle our anger?"

"No." But he didn't give more. He had a feeling the anger was more directed toward Cole than the device. He opened his mouth to probe further when the fire alarm started blaring in the kitchen.

Susie ran to the kitchen. "My goop!"

Cole hurried after her. He opened the oven, and sure enough, dinner was ruined. He glanced at Susie, tears welling in her eyes.

Why did he think he could fix anything with Fallon? He couldn't even fix the problems in his house. He reached up to pull the smoke detector from the ceiling and end the ear-piercing racket.

Add dinner to the list of things he couldn't fix.

six

THIS FELT ALL WRONG. FALLON STOOD IN FRONT of Cole's door with her bag in hand and her pillow tucked under her arm. She lifted her hand to knock but didn't move. But after running out of here last night like something was chasing her, she really didn't want to face him today.

She had overreacted. That was clear the moment she'd started her car last night. But it wasn't like she would walk back in and say, *Sorry about that. I thought for a moment there that we were getting too close again. False alarm, we're good. I'll take some goop after all.*

She lowered her hand and walked to the edge of the porch. The sun was getting low but still peeked above the buildings, which meant she had a little time before she had told Cole she'd be here. Maybe she should go back to her house.

She went down two steps but stopped. By the time she drove home, it would be time to drive back. She sighed and let her head fall back and the crisp air wash over her.

She'd left early because of the few snow flurries that were starting to fall. But that hadn't panned out into much. The snow had already stopped and the sun had come out, which left her here early. Cole wouldn't care—she just needed to go in.

It was as if all the sharing had cracked the wall that had stood between them all these years. But neither had a plan for what it would mean if it finally came down.

She walked back to the door and lifted her hand again. This time it flew open before she could even knock. Susie stood before her, dressed in a Cinderella dress over a pair of jeans and pink shirt, grinning. "I got tired of waiting for you to knock."

Susie pushed open the screen door and grabbed the pillow from Fallon's hand. "Did you bring your paints?"

"Uh . . . no." Shoot, she'd forgotten she'd agreed to that in her haste to leave. Maybe Susie would forget about them. Because how was she supposed to explain to a seven-year-old that she couldn't paint anymore?

"That's all right. You can bring them next time." The absolute certainty in Susie's voice erased any hope of her forgetting. Susie motioned for Fallon to follow. "I'll show you to your room."

Fallon gave a glance around the living room, but Cole was nowhere in sight. At least he hadn't seen how neurotic she'd been acting.

Fallon followed Susie up the stairs and into the first doorway on the right. Susie ran and jumped on the queen-size bed. The room was small but exactly what she would expect from a guest room. Just a bed, dresser, and side table. By the closet there was a pair of Cole's shoes he must have left in here, but that was all. Oh, and a shoebox on the dresser.

"Come on." Susie flopped onto her back on the bed. "This is the most comfortable bed in the whole world. You'll love it."

Fallon set her bag by the wall and sat on the edge of the bed and flopped back next to Susie. "Very soft."

"Soft? It's amazing." Susie wiggled with her arms spread out.

Susie was right—it was like the mattress sucked all the tension from her shoulders. She drew in a slow breath and closed her eyes. She couldn't quite put her finger on the musky scent, but it was rich and soothing. Maybe this weekend wouldn't be so bad.

"Susie, when Fallon gets here—"

Fallon sat straight up. Cole was three steps into the room, frozen misstep. His left hand paused in the middle of buttoning his right cuff. The rest of the navy dress shirt was still unbuttoned, and today there was no white undershirt.

Oh my.

With his bare feet and damp hair, she guessed he'd just hopped out of the shower.

"Are you going to finish your sentence?" Susie's giggle seemed to snap him out of it.

He angled away as he started buttoning his shirt. "Sorry, I didn't hear you arrive."

Fallon blinked around as he stepped over and opened the closet door. Shirts and pants hung neatly, each about an inch apart. His shoes in a perfect row on the floor. This wasn't the guest room. This was *his* room. She practically jumped to a stand. "I can sleep on the couch. Or the recliner."

He shook his head as he finished the last button then moved to his left wrist as he turned back toward her. "The couch is too small, and the recliner stopped reclining yesterday. I'll have to look at it when I get back. But I washed the sheets, emptied the nightstand, and even cleared a space for you in the bathroom. Think of it like a hotel."

"Sure." If a hotel held the heady masculine scent of the man who was trying to occupy her thoughts these days. Now that she thought of it, that wasn't the scent of a guest room. That was the scent of Cole.

The look he gave her telegraphed he tried to think through every alternative as well.

Fine. She nodded, and he gave her a tight smile.

"Thank you." He glanced at his watch. "I have to get going. There's some traffic on 31—probably an accident. And I don't want to miss my flight." He held out his arms. "Come give me a hug, little bug."

Susie stood and launched herself off the bed into his arms.

Suddenly everything felt a little too domestic. Too perfect. Too much of the life she'd always dreamed of but would never have. Fallon glanced away, her gaze landing on his dresser. An open shoebox sat on top with a few old photos next to it.

Wait. Was that her old horse in the top photo?

She took a step toward the box but Cole blocked her path, scooped up the photos, and slid them all in the top drawer. "Sorry, I hadn't realized I left it a mess."

"No problem." And now he thought she was being nosy.

He looked about ready to say something, glanced at Susie, then moved toward the door. "All the emergency numbers are on the fridge. Feel free to text or call. If I can't answer, I'll call back as soon as I can."

"Don't worry about us. We'll have fun." Fallon followed him to the bedroom door. "Where's Zane?"

"At his friend Jimmy's. He should be home soon." Was that tension in his voice? Over Zane or—he turned back toward Fallon as if to . . . what, hug her? Shake her hand? He seemed to be at a loss as well and settled with a nod and hurried downstairs and out the front door.

"My dad was acting weird. Probably because of Zane?"

Okay, so maybe she'd been reading into it.

She glanced around the quiet house. With Cole gone, she could breathe for the first time. Maybe it was still Cole's house and Cole's kids, but she could pretend for a moment she was just a babysitter in a strange house watching two kids she adored.

Adored? Where had that thought come from? But it was true. Somehow the kids had wormed their way into her heart and she'd found herself looking forward to this weekend. Susie was nothing short of a darling. And even though Zane could be a pill, there was a touch of vulnerability to his face that made her want to reach out and hug him. He might come across as angry, but the kid just needed to know that he wasn't alone. So much like his dad at that age.

She looked at Susie. "What's up with Zane?"

"It's not you." She held up her hands as if to reassure Fallon. "Don't tell him I told you, but I can tell Zane was excited you're coming. He was just mad at my dad for leaving again."

Fallon couldn't stop herself from pulling Susie to her side and kissing the top of her head. "I know your dad would rather be here with you two also."

"Too bad you can't come to stay when my dad isn't leaving." She walked out into the hall. "Or maybe you could. Dad said I could start having sleepovers with friends after I turn eight. And you're my friend. That would be super fun."

Um, time to redirect. Fallon followed her out of the room and down the stairs.

They had just reached the bottom when Zane burst through the door. He tossed his backpack on the floor and flopped on the couch. She pointed to the backpack. "Take that to your room, please."

Zane looked almost ready to argue but stopped, picked up the bag, and disappeared up the stairs. When he returned, he stopped at the bottom of the stairs. "What's for dinner?"

"Aren't you making us pizza?"

His face lit up as his shoulders lifted. "Right! I'm really good at pizza."

"I bet you are. Can I help?"

He nodded and couldn't keep back a slight smile.

He started pulling cheese and pepperoni from the fridge.

Fallon washed her hands and reached for the towel. "What would you like to do this weekend, Zane?"

He shrugged. "I think hanging here with you would be fun."

Fallon bit her lip to keep tears from her eyes. His kids had been through a lot and she was happy to be there for them in any way she could. Maybe this wasn't so wrong after all.

However, hours later as she stared at the ceiling of Cole's room, the unsettled feeling was back. It had resurfaced the moment she'd tucked the kids in and placed her toothbrush in her own mini drawer.

Why couldn't she just think of this as any babysitting job she'd once had? It was different because now this was what she wanted. She wanted a house. She wanted a family. She wanted a husband.

Fallon flung back the covers, walked back to the bathroom, and got herself a cup of water. She stared at her mini drawer then opened it. Shut it and opened it again. She pulled out the toothbrush, set it next to the sink, then shut the drawer yet again. Maybe this all felt weird because it wasn't just that she just wanted a family. She wanted *this* family. And she didn't just want a husband. She probably should admit the truth. She wanted Cole.

Maybe the problem wasn't that it felt wrong. The problem was it felt right, and this right wasn't possible.

Ever.

Even if she did believe him now about everything back in high school, the vague way he had answered her yesterday about Tiffany left little doubt there were still things she didn't know. Like it or not, she had a feeling Tiffany would always be between them, and she wasn't sure she could live that way.

One thing about working with Walker, it was never boring. Cole studied the bank of monitors before him, searching for anything out of the ordinary. But in a wide-angle view of a crowd, assassins, political supporters, curious bystanders, and pickpockets all looked exactly the same. Anyone and everyone on that screen could be a threat.

Fighting the jet lag that came with crossing half the globe wasn't helping his brain sort through the images either. He could barely remember it was Saturday. Maybe he should have said no once Walker explained the job, but money talked. Talked loudly in this case. This oil tycoon had cash to burn, including hiring security experts for his political rally.

Why Moneybags had chosen this spot was beyond him. It was an operational nightmare. The heavy civilian traffic was bad enough, but a shooter in any one of these buildings would have line of sight on either the stage or the motorcade's arrival point.

He respected that the guy was trying to unite his small country against the corrupt politics that had plagued it for decades, but he wasn't sure this was the best approach. The current regime had an awful lot to lose if the election went against them. Which meant they had an awful lot to gain from removing Cole's employer from the equation.

"It'll be fine. His own security is everywhere. We're just the insurance policy." Walker adjusted one of the monitors then sank back in his chair. "Seems like overkill, but I wasn't going to say no to that paycheck. Now relax."

"This *is* me relaxed." Cole studied monitor seven then picked up his radio. "Evans. There is an alcove thirty yards south of you. By the market, east side of the road. I don't like the looks of it."

"On it." Evans's response was professional, but Cole could hear the boredom behind it.

Cole set the radio back down, but Walker wasn't done. "You were my first choice 'cause you never get rattled, but if you clench any harder right now, you're gonna hurt yourself. What's up? Tiffany call again?"

"Nope. Radio silence for six months." He hated that she always seemed to be lurking in the shadows, resurfacing to torment him all over again. "It's fine. Life just feels off right now." He tried to will the tension from his muscles, but it wasn't happening.

"Is it the kids?" Walker leaned back in his chair, rocking slightly back and forth.

Cole shrugged. "Zane is . . . a teenager."

"That'll do it."

"I thought he was torqued about me spending time with Fallon, but it's gotta be more than that." Cole rubbed at his forehead, his eyes still shifting to every new movement on the screens.

"Hold on." Walker's gaze snapped to his profile. "Who's Fallon?"

"She's watching the kids while I'm here."

"Your babysitter? Cradle robber."

"It's not like that." He glared at his friend. "Besides, she's our age. I went to high school with her. We were . . . friends."

"And now you're *friends* again?" Walker gave him a look that didn't need to be explained.

"Get your mind out of the gutter. I said it's not like that. I'm helping her at her parents' place and she's helping watch the kids while I travel. That's all."

"You do the honey-do list and she stays home with the kids? So you're basically a married couple."

"No. Well, sort of, but definitely no."

"If it is really *no* . . . then maybe that's your problem, chief."

"What is that supposed to mean?"

"It means you're obviously into her, but you're trying to convince yourself that you're not. And until you're honest with yourself that you actually like her, everything will always *feel off*."

"All clear." Evans's voice came back over the radio.

Cole relaxed in his seat.

"Wait. Stand by." Evans again, and this time his voice was anything but bored.

Cole stood and grabbed the radio. "What do you see?"

"Possible shooter. He's in your building. Third floor, third window from the north end. I caught a reflection, could be off a scope."

"Trenton." Cole spoke to the guy in the building across the square. "Can you get eyes on him?"

"Hold on . . . got him. That room was clear a minute ago. I think he's alone but I can't see the whole room. Subject is setting up a bipod. Long rifle. We've got a confirmed shooter, boss."

What he wouldn't give for Trenton to be a sniper. That's what he would be if they were dealing with a fully operational SEAL team. But they weren't, and Walker might have bitten off more than he could chew with this job. But still. No one would die on his watch.

Cole checked the time. Their guy was set to take the stage in less than five minutes. They didn't have time to plan it. "I'm going up."

Cole bolted for the stairs, the hallway echoing with Walker's tense but clear voice updating the local security head over the radio. "Cole—"

He didn't think, just let his instincts take over. Taking the concrete steps two at a time, until he came to a section of missing steps. All that remained was a grid of rebar. There was a reason this building was empty. He tested the metal. Checked his watch. Four minutes. He scrambled over the rebar, praying he didn't hit a weak point.

It had been over a year since he'd done a live op, but muscle memory kicked in as if he'd never left. Once he bridged the gap, he didn't slow until he hit the landing three floors up. He cracked the door and used his mirror to check the area. The space was dim and debris littered the path, but the floor was empty. He glanced back down the steps. Walker was no doubt doling out orders before he gave him backup. He checked his watch. Three minutes. Less if the motorcade arrived early. He couldn't wait.

Cole slid through the door, counted three doors from the end. Bingo. He pulled his weapon and maneuvered down the hall, breathing evenly with practiced calm. He kept his back as close as he could to the inside wall without getting snagged on the mess of cracks and missing sections of sand-colored paint.

He paused a foot from the target. Light under the door flickered, like someone had walked in front of it then stopped. Maybe he hadn't been as quiet as he'd thought. He should wait for backup. Where was Walker anyway? It must be taking him longer to navigate the broken steps than Cole had anticipated.

The doorknob turned.

Waiting for backup was no longer an option.

Cole froze. *What am I doing?*

This wasn't the first time he'd put himself in danger, but before, the kids had Tiffany if anything happened to him. And his risk was for the betterment of the world they lived in.

Now?

Now, neither of those things were true. He'd leave them alone and for what? A few more dollars in his pocket. His stomach felt like lead. Why had he let Walker talk him into this?

No.

He had to stop this way of thinking. Distractions would get him killed. He shook thoughts of family from his head, eased into a ready stance, and waited.

The door finally cracked open and a heavily bearded man with a gun at his chest stuck his head out. The would-be assassin looked to his left. Thank God for small favors. Cole grabbed the guy behind his head. Yanked him into the hall and threw him to the ground. Unable to get his hands out to brace his fall, the man hit face-first, hard. Cole jerked the weapon out from under the dazed shooter and pressed his knee into the middle of his back while pulling zip tie cuffs from his tactical belt.

A gun cocked in the doorway behind him, sending an icy chill flashing through his veins. *Second shooter.*

Cole didn't need to speak the language to understand the meaning of the words the second man yelled at him. Cole dropped his weapon and held his hands out, trying to look as harmless as possible, while still positioning himself to try to disarm the man. But kneeling on a half-conscious prisoner with the gunman behind him didn't give Cole much of a chance. To make matters worse, the first guy was waking up.

His chest tightened in a vise. He could barely breathe. How could this be the end? Even as he tried to focus on the details of what he needed to do, he couldn't stop his resolve from melting away. All he could think about was Zane. Susie. Fallon.

And in that very moment, everything was clear.

He knew what he wanted. Wanted more than life itself.

Time.

More time to watch Zane become a man.

More time to hear Susie laugh.

And more time to make things right with Fallon.

A fear unlike anything he'd ever known flooded over him. How could he have thrown all that away like this? For money. He was a fool.

The boot to the back of his head sent him crashing to the floor. He rolled with the momentum and started to rise, glancing up just as his killer leveled a handgun at Cole's head, his finger starting to squeeze the trigger.

Then a shadow flew past.

A crushing force drove him to the floor on his back.

A deafening thundercrack hammered his ears.

Pain exploded through his chest, and his vision went black.

For a moment, he was aware of nothing but immense weight, unable to breathe, unable to hear. Unable to see. Then the ringing started.

The ringing in his ears drowned all other sound out, but he could sense the thrashing and grunting nearby. Pushing through the pain and disorientation, he levered himself up on an elbow, still seeing stars.

Walker had the second gunman on the floor in a hold and was desperately trying to kick a gun out of reach of the first man, who was struggling to his knees, wincing and holding his ear with one hand.

Cole's ribs screamed in pain, but he forced himself to draw in a breath. His vision slowly cleared and started to rise. Before he could lunge forward, Evans and two other guys—local security?—threw themselves on the first subject and pinned him down. Two more raced through the doorway to clear the shooters' room. Cole fell back in relief, then grunted in pain.

Game over.

Cole shuddered. Those words had almost had an entirely different meaning.

Walker bent over him, the weight of what it had almost cost them in his eyes. He poked his finger through the hole in Cole's shirt.

"At least we know your vest works." Walker was trying to play it cool, but Cole had never seen him this shaken. Walker closed his eyes, his voice barely a whisper. "That was too close."

"Maybe we should stick to testing security systems. Near Heritage," Cole croaked out. His own voice sounded odd and far off to his still-ringing ears.

Walker smirked. "Sounds like you figured out what you wanted."

Had he? He had at least admitted to himself that he did in fact like Fallon, but now he had to figure out what to do about it.

Because he wasn't so sure Fallon was on the same page . . . at all.

seven

FALLON HAD BEEN HOPING AND HOPING THAT the weekend would reset her perspective. That this whole situation was a means to an end. That she simply needed help and Cole just needed help. That there was nothing special about him. But as she put away the last of the clean dishes in his kitchen Monday morning, her perspective felt more skewed than ever.

It was as if playing house for a weekend had resurrected a desire that she'd buried so long ago and so deep that she'd forgotten how bad she wanted it. She had wanted a future with Cole so desperately once upon a time that she convinced herself that it could happen.

A home with him. Kids with him. A life with him. And being here eating at his table, tucking his kids in at night, playing game after game of Sorry with them, sleeping in his bed . . .

Emotions had resurfaced—desires she'd thought she'd left in the past. Because it wasn't just that she found him attractive, which was a given. It was that he had a way of bringing out her fun side, which, she had to admit, had been pretty much non-existent for a long time. Helping her enjoy life and yet taking every dream she had seriously. No one had ever believed in her like Cole. And the way he was with his kids? She could never have imagined how good of a dad he'd be.

But by the way he'd hurried out of here the day she arrived, she was pretty sure it wasn't a mutual thing. She had to pull herself together. Because as much as she longed for this, something in her resisted just as much. She wasn't exactly sure why, but she didn't trust he wouldn't hurt her all over again.

The front door opened, and Fallon wiped her hands on the towel then walked out of the kitchen. Cole stood by the front door, his duffel in his left hand. He finally spotted her. With a face full of scruff and hair that looked like he'd tried and failed to sleep on the plane, she had to restrain herself from rushing to him and wrapping him in a hug to welcome him home. Not the best start to pulling herself together. He dropped his pack by the door and blinked at her for a long moment.

If she didn't know that he was probably severely sleep deprived, she might be tempted to read something into that look. Unless—

"You're still here?" His words came out a little gravelly.

Right. Because with the kids at school and him getting home before they did, she didn't need to be here. So much for *unless*. Her mind had been playing tricks on her all weekend and she needed to get out of here before she did something really dumb.

She lifted her coat from one of the dining room chairs and slid it on. "Dinner is in the fridge. It isn't much, but I figured you wouldn't want to cook after your long flight. Just put it in the oven at 350 for thirty to forty minutes."

"You're leaving?"

Seriously, he was irritated she was here and irritated she was leaving? She stared at him for a moment. She wasn't a hundred percent sure what she was seeing in his eyes. Jet lag? Probably.

Fatigue? Definitely. Longing? Probably not that. She needed to stop projecting her emotions on him.

"I have a ton of work to catch up on after spending the weekend here. And you look as though you're about to fall asleep on your feet."

He opened his mouth but then nodded and ran his hand roughly through his hair.

She grabbed her bag and pillow. He stepped aside as she walked to the door. "The weekend went well. We really had a lot of fun. And even if Zane doesn't show it, he missed you."

She hurried out of the house, letting the door click behind her. She made good time of getting home. She shoved the car into park, got out, and hurried up the steps. No one was in the living room, but from the laughter coming from the kitchen, she supposed both her parents were in there.

"Hello?" She pushed through the door just as her father was pulling back from a kiss with her mom.

"You're back." Her mom playfully swatted her dad's arm. "Good. Now get this man out of here. He is distracting me from making more cookies."

"More cookies?" Fallon took in about five cooling racks of sugar cookies, half of them decorated.

"The postcards you ordered that outline the benefits of natural trees arrived. I thought if we tied them each to a cookie and gave them to patrons of Donny's with a meal, people might read them."

"I love that." Fallon snagged a bit of cookie from the broken pile. "Do you need help?"

"What I need is this man distracted so I can get more done." Her mom ushered them both out of the kitchen.

"What can I say? The doctor cleared me to get off bed rest."

"Good, then maybe we can finally catch up."

They walked over to the couch and Fallon settled on one end while her dad chose his regular spot on the recliner.

He extended the footrest with a slight wince. He wasn't fully back yet. "How did things go this weekend?"

Fallon tucked her legs up under her on the couch. "Good. Really good, actually."

"Then why do you look like someone tipped over your Christmas tree?" That was always her father's favorite saying.

"Tired." She *was* a little tired, but it was the easy answer. Because what could she say? She was falling in love with a man who wasn't right for her?

"It was good to see you in church this weekend with the kids."

A twinge of tension pinched in her neck. That was the whole other stress to her weekend. But that was a stress she might be ready to talk about. "How do you believe it all, Dad? I know what I was raised to believe, but sometimes it's like this fog I can't quite see through. I mean, for a long time, I blamed God for Robert's death, but if I'm being brutally honest, it sort of makes sense. I stopped doing what God wanted me to do and Robert died. But you and Mom are some of the most faithful people I know and yet you're on the verge of losing this place. Why would a good God allow that?"

"Whoa. Back up. God didn't take Robert to punish you. God didn't cause his death. A very bad man with a gun did. God could have stopped it and didn't, true. And we may never know why. But I do know that He can still use it in your life to draw you to Him if you let Him. But He *is* a loving God. He's not waiting to punish us when we mess up. But when we do mess up or the ugliness of sin finds us, He is there. Always there to walk us through it."

"Doesn't the fact you might lose this place make you doubt your faith at all?" She sank back into the couch and ran her hand through her hair.

"I want to say no, but that'd be a lie. I have spent a lot of time in that bed lately and I have spent many hours in prayer for this place. But I had spent many hours over the past few years in prayer over this place and nothing seems to make a difference."

"Then how can you still trust God? How can you still pray if it doesn't work?"

"Oh, prayer does work, my love. Time after time I have seen God move when I pray. But this time, I don't know." He reached out and patted her hand. "I do know that if God *always* did what I wanted, then He would be serving me, not the other way around. I serve Him because I love Him, and I love Him for who He is, not what He does for me."

She had never thought of it that way.

"I hope you don't give up on Him. God wants you to depend on Him."

"For a while after Robert's death, I was so angry I pushed God away. I think He is just gone. I can't even paint anymore." She hadn't meant for that last bit of confession to slip out, but it was true. And it was a little freeing to say out loud.

"First, you can never run farther than God can chase you. Second, I'm sorry painting is a struggle right now. But don't give up. I believe you *will* find your way back. Third and finally, you just said that you weren't living how you should before Robert's death. If you want to find your way back to God, then maybe figure out what made you first push Him away and start there."

Fallon stared out the big bay window, her eyes going to the porch swing. And just like that it was clear. She had pushed God away right there. Right there as Cole sat next to her, broken after finding out Tiffany was pregnant. Broken by the fact that the future she'd hoped for was gone.

She'd been so young. So immature. All she had seen was betrayal. Betrayal by God. Betrayal by Cole. He'd begged her to believe him—believe that he hadn't been pursuing Tiffany behind her back—but she hadn't.

God had taken everything she wanted in an instant. Everything she'd prayed for dissolved with Cole's confession. The worst part, Cole was only at that party because she'd had a fight with him about something so dumb she didn't even remember what now. God could have kept them from fighting. God could have kept him from the party. God could have done any number of things, and yet . . . He didn't.

He had failed her.

And maybe that was what terrified her about a future with Cole now. Not just that Cole would fail her again. But that God would fail her again. And she didn't know if she could trust her heart to either of them.

What were the chances Cole had enough food at home to scrape together even the most basic meal? He slid out of the truck and tried not to wince at the shift in his three bruised ribs. He was still beating himself up three days later for how close it had been. He'd arrived home yesterday morning ready to move forward with Fallon by—what?

Pulling her into his arms and kissing her like he'd been thinking about since that bullet hit his chest? Probably not. But at least talking to her.

But he deserved a medal for the restraint he'd shown when he'd walked through that door. Coming home had never felt so good. If there'd been even a shred of doubt left, it had vanished the moment he'd seen Fallon standing in his house waiting for him. Only she had taken one look at him and raced out of his house as if she feared he might chase her. But he had no desire to chase someone who didn't want to be caught.

He'd hoped to see her today when he worked at the tree farm, which had been way more painful on his ribs than he'd anticipated, but he hadn't seen her once. She'd been gone the whole day with Sadie. He'd stayed as long as he could, but the kids needed dinner.

A dinner he now had to come up with. What he wouldn't give for a pizza place in town right about now.

Cole let himself in the front door but before he could even shed his coat, Susie wrapped her arms around his legs. "You're home!"

Zane, who sat on the couch staring at his phone, glanced up out of the corner of his eye and then back at his phone. Cole had hoped his anger would lessen now that he was back, but the kid was as stubborn as he could be. Guess the apple didn't fall far and all that.

Cole bent over to lift her in his arms but stopped as the pain stole his breath. The kids didn't know about the ribs, and he didn't want to worry them. He squatted down to meet her eyes instead. "How was your day at school?"

"Great, we had a party because there's no school tomorrow."

"No school?" His gaze darted to Zane and back to Susie.

"Thanksgiving is Thursday so we get Wednesday off too." She ran to her bag and unzipped it before removing a roughly constructed turkey and slid it on her head. "I was a turkey in the program today."

Program. He closed his eyes as the memory surfaced of the orange paper she shoved in his hands while he was warming up dinner last week.

He knelt to one knee and laid his hand on her shoulder. "I'm so sorry I missed it, sweetheart. I completely forgot."

She shrugged and turned away. "Mom always missed them too."

The barb found its home. He was trying to do better but was failing left and right.

"What are we doing for Thanksgiving?" Zane spoke up for the first time from the couch. "Or did you forget about that too?"

He stood and glanced at Zane, ready to deny it. But what was the point? "I didn't forget. But I didn't think to plan something either."

"We can go to Grandma and Grandpa Smith's." Susie dropped the turkey and began twirling around the room.

Cole walked over and sank into the broken recliner. "They're in Florida, remember? They can't come back until the weather warms because of Grandpa's health."

The kids didn't even suggest his mother. They had only met her once in their young lives. The whole interaction had been painfully awkward. The choice he'd made with Tiffany had a large ripple effect, and one of those seemed to be being alone for the holidays.

"So it will be just the three of us." Cole clapped his hands together once, as if that made it less pathetic. "We can do a feast for just us."

"That'll be fun," Zane mumbled from the couch.

Susie climbed up on his lap. "I'm sure you'll do great at making the turkey. Then again, you did burn spaghetti and Grandma Smith said she didn't even know that was possible."

Cooking was not his thing. And a turkey didn't sound simple. But Cole had never backed down from a challenge and he wouldn't start now. Maybe Donny's offered a Thanksgiving take-out option.

"What's for dinner?" Susie laid her head on his chest.

Right. The original problem—tonight's food. "What do you think about going over to Donny's?"

Then he could ask about their Thanksgiving options as well.

Susie climbed off his lap and ran for her shoes. "I love Donny's. They have the best burgers."

He glanced at Zane, but the boy didn't move. Cole wasn't in the mood to play this game, so he stood, walked over to the table, and started fingering through the mail.

"Why can't we eat here?" Zane finally mumbled from the couch.

"I was working all day and didn't have time to go to the store." He opened one of the credit card bills Tiffany had left in her wake. He was only halfway to paying this one off, and there were two more.

"You're always working."

What could he say to that? It was true, but he was working for them. Working to pay off this dumb debt. Working so they could have a great Christmas. But Zane was looking for a fight and he wasn't going to give it to him.

Cole added the bill to the file and pulled his keys from his pocket. "You want to come with us? Or we can bring something back."

That seemed to perk Zane's interest. Not that he wanted to stay, but his teenage son seemed to thrive most when he had options.

Zane finally shrugged. "I'll go."

When he still didn't make any effort to move, Cole took a step toward the door. "Then grab shoes and a coat, we're leaving."

The boy pushed off the couch and slipped on his shoes but ignored the coat. It had to be dipping close to forty degrees out there, but if Zane wanted to freeze on the walk over, that was his choice. After all, if they cut across the square, it was only a few minutes' walk.

Susie lifted her pink coat from the hook and slid it on. The sleeves didn't quite reach her wrists. She must have had a growth spurt. One more thing on his list to buy.

It was a clear night and the stars seemed unending. The air was still but crisp, and every breath was accompanied by a white plume of fog highlighted by the streetlights. Susie ran ahead, making a beeline for Otis next to the gazebo. She jumped on his back then slid down his nose. Then again. Then she stood on the brass back and stared at Cole. When he got about three feet away, she had that familiar twinkle in her eye.

Oh no.

"Susie, w—" It was too late. She launched herself off Otis toward him with a hundred percent confidence that he would catch her. He did. But the action stole his breath as pain shot through his ribs. He set her down and took slow breaths, willing the pain away.

Susie laughed, completely oblivious. But Zane's eyes narrowed on him. "What's wrong?"

He hesitated a moment then nodded toward Donny's and kept walking. "Bruised a rib, but I'm good."

Zane gave a slight shake of his head before stomping past him and crossing the street toward Donny's. Did he even look? Granted, the cars were few in a small town, but still. Susie, on the other hand, waited for him on the sidewalk and grabbed his hand before they crossed.

They claimed the first booth available, and a waitress named Gina hurried over and handed them menus. "I'll be right with you, but just so you know, the James Tree Farm dropped off some special cookies. Every meal comes with one sugar cookie shaped like a tree."

"Maybe they're the ones I made." Susie's face lit up and she sat up on her knees.

Zane shook his head. "Those were all gone."

"I think Mrs. James was working on a batch when I was there today," Cole said.

"Miss Grace. Miss Grace." Susie waved her hand violently in the air to her ballet teacher, who had just walked in with her husband, Seth. Seth had taken Zane under his wing over the summer because Cole had been busy with two jobs.

The couple stopped at their table. Grace turned her blue eyes on his daughter. "Are you excited to be out of school for a few days?"

"Yup. I have been practicing my turns a lot."

"Good to hear."

"What about you?" Seth focused on Zane. "Getting any lifting in? I know you had basketball, but that's over now, right?"

"It's over." The kid shrugged. "Just been busy."

Cole eyed his son. Busy? Doing what? Holding the couch in place? Zane narrowed his eyes at his dad. Maybe he wouldn't call him out here.

Seth slipped his hand back into his wife's as he met Cole's gaze. "Don't forget the invitation for you is still open too."

Cole did miss his workouts. He had a few free weights in their basement, but being able to do a full workout would be nice. "I might do that. Maybe we can come together."

Zane's gaze darted back to his, but he couldn't quite read the expression. Interest? Annoyance? The two didn't look that different on the surly teenage mug.

Just as the two walked away, the door to Donny's jingled, and Fallon walked in, carrying a large box. The kids waved her down and she stopped at the table but kept her eyes fixed on the kids. "Are you having a good evening?"

"Yup." Susie bounced up and down on the seat until Cole tapped the table and she stopped.

"Oh, Zane, I have to show you." Fallon reached into the box and pulled out a colorful card with the words "Why the Earth Loves Real Christmas Trees" printed on one side and an advertisement for the Christmas Kickoff Extravaganza on the other. "I took your advice, and now everyone gets a card and a free cookie with their meal today and tomorrow."

Zane took the card in his hand and turned it over. He seemed to be trying to look indifferent, but there was a glint of pride in his eyes that hadn't been there before.

"Maybe you should go into PR." Fallon sent him a genuine smile, and something about it gripped Cole.

She had just turned away when Zane blurted, "Can we have Thanksgiving with you?"

Cole nudged his foot under the table and spoke to his son through gritted teeth. "You can't invite yourself over."

He cast a glance back at Fallon, but she had the deer-caught-in-the-headlights thing going on.

He opened his mouth, trying to figure out what to say when Deb appeared at Fallon's side, holding her own box. "What did I miss?"

Susie jumped right in. "Zane asked if we could have Thanksgiving with you guys, and Dad said that it was rude to ask. But we don't need to come over because my dad said he'd make Thanksgiving for us, turkey and all. Though he isn't that great of a cook so pray for us."

"Fine," Zane grumbled, then looked at them with an overly innocent face. "I mean . . . I don't think we'll die if you don't invite us. People live after food poisoning, right?"

Zane blinked his blue eyes up at Deb with such innocence. Innocent his foot. Cole nudged him under the table again. "Zane—"

"Of course you're invited." Deb patted Cole's shoulder. "You're practically family."

Fallon finally moved as she shot her gaze to her mom's, clearly not pleased with that statement. But Deb didn't pay her any attention. "Our table is your table. Now we need to drop these boxes off and we'll see you guys Thursday at eleven. How does that sound? Good? Good."

With that, she pushed Fallon toward the counter and away from them.

Cole stared at Zane. "Seriously?"

The boy didn't look apologetic at all. "Hey, I saved us from eating raw turkey."

Cole opened his mouth to argue but Susie's hand landed on his arm. "You know he's right. Face it, he just saved our lives."

His gaze found Fallon again. Yeah, they'd all be just fine.

But as much as he'd come to the conclusion on his trip that he wanted her, she seemed to have come to the opposite conclusion. Which meant spending a full day with her was the last thing he should do.

eight

IF SOMEONE HAD ASKED FALLON A MONTH AGO how she might spend Thanksgiving this year, playing Twister wouldn't have even made the list. She stretched toward the red circle with her left foot while struggling to keep her right hand on the yellow. She flipped her blonde hair out of her face, but that was a mistake because Cole's face was just a few inches away. How had that happened? When the kids had begged her to play, she carefully positioned both Susie and Zane between her and Cole for this very reason.

The entire day had been a catastrophe in the making. Ever since her mother had completely betrayed her and invited the family over for Thanksgiving, she'd been in a mild panic.

No, full out panic.

Cole, back in her life, back in her thoughts, maybe even her dreams. Finding his way into her heart, and bringing his children with him, to boot.

It seemed she was powerless to stop them from bulldozing over all her defenses.

And now, Cole's eyes locked with hers. There was a touch of

energy that had seemed to hum between them all day. She turned her head and dropped her knee to the mat.

"I lose." Fallon stood and straightened her shirt. "I'm going to work on the dishes."

"First we are going to paint." Her mom walked to the cupboard and rummaged around as Susie began to cheer and jump around.

Paint? She knew she couldn't put it off forever, but today in front of everyone wasn't that day. "I would but you need special paper and—"

"And I bought some." Her mom pulled a pack from a Hobby Lobby bag. "And a few sets of watercolor palettes."

Before Fallon knew what was happening, her mom had lined the table with newspaper and set up a little station for everyone.

She was about to make another excuse to escape when Cole spoke low, right by her ear. "What are you so afraid of?"

Besides losing her heart to him? That any painting she attempted would turn out bad. That she'd never measure up. That she'd wasted her gift and there was no going back. That it would show everyone that God had really abandoned her. Her paintings were the only place where she'd connected even a little bit with God over the past several years, and that line had been severed.

Cole picked up a brush and handed it to her. "Just have fun."

Fallon settled into a chair and dipped the brush into the water. When was the last time painting had been fun? "I don't even know what to paint."

She started to rise but her mom's hand touched her shoulder. "Paint the farm. For me."

She dipped her brush in the green and mixed it to the right shade.

"I'm going to paint the farm too." Susie dragged a stripe of green across the paper.

Fallon started with thin strokes but the whole thing felt awkward. The brush felt wrong. Maybe the color wasn't right after all.

And it didn't help that she felt like she was under the microscope of everyone at the table. All waiting for a masterpiece that she couldn't make.

Fallon dropped her brush, pushed away from the table, and stood. "I better get to those dishes."

"I'll help." Cole stood too.

She sent a dismissive wave as she walked toward the kitchen. "I got it, thanks. Keep painting with the kids."

But her mom was clearly not on her side because she passed him a stray dish. "Thank you, Cole."

Et tu, Mom?

Fallon walked through the swinging door that led to the kitchen, then over to the sink, and turned on the hot water. She added a fair amount of dish soap and set the antique china dessert plates in the bottom, letting the water fill around them.

Cole stepped into the room and stopped next to her. "If you wash, I'll rinse and dry."

He undid the buttons at his wrists and rolled up his sleeves, revealing strong forearms and a tattoo of an eagle, anchor, gun, and trident. There were some words too, but she was a little too distracted by the definition of his forearms to read anything. He paused his movements and she glanced up to find him watching her watch him.

She focused back on the water. "Nice tattoo. Military?"

He ran his thumb over it. "It's the SEAL trident. It represents that we fight by air, water, or land." He pointed at the words on his arm. "And that is one of the mottos. 'The only easy day was yesterday.' I got it after I separated from the military. Just a memento."

"You know what? I can handle these few plates. Go relax." She turned away with more speed than she intended, knocking over the short stack of dinner plates. They clattered on the counter, but none seemed to have broken.

Cole didn't seem fazed at all. "Tell me about Robert. What

was it like to be married to a Winterbourne of *the* Winterbourne Industries? Kings of Christmas. Movies. Ornaments. Isn't there even a small theme park?"

"Winterbourne Wonderland: Where all your Christmas dreams come true." Fallon shut off the water and started scrubbing the first plate. "Robert and I met when I was one of the lead designers. Have you ever seen one of their Tiny Angels ornaments?" She dropped the plate in the rinse water.

He lifted it out and reached for a towel. "Tiffany was obsessed with them."

"I designed and painted that whole line. I bet she'd love to know that."

"Wait. I'm so confused." He paused midway through drying the plate. "Didn't you inherit Robert's estate? I don't mean to be rude, but couldn't you buy this place outright? Or hire a whole crew to help?"

"It's complicated." She picked up another plate and scrubbed it clean.

"I bet I can follow along." He took it from her and rinsed it.

Fallon drew in a deep breath for a strong refusal, but it fizzled. Something in her wanted to tell him. How did Cole do that to her? She'd never wanted to open up to anyone. Until Cole.

"The first year after his death was hard. Really hard. I lost the desire to paint, and I took a step back from the company. When I was ready to go back, his brother Bryce told me there was no space for me. I think he was always jealous of Robert, who was set to inherit the controlling shares of the company. He couldn't take it from Robert, so he took it from me."

"But what about what Robert left you?"

"Turns out all of our accounts, the house, everything was in his family's name or the company's name, not his. So when he passed away, it all reverted to the company. Well, not immediately. They revealed that information bit by bit."

Cole's jaw slackened and he nearly lost control of the plate in his hand. "Are you kidding? The family didn't give you anything? What about his parents?"

"His dad never cared for me—always thought Robert married below himself. His mom was sweet, but she was very caught up in her own world. She joked that the only thing she wanted to know about the financials was how much she could spend. And after Robert's death, she pretty much escaped to their house in France." Fallon pulled the drain, and the water started to go down. "All I know is that at the three-year anniversary of his death—which was the week before I arrived in Heritage—Bryce gave me an eviction notice."

He finished drying the plate but didn't put it down. "What?"

She pulled off her rubber gloves. "He informed me that I needed to leave the estate, only taking personal items with me."

Cole's face reddened as his knuckles whitened. "You didn't fight it?"

"Let me take that." She pulled the plate from his hand. "And spend money I don't have in the courts? For what? They had all the documents to back it up. As far as I can tell, it's legal. Disgusting, but legal. Besides, you don't go against Charles Winterbourne. The world sees him like Father Christmas. To the family he is more like the Godfather—without the killing. At least I'm pretty sure there is no killing."

His grip shifted to the edge of the sink. At least he couldn't break that. Probably. "It's not okay. Is that why you don't go by Fallon Winterbourne?"

"No, actually, I never took his name. I had already established myself with my art as Fallon James and honestly, I think his father was relieved. They're very particular with their name being handed out."

"Robert didn't care one way or the other?"

"Robert only had opinions on the business and his racecars."

Cole looked about ready to say something but just shook his head.

"The worst part is I lost the rights to my Tiny Angels collection and that feels like losing a part of me."

"The Tiny Angels. All those ornaments—your designs."

"Yes. All mine. But not anymore."

"No wonder it hurts to paint." He raked his hand over his hair as his voice caught on the word *hurts*.

"It's like that piece of me is just gone." She picked up the turkey platter to put it away for another year. She opened the door to the china hutch but couldn't quite reach the top shelf. "I used to think my painting ability was a gift from God."

He took the platter from her and slid it on the high shelf. "And now you don't?"

"If it is, God took it back."

He stared at her, frowning. "Or maybe you just need to let yourself paint badly for a while. Get out your anger."

"I'm not angry." She headed back to the sink.

"What? Yes, you are. You're angry at Robert for not taking care of things like his estate, and if I read you correctly last week and a moment ago, you're angry that he chose his adventures over what you wanted . . . a family. And I think you're angry at your in-laws. And most of all, you're angry at God because life was not supposed to turn out this way."

She stilled. The words pulled an ache from her chest she hadn't known since the funeral. She was definitely mad at her in-laws. But was she mad at Robert? Was she mad at God?

For a while after Robert's death, I was so angry I pushed God away. Maybe it wasn't past tense. Maybe she was still mad.

She fought against that idea but maybe that was the root of it all.

She squeezed out the rag, her throat thick.

Cole leaned his hip against the counter, folded his arms, and dropped his voice low. "And you're still angry with me because of everything with Tiffany."

The words hit her full force and she closed her eyes. Aw, shoot, now her eyes burned.

"If it makes a difference," he said, his voice still devastatingly soft, "I'm angry with myself for everything that happened with Tiffany too."

No, no—she opened her eyes and turned her head but kept her body facing the empty sink. "I didn't think it was possible, but she's even worse than I thought."

Cole released a humorless laugh. "And you don't know the half of it."

"Oh, I bet I could imagine." Fallon willed her emotions back into control. "Did you know we were best friends until the third grade?"

"What? You two hated each other." He leaned his back against the counter.

"Not always." She shifted so her back was against the sink. "We used to live over on Woodlawn next door to her family and we were inseparable. When my parents inherited the tree farm, we moved here and a new family moved into our old house. They had a girl our age. Suddenly she was the new best friend and I was out. She told everyone I smelled like manure because I had moved to a farm."

He stretched out his long legs, crossing one foot over the other. "You smelled like Christmas tree manure?"

"We were in third grade. Kids don't think things through. It got so bad I wanted to change classes, but my parents were both teachers and didn't want to seem like they were asking for special treatment. They told me to grin and not let it get to me. It was a rough year. The worst part was it felt like my parents had taken her side even though she was the one being mean."

"I'm sorry."

"Anyway, it started about that, but it seemed to become so much more. It became about everything. If we both went out for the school play and I got the lead, she accused me of turning the theater teacher against her. We were mortal enemies. I actually started her nickname Regina."

"You started that? I never understood it. I just knew it made her mad."

"It was a *Mean Girls* reference. I hadn't meant to start it, but we were arguing one day in English because she took my seat to sit next to Ted. Didn't even ask, just tossed my stuff on the floor. I called her Regina as a joke. The kids around us laughed and ran with it because it was really fitting. She was determined to make my life miserable."

"And I got caught in the crossfire." He rubbed his hand across his forehead a moment, giving nothing away.

"What are you talking about?"

He finally looked up and met her gaze again. "Remember when I came to you and told you . . . everything. I had insisted that I hadn't pursued Tiffany."

Her breath caught. She could still see him in her mind, broken, telling her that he'd gotten Tiffany pregnant at a party he barely remembered. And she had just been so mad. So betrayed. "And I said I didn't believe you."

He offered a half shrug. "Well turns out, she'd planned the whole thing just to get to you. Only she hadn't planned on getting pregnant."

"What?" The air whooshed from Fallon's lungs.

"One night I came home from an op, Susie was just over a year old. Both kids were asleep and Tiffany was sitting on the porch nursing a bottle of vodka, staring at your wedding photo that made the news. When I was trying to help her to bed, she glared at me and said, 'I got you drunk and slept with you to make *her* mad. Now I'm a wife and a mom living in this dump. And her? She's marrying a billionaire. Guess the joke's on me.'" Cole pushed away from the counter. "Seems more like I was the joke."

The raw vulnerability in his face was more than she could take. She stepped closer and placed her hand on his arm.

"You weren't a joke. You *aren't* a joke."

"No? She was *stuck* with me. Her words. I don't claim to have been the perfect husband and we both know things didn't start with us the right way, but I tried. I provided for them. I never walked away. I just couldn't fix it." His head tilted back as his jaw muscle twitched. Then again. "You had a lot of guy friends in high school. I still can't figure out why she picked me to get to you."

"Because . . . I liked you." Fallon closed her eyes a beat. So much for staying to safe topics. She opened her eyes and looked at Cole. His eyes were back on her and his whole body still.

His intense gaze lingered somewhere between uncertainty and want. "You liked me?"

Here went nothing. "According to my journals, back then I was in love with you. But you know seventeen-year-olds can be dramatic. Anyway, I think she wanted to prove she could have something I couldn't."

He pushed away from the counter and stood up straight, his brows rising slightly. "You. Liked. Me?"

"Why does that surprise you?" He really needed to stop with the molten stare before she melted right in front of him. "Half the girls at our school were crushing on you. You were just too focused on your studies to notice."

"I wasn't too focused on my studies." He sighed and stared at the ground a moment as if weighing his next words. Finally, he swallowed and lifted his gaze. "I was too focused on hiding my feelings from the girl who didn't see me as more than a friend. Her best friend."

Her smile faded as her mind tumbled through it, processing what he was saying. Wait—*what?*

And just like that, they were well beyond safe waters. They were in deep.

～

With one confession Fallon had tipped Cole's world sideways. She had liked him too. Life could have turned out so differently.

She blinked, breaking eye contact before reaching for the towel. She dried, redried, then re-redried her hands. Finally she stepped over to the stove and tried to hang the towel back up. "That's not true. I'd have known."

"Not true that I had a crush on you in high school? Oh, it is true." He took a step closer, his chest nearly brushing her elbows. The hum between them seemed to vibrate off her skin. "You don't know because I didn't let you know. You had friend-zoned me—or I thought you had."

"I hadn't. I was just . . . young." She was still having no luck with the towel.

"We both were." He took the towel and hung it up for her. Then turned back to her. She hadn't moved and now her arms were an inch from his fingers. As if by its own will, his index finger brushed across her forearm. When her only response was the slightest intake of breath, his other fingers found her arm as well. Nothing had ever felt more right in his life. Every nerve coming to life with every touch.

Her tentative fingers found his sides. "If you had known—"

"If I had known . . . " His voice had gone rough and he cleared his throat as he ran a finger up her arm. "I would never have gone to that party." He traced the curve of her shoulder. "I would have never been tempted to escape into that drink." He followed the line of her neck, then her jaw. "I would have been with you. It was always you I wanted." A tremor passed through her body, and it took every ounce of his training to not rush the moment.

"Is that so?" Her voice had gone breathy.

"You were everything to me." He tilted her chin up, putting her lips just a breath from his.

"And I walked away. Breaking your heart." Regret laced her eyes again.

"Only after I broke yours." His thumb traced the edge of her bottom lip. She was soft. Almost too soft for him. But he lowered his mouth toward hers.

"I forgive you." The edge of her lips brushed his as she spoke.

"And I forgive you." He slid his finger to the back of her neck, then into her hair.

"Are you ever going to kiss me?" A beat while she took a shallow breath. "Or just tease me?"

"I didn't want to move too fast." He brushed his lips across hers in a feather-light touch.

"I know it's been a while since you dated, but if you moved any slower, we'd be—"

He pressed his lips gently to hers. He'd meant what he said, he wanted to take things slow. But as soon as she sighed into him, all sense of control left his mind. He deepened the kiss, taking time to taste and savor every moment.

It'd been some time since he'd kissed anyone, but he didn't ever remember it being like this, feeling like this. It was more than just where their lips touched. It was as if every nerve, every cell, every part of his being was content while at the same time hungering for more.

But he needed to slow this down. He wanted more, so much more. There was a lot they needed to figure out. He started to pull back, but when she released that slight whimper of protest, it destroyed any resolve he had.

Her hands traveled up his back then down again. He might combust. Because it wasn't just about this moment—it was about all the years he'd pined for her in high school. All the years he'd had to block out the memory of her. About how he'd wanted to do this from the moment he saw her standing at her parents' front door with fire in her eyes three weeks ago. It was a culmination of everything he'd been longing for and the hope of more to come. This was his Fallon, and in that moment, he knew he wanted her to always be *his* Fallon.

Her hands slid up his chest, tentatively at first, then with more pressure.

"Ah!" He jerked back. He should have been ready, but he was so caught up in the moment—in her—that he wasn't prepared for the pain that shot through his chest when she hit his cracked rib.

Fallon's eyes rounded as she pulled back her hand. "What?"

"Sorry." He winced as the pain slowly eased. Slow breath in. And out. "Injury from the weekend."

He must have failed at sounding nonchalant, judging by the way something dark clouded her features. "Is it bad?"

"Just a bruise."

"This job you fly off to. It's dangerous. Isn't it?"

Talk about a misstep. Her husband had put his love of danger above her wants and needs. Her husband who'd been shot and killed in a mugging. He'd looked up the ugly details on the flight home. Shot three times to the chest on a street in LA. The mugger had gotten a fair amount of cash but nothing worth killing for. It had all been a waste.

She still waited for his answer, and he refused to lie to her. But there was so much she already carried, and he didn't want her to carry the weight of his job too. Besides, Walker had said they wouldn't take another job like that. "We are very good at what we do. And what I did as a SEAL was much more dangerous. Now I'm just a glorified security guard for the elite."

"But you carry a gun."

"I'm an analyst. Who sometimes carries a gun." Sometimes two, actually, but he wouldn't mention that. "For the most part, we're working to find the weak point in security systems. The night I showed up at your mom's, your first night here, we had just done an infiltration exercise on a new four-million-dollar home built up in Traverse City. All guns were empty. Walker wanted to see if the system he set up was as strong as he thought."

"Was it?"

"I broke in six times, the first time in under ten minutes."

"So it wasn't as strong as he'd hoped."

He snagged one of her beltloops and pulled her to him again. "Maybe I'm just really good."

She ran her hands up his arms, steering clear of his chest. Stupid wound. "And so modest."

"That's my middle name."

"So you never carry loaded guns."

He slid his hands around her waist. "We do if the situation calls for it, but we are very careful. And we are good. We don't take careless risks." At least he never had before. The click of the gun echoed around his memory. He waited until she met his gaze. Reached up and tucked a strand of blonde hair behind her ear. "Trust me."

He'd meant for the whole action to be light and playful, but the words came out deep and a little rough. And with her wide eyes staring up at him, he had no doubt that he really needed her to trust him. To believe him. Her failing to believe him had been a huge fracture in their friendship the first time. He wanted things to be different this time.

"I trust you."

With that, his lips found hers again. But this kiss wasn't the hesitant exploration of the first. It was a promise. A promise from him to her and her to him that they would figure this out together.

"Daddy, Daddy!" The joyous yell gave them just enough warning to yank apart before Susie burst into the kitchen. "It's snowing big flakes! Come see."

She grabbed his hand and tugged. He wiped his mouth with his free hand and cast a small smile at Fallon. "Can Fallon join us?"

"Of course." She tugged again. "We like Fallon."

This time he let himself be pulled away but not before motioning Fallon to follow. "Yes, we do, sweetheart. Yes. We. Do."

nine

IT HAD BEEN TWENTY-FOUR HOURS SINCE COLE'S kiss and Fallon could still feel it through every inch of her body. In all the times she'd imagined what it might be like to kiss Cole, she hadn't even come close to the reality. The strength of his lips contrasted with the tenderness of his hands. She had never felt so protected, so cared for, so wanted. So safe. So—

Fallon drew a deep breath and lifted her legal pad. She didn't have the time to think about kisses. The Christmas Extravaganza kicked off Saturday at ten in the morning. Which meant she had just over fifteen hours to get any last-minute items done. She ran her finger down her list but everything had been checked off.

The Sugar Shack had been transformed into the North Pole for Santa. Edison lights had been strung around the tree lot. Cole had even cut extra trees and had them waiting for those who didn't want to search for their own. They were ready, and she needed to relax.

Easier said than done. In the past, painting had always been her go to for respite, but now? She walked over to where she'd laid out a piece of watercolor paper and settled into the chair. She blinked at the paper in front of her, trying to summon inspiration to paint the farm like her mom wanted, but her mind was empty. That wasn't exactly true. It was just empty of anything useful for painting. Half of her mental space was spinning with the details for tomorrow and the other half was taken up with the memory of that kiss. The warmth of his lips, the feel of his breath, his solid arms that had wrapped around her and made her want to trust him with everything.

Her phone buzzed with an incoming text.

JAN

Is this still you, Fallon?

She hadn't heard from her old friend in six years. Not since Jan had left Winterbourne to work for Hallmark. Losing touch hadn't had anything to do with her going to work for the competition as much as life simply got busy, and with the headquarters for Hallmark being in Kansas City, Missouri, it wasn't like they could get together for coffee.

FALLON

Yes! Jan, how are you?

JAN

Married with two kids.

A photo followed of two kids. There was a girl about three with hair as red as her mama's and a newborn baby boy, who looked like a cross between Yoda and Dobby. But she expected he'd grow out of that. She waited for the well-known pinch of regret, but it didn't come. Instead, the image of Cole and his kids filled her mind.

FALLON

They are beautiful.

JAN

I heard you are no longer at
Winterbourne.

She'd expected the rumor mill to do its work but not this fast.

FALLON

You heard right.

JAN

That is why I reached out. I talked
to the VP of Design and he wants
to interview you and see a recent
portfolio of what you're working
on these days.

Fallon stared at the text. Hallmark was her dream job. An impossible dream. But a recent portfolio? She looked over at her blank piece of paper in front of her. That would be one short meeting.

FALLON

Can I let you know?

The doorbell rang as she hit send. Her parents had gone out for the evening, so who could that be? She set her phone aside, stood, and hurried to the door. Cole and the two kids stood shivering on the other side.

"Surprise!" they all said together.

"We brought you pie," Susie said as she brushed past her through the mudroom and into the house.

Cole winced an apology but lifted the foil wrapped container in his hand. "Hungry?"

She tried to hold back the smile but couldn't as she stepped aside, holding the door.

Zane entered next and headed straight for the couch. Cole secured the door but then stayed in the mudroom next to her. His fingers found her waist but his action was still hidden from the kids. His voice lowered. "Hi. I hope you're up for some pie."

Her mouth went dry. "Pie sounds good. I really like . . . pie. I have thought about . . . pie all day actually."

His eyes took on a heady quality as he stared at her lips. "Me too."

"What is taking you two so long?" Susie poked her head in the doorway.

Cole dropped his hand and handed Fallon the pie. "I'm just removing my coat."

He shed his coat and hung it up. Then picked up that pie from Fallon's hands and walked it to the table. He paused by her art supplies spread out on the dining room table and lifted one brow at the blank page. "Painting?"

"I have been working on it all day. Isn't it marvelous?" She stepped up next to him, propping her hands on her hips.

"Inspired."

"I don't get it." Susie leaned toward the page. "I don't see anything."

"Can't you?" Cole moved down to Susie's level. "It's a polar bear building a snowman in the middle of a blizzard."

"Oh, I see!" she said, leaning closer.

"You do?" Cole stared at his daughter.

"No." Susie gave a dramatic eye roll. "And you can't fool me. I'm not a baby anymore. I'm seven and a half now."

"You'll always be my baby." He tapped her on her nose.

Then without warning Cole stood and picked up the brush, dabbed in the blue watery pigment, and splattered it on the paper. "There."

"What are you doing?" Fallon took the brush.

"I'm taking away the blank page. Now, move forward without the pressure of it being perfect on the first try." Cole's face became serious. "Redeemed mistakes can lead to something more beautiful than perfection."

"Wow, where did that come from?" And why did it sound so familiar?

"I just thought of it." Cole tapped the side of his head. "I *am* quite deep, you know."

"You're deep, yes, but poetic?" She was still studying his smirk when Susie began to laugh and pointed to the wall.

There it was scrawled under a photo of a Japanese Kintsugi bowl. Her mom had hung it there years ago. So long ago that Fallon had stopped even noticing it. But there was a lot of truth to that. The gold line that repaired the broken pottery made it true art instead of just a serving dish.

Fallon sat down, dipped the brush in the green, and splattered the paint much like Cole had.

"Perfect start," Cole said low in her ear.

It wouldn't be perfect. It probably wouldn't even be good, but maybe it was what she needed.

Cole lifted the pie and reached for Susie's hand. "Why don't you and I serve this up. Then maybe you and Zane can watch the movie we brought, and Fallon and I'll do dishes."

Cole sent her one meaningful look before disappearing into the kitchen with Susie.

Her phone flashed with an incoming text as the door shut behind them.

JAN
____

Yes, but don't wait **too long**.

She picked up her phone again, her fingers hovering over the screen. How could she pass this up? But how could she not when everything she really wanted seemed to be right here?

A distant buzzing sounded by the door, then again. What was

that? She stood and followed it to Cole's pocket. "Cole, your phone is ringing."

He poked his head out of the kitchen. "Can you answer it and bring it here?"

She pulled out his phone. "Walker" displayed across the screen.

She accepted the call and started walking toward the kitchen. "Hi, just a second, let me grab Cole."

"Wait." Walker's voice came through the line. "Is this Fallon? The one who was watching his kids?"

Fallon slowed. "Yes."

"Heard a lot about you. All good, of course."

She stepped into the kitchen and met Cole's gaze. His brow lifted in question, and she mouthed the word *Walker* to him.

Cole rolled his eyes as he continued dishing up the pie. Then raised his voice loud enough to be heard. "Be good, Walker."

Walker's chuckle came over the line in her ear. "Oh, the stories I could tell you. But I won't. Seriously, just checking to see how he's doing. But if he's hanging with you, I'm guessing he's doing all right. I promise we don't test our bulletproof vests very often."

Walker's words were like ice water over her head. "What?" Her voice was small even to her own ears. Her gaze whipped to Cole's. "Your what?"

Walker swore in her ear then apologized. "I should have guessed he'd BTF his way through it."

Cole closed his eyes a moment. Opened them and handed two plates to Susie. "You two start the movie. Fallon and I will be right out."

He took the phone from Fallon, said something to Walker, but she didn't follow the conversation. All her brain circled on was bulletproof vest and the way he'd pulled back yesterday during the kiss. The casual way he'd said *Just a bruise.* The way he'd avoided answering her questions about the dangerousness of his job directly.

Cole set the phone aside. "Fallon?"

"Unbutton your shirt."

He smirked. "Well, that is moving a little—"

"Unbutton. Your. Shirt." Her tone was flat and demanding but she had to know. She had to see it.

Any last bit of humor faded from his face as he reached up and undid his shirt. Each undone button revealing more and more of an angry deep purple bruise on the upper-right side of his chest that spidered across his sternum and over his shoulder.

Finally she met his gaze. "What is BTF?"

"What?" Cole started rebuttoning his shirt.

"When Walker realized I didn't know, he said he should've guessed that you'd BTF your way through it. What is—"

"Big Tough Frogman. It's a SEAL saying. Basically tough it out, don't show weakness."

"You mean lie."

"I didn't lie."

"You said you didn't take unnecessary risks. Was what you were protecting worth risking your life? Leaving your kids?"

"Yes. No. It's complicated, but we aren't taking those kinds of jobs anymore. That's why I didn't mention it. I didn't want to worry you."

"So you kept it from me."

"We aren't even officially dating."

The words were like a slap. "Right."

"I didn't mean it like that. I just mean—"

"No, it's fine. I get it."

"Fallon."

"Cole. I'm being serious. I'm okay. I just wasn't expecting that. Give me a minute to take it all in." When he only stared at her, she picked up a piece of pie and handed it to him. "Join the kids. I'll be there in a moment. Please."

As soon as the door swung shut, Fallon gripped the side of the table. He'd almost died. How had she let herself get attached to another person who preferred danger to her love. Love? The word did strange things to her. Then again, maybe it didn't matter.

We aren't even officially dating.

So maybe she was dreaming of happily-ever-afters and he was having fun for now. But that wasn't what she wanted. She wanted it all or nothing.

She slid her phone from her pocket and stared at the texts from Jan again. Hallmark. Her dream job was open and she was waffling about the interview because a guy kissed her. What was wrong with her?

FALLON

I am helping my parents through the Christmas season at their tree farm. Can we schedule it for after that?

JAN

A tree farm? Maybe I should send you to Hallmark Media for an interview.

FALLON

Funny.

Now she had to figure out how to make a portfolio when she couldn't even finish one piece.

She pocketed her phone, lifted her piece of pie, and walked to the living room, but she wasn't really hungry anymore.

The overwhelming scent of pine in the evening air surrounded Cole for the hundredth time today as he lifted a tree on top of a silver minivan. He schooled his face against the pain in his chest. Though the rib was better, it would be a bit before he was a hundred percent.

He knew he should have been more forthcoming with Fallon about his injury. But why couldn't she see that he was trying to protect her?

He stretched and tossed the yellow nylon rope to the other side. Glanced at Fallon who stood talking to a group of people by the entrance of the Sugar Shack. Her eyes lit with laughter, and long blonde hair curled out from under her pink stocking cap. Everything on the surface seemed normal. But she hadn't said anything more about his injury.

Who was he kidding? She hadn't really said anything to him about anything last night. No more flirting. No more banter. He needed to fix this—he just wasn't sure how.

Cole stepped up on the running board and secured the yellow nylon rope to the luggage rack, then tossed it to the owner on the other side once more. The man set to tying his side before tossing it back. Cole caught the rope and secured it for the final time. He stepped off the running board and tapped the roof. "You're all set."

"Cole." Fallon appeared next to him but kept her gaze on her clipboard. "When you're done with that, a family is waiting over by the fifteen-footers."

Fallon's professional, polite tone grated on him. Maybe it was for the sake of a couple dozen customers who stood around eating Deb's cookies. Then again, probably not.

"Sure thing." His words plumed in the frosty evening air as he headed toward where they'd lined up the tallest trees behind the Sugar Shack, a snowy path of lit-up candy canes leading the way.

He cast a glance inside the Sugar Shack as he passed. Wall-to-wall people were buying up the cookies or waiting for Santa. The cookie promo plus advertising about Santa and the benefit of real trees seemed to have brought in a fair number of people. Though he wasn't sure it was enough to save the place, they'd had a steady flow of buyers for Black Friday and today.

He caught a glimpse of Zane collecting payment for a photo

with Santa. The kids were thriving here. He couldn't hold back a smile. That was all he'd wanted for them. Life had been unstable since Tiffany took off, but now? Things seemed to be finally turning around.

He made his way around the corner of the building to the taller trees.

"Look over here, Lincoln." The woman who he assumed was the mother followed a kid with her phone videoing his every move. He looked about Susie's size. But as the kid wound through the trees screaming in what hopefully was joy, Cole couldn't imagine him sitting through a school day. Then again maybe it was one too many cookies at the Sugar Shack.

A man, who Cole assumed was the father, leaned against the shack next to the trees. He was pretty good-sized and should be able to help move the thing. That was a bonus.

He waved at the man. "Are you the family waiting for one of the fifteen-footers?"

"That's us." The dad pushed away from the wall but stumbled and lost his balance and braced himself on the closest tree.

The tree shifted and pushed against the next one, causing that one to slide. The next tree picked up momentum toward the next then the next. Cole was three steps ahead, scanning to where the final tree would fall. And the boy's trajectory. He broke into a sprint, grabbed the boy, then tucked and rolled just as the final tree crashed down in the path.

The tree landed with a loud thud but the noise was mostly drowned out by the mother screaming. "My baby!"

He untucked the kid from his arms and lifted him to his feet. "You okay?" The last time he'd saved someone like this, it was from gunfire, but the enormous tree seemed just as dangerous to a kid this size.

The wide-eyed kid nodded.

The mom dropped to her knees and grabbed his arms, looking

him over once, then again before pulling the boy into her arms and looking at Cole. "How can we thank you?"

"No thanks necessary." He'd been the idiot who'd lined them up like that.

The boy leaned up as if to tell his mom a secret, but he wasn't very quiet. "I think he's Superman!"

"No." The mom's laughter rang out as she reached up and brushed away moisture from her eyes. "He has dad reflexes."

No doubt the SEAL training had helped more than being a dad, but he'd go with it. He stood and brushed off his jeans. "I have two kids of my own. Do you know which tree you want?"

The dad walked over and picked up the kid, ruffling his hair. "What do you think?"

"That one." The kid pointed to the one on the bottom.

"The one that almost squished you? Way to look danger in the face and not blink." Cole tried to make a joke of it but was just thankful they didn't seem more upset. Lawsuit or bad publicity wasn't what this place needed. And definitely wouldn't get him back in Fallon's good graces. He walked over and began moving the heavy trees off the one they wanted.

As soon as he got them safely on their way, Cole went in search of Fallon. She needed to hear about this firsthand, not to mention he wanted to smooth things over with her before he had to leave to get the kids home to bed.

His phone rang and he pulled it out. Walker. He accepted the call and put it to his ear still looking for Fallon. "This is Cole."

"How quick can you get on a plane?" The words were muffled as if his buddy was packing while making the call.

When he didn't see Fallon in the Sugar Shack, he moved toward the parking lot. "Not tonight, that's for sure. What's the job?"

Walker hesitated. He hadn't given op details on the last two until Cole had arrived. "Guarding a birthday party."

Didn't sound too hard. Not up their alley either. "And?"

"It's in Venezuela."

His tone flattened. "And?"

"The kid's father might be hiding from the cartel."

"No."

"We are a new company, Cole. We have to take what we can get. It's good money. It's even more than the last job and—"

"No. I'm serious." Cole rubbed at his bruise. "I love working with you, Walker, but I need to put some limits on it. No more overseas. No more unnecessary risks. At least not for me."

"That's where the really big money is."

"I know, but my family is more important." His possible future with Fallon was more important.

"All right." There was defeat in Walker's tone but a touch of respect too. "Are you up for testing another security system out in Detroit this coming weekend?"

"I'll see if I can make arrangements for the kids and let you know by tomorrow."

He hung up just as he finally spotted Fallon talking to Sadie under the Edison lights in the yard. He moved that way, their laughter and words carrying across the stretch of snow-covered yard.

"Hey, Fallon, do you have a second?"

When she didn't immediately respond, Sadie's gaze bounced between her and Cole. Finally, she glanced at her phone. "Look at the time. I better go find David." With that she disappeared into the night.

Cole took a few more steps then stopped in front of Fallon.

"So another job came up—"

"Is the job dangerous?" She stiffened as fear returned to her eyes.

"No. I told Walker I didn't want to test any more vests. This is stateside. Just down in Detroit actually." His hand landed gently on her arms. "It also means that I won't be here this weekend to help, but I'm going to tell Walker no more traveling until after Christmas."

She nodded but the wariness in her eyes killed him. He'd finally gotten her to trust him only to destroy it with one dumb move.

"I better get the kids home."

She held the clipboard in front of her, verifying there would be no goodnight hug in his future. He walked away and went in search of his kids. Shoot. He forgot to tell Fallon about the trees. But if he turned around now, he might beg her to trust him again, and that probably wouldn't be a good look. He'd prove she could trust him again. He just needed time. But with Christmas looming close, he wasn't sure he had enough time.

ten

THE MAJORITY OF HERITAGE HAD SHOWN UP FOR the Christmas Kickoff Extravaganza, so why were their sales still so mediocre? Fallon sipped her coffee and retyped the numbers from the weekend's receipts into her dad's old adding machine. But no matter how many times she re-added them, they always came out the same—not enough. She rubbed her eyes from the lack of sleep over the weekend. This was why people hated Monday mornings.

Her mom slid into the chair across the table from her, coffee in hand. "I know that look. I saw it too often on your father's face the past few years."

"How can we have only sold this much?" She angled the adding machine toward her mother. "Over half the town was here."

"Half of a town that is only a few thousand strong is not very many. At least not when it comes to a business."

"Then how did you and Dad do it before?"

"People used to drive two to three hours to pick out their tree here. We could never have survived on business from Heritage alone."

Fallon sank in her chair and let her head fall back with a sigh, then looked at her mom. "I can't drive cookies to all the neighboring towns."

"No, you can't. We could never afford much advertising. We depended on the tradition of it. Happy customers came back year after year and told their friends. Our sales in 2020 dropped to maybe a fourth that year and it was like people forgot about us."

"Then what are we going to do?"

"If I knew that answer then we wouldn't be considering selling. We need to get the word out, but we can't afford the advertising it would take to get us back on the map." She pushed to a stand and lifted her coffee. But paused by Fallon's painting of the tree farm. "This is lovely. Are you done?"

She had spent the last couple nights working on it after they closed. A hint of the splatter Cole had made still could be seen, but rather than being distracting, it added character and texture she hadn't anticipated.

"You know people still want ornaments from you. I got asked more than two dozen times last night if you had any for sale. You could make this an ornament."

Fallon stood and walked around the dining room table. It definitely had her Fallon James style but rather than cute little angels, it was more serious. More peaceful. But ornaments? "That seems like a stretch. It's not like I have access to the Winterbourne factory."

"I did some searching on the internet yesterday and found several print on demand companies that might work. They wouldn't have the quality of the Tiny Angels line, but I think people would still enjoy them. Might be enough to bring a few more people to the farm."

Print on demand. She hadn't even considered it. She also had a few connections in the industry, assuming anyone would still touch her after her separation from Winterbourne. Then again,

Hallmark seemed willing, so maybe others would be too. "I don't know, it just feels too much."

"This sounds like something we need to pray about. The ornaments and our solution to this place."

Honestly?

Praying about it was always her mom's solution.

Her mom carried her mug to the sink. "I do some of my best praying while cleaning, so I'm off to clean the basement. If your dad wakes up, tell him where I went."

Fallon reached for the pot, refilling her coffee as her phone buzzed on the table. Then it buzzed again. And again and again. What in the world?

She lifted her phone and scanned it. Four texts from four different friends in a matter of seconds, and everyone pointed her to Instagram. She tapped the link and opened the app set to the James Tree Farm account. Over two hundred notifications?

She focused on the video, trying to figure out what she was looking at. A boy was running around at a tree farm. Wait, that was this tree farm. From this weekend. Maybe she should have checked her socials yesterday.

All of a sudden the trees began to lean and fall. This was bad—very bad. Then Cole appeared in the frame out of nowhere, scooped up the kid, and rolled out of the way of the falling trees. Frantic mom. Hugs. Then everyone was smiling. And Cole was a military hero in the flesh. How had she not even known this had happened?

She tapped on the notifications and chose the top one. It was the same video of Cole's rescue, but it was side-by-side with someone's reaction. The Instagrammer was a girl in her twenties who was a mix of girl-next-door and runway-ready. When the split screen showed a screenshot of Cole flashing an easy grin to the kid followed by a slo-mo of his tuck and roll, the girl in the other half of the screen fanned herself. "Seriously? Wow. Is Michigan too far to drive from Arizona to buy a tree? I think not."

Fallon clicked another link. This one had added a sticker of a Santa hat on Cole at the end with the words "Hot Santa" flashing at the bottom.

They had all tagged James Tree Farm, and the original already had over three hundred thousand views. What was happening?

Before she could even process all of this, the doorbell rang, and she walked over and pulled the door open.

Cole stood there in black-and-red flannel, wide eyes, and jaw so tense he might break a tooth. She held up her phone. "Have you seen this?"

He nodded and walked in past her. "I'm so sorry."

"Sorry?" She shut the door and followed him. He was pacing the length of the living room, looking a little like a caged lion.

She blocked his path. "You saved the kid. Good job. Any day that doesn't end with death on the James Tree Farm is a good one."

"I'm the one who stacked the trees." He pressed both hands to his head a moment, then dropped them. "We are lucky the parents aren't suing."

She hadn't thought of that. That could have been very bad. She shook the idea from her mind and laid her hand on his arm. "But you were there, they aren't suing, and the world—especially the female population—seems to love you."

His face reddened slightly, which probably meant he had seen the Hot Santa one.

Before she could say more, her phone rang with an unknown number.

She tapped her screen. "James Tree Farm."

"This is Channel 10 News and we were wondering if we could do an interview segment on your tree farm." They wanted to put her on the news? She glanced at the table and the lack of receipts.

This was all happening too fast to keep up, but maybe this was what they needed.

"I'm Ms. James. I'd be happy to give an interview."

"We were hoping to interview the guy who did the rescuing. Does he work there?"

"He does . . ." She met Cole's gaze.

He shook his head and took a step back, mouthing *No*.

"Can I call you back?" She took the number and ended the call before turning to Cole. "This free publicity might just be what we need."

He shook his head again.

"Are you afraid of the camera?" Even now at eight in the morning with a thick layer of scruff and hair askew he would get the ladies' attention. "You'll do fine. Any publicity is good publicity, right? And trust me, we need publicity."

"Need I go back to the point that I'm the one who stacked them there?" He leaned on the back of a chair, his knuckles whitening as his shoulders tightened. "I'm the villain in this story, not the hero."

All of a sudden, the pieces of what he'd said over the past couple of weeks fell into place. "Wait. Is that how you see yourself?"

He loosened his grip on the back of the chair, but as he met her gaze, there was a slope to his shoulders that wasn't usually there. "What?"

"You see yourself as the villain of the story. Of your kids' story. But you're not."

"No?" He pushed away from the chair and walked to the mantel, resting his hand on the top. "I should have been home more. I should have tried harder in our marriage for their sake. I should never have even gone to the party or trusted Tiffany."

His voice cracked on the last words. He walked over to the couch and sank into it, his head in his hands.

Oh, Cole. "Maybe. But that doesn't make you the villain. We all have made mistakes—some pretty big. And I'm guessing we aren't done making them." She sank next to him but pulled her knee up so she could fully turn her body. "Remember, redeemed mistakes can lead to something more beautiful than perfection? Or did that only apply to paint and paper?"

When he didn't answer, she pushed on. "It's what you do after you recognize that mistake that makes you a hero or a villain. Maybe you shouldn't have gotten into a relationship with Tiffany, but you did try to love her, provide for her, and protect her. You're still protecting her by not being fully honest with the kids. Maybe you could have been home more with your kids, but you were sacrificing to serve the country, and when you found out your kids needed you, you upended your whole life for them—bagging groceries of all things so they didn't have to start over yet again. You aren't the villain, you're the hero."

"I thought that I didn't take care of my responsibilities." He lifted his face, his gaze on her. There was a teasing tone to his words but a desperation in his gaze too. A desperation to know that someone saw him. That she saw him.

"I was wrong." She reached up and laid her hand on his shoulder, letting it slide softly down his arm toward his elbow. "I don't think I have ever met anyone who takes care of their responsibilities plus other people's more."

When she started to pull her hand back, he snagged it with his fingers. "I was still the one who stacked the trees there. Villain."

He turned her hand over and trailed his thumb across her palm. Fallon took a slow breath, trying her best to focus on the words and not how every cell in her body was coming alive. "You were also the one who put yourself at risk to save him. Hero."

"Why are you determined to see the best in me?" He dropped her hand, stood, and walked a few paces away. Laced his fingers over the back of his head.

"Because you see the best in me. You were so confident I could paint. Even when I wasn't." She stood and stepped over to the dining room table a few feet away, lifted the piece she was looking for, and walked back. "It isn't perfect. But it is something."

"This is amazing." He gently lifted it by the corners, studying it. "Are you going to frame it?"

"No. It's just dipping my toe in. My mom said I should put it on ornaments to sell, but there is no—"

"You have to." He met her gaze and his eyes were alight with ideas. "If you want more business. Let the world know they can get a new Fallon James ornament here this Christmas."

"This is not—There's no way—I couldn't do—no. Just no."

"Don't think I didn't notice you introduced yourself as Ms. James when you were talking to the news station. Maybe I'm not the only one determined to punish myself." He balanced the painting on the mantel then walked up to her. "I'll do the interview. As long as you do it with me, and show them what you can do. As Fallon James the artist."

"I can't." Her whole world began to shrink with the idea. "I'm not ready to show my art again. What if this was a one-time thing?"

"You'll show them that painting and tell the viewers that they can get ornaments of the painting here when they buy a tree."

She sighed. "Okay. I'll do it. When?"

"ASAP. Remember, I need to go away again this weekend."

"Right." A touch of fear traveled through her again.

"I'll be safe." He reached for both of her hands. "I need you to trust me."

She stared at him. He had never lied to her, but he was the master at evading. But that was a direct response. And hadn't she been the one trying to convince him he was a hero?

How could she not back that up now? She closed the remaining distance, her hands gripping his shoulders. "I trust you."

A weight seemed to lift as he slid his hands around her waist. "Well, you know—"

The door to the basement opened and he dropped his hands

as they both took a quick step back. Fallon turned toward the window, blinking rapidly as she drew a breath.

"Cole, I hadn't heard you arrive." Her mom's voice was slightly out of breath from the stairs. "I was vacuuming."

"Good to see you, Deb." He offered her mom a wave then pointed to the news station's number on the table. "Let me know what time I need to be there for the interview. I have to call Walker. Then we can make a plan for what you need done here at the farm before I leave. Oh, I should have clarified. It's Thursday to Monday. Does that work?"

When she nodded, he hurried out the door and was gone.

Her mom looked at her. "What was that about?"

"A video of Cole saving a kid at the tree farm went viral. Channel 10 News called and wants to interview him."

"What? What happened?" Her mom's brow furrowed.

Fallon played the original video for her, the number of views still growing by the minute.

"Wow, that's incredible. Talk about free advertising. God answered those prayers quickly." Her mom threw a triumphant smile over her shoulder as she disappeared through the kitchen door.

Fallon followed after her. "The viral video happened before you went downstairs to pray, Mom. I'm not sure that counts."

"God knew I was going to pray." She started pulling cans of beans from the cupboard. "He's big enough to start answering even before I opened my mouth. Can you get down the Crock-Pot? Thought I would put soup on for lunch."

Fallon reached up and pulled the appliance from above the fridge. "Then why does He need you?"

"Need me? I'm not sure He needs me. But He sure likes to involve me." Her mom grabbed the can opener and opened one can after another. "Because when He involves us, it allows Him to do His favorite thing."

"Which is?"

"Pour out His love in a tangible way. And this time that tangible way is free advertising."

"Then why didn't He do this last year? Or the year before? Are you going to tell me this is the first time you've prayed about it?"

"Of course not. I have been praying about what to do for years. Why is He answering now? I don't know. He doesn't run by our timetable. Maybe He needed your dad and me to trust Him more, or maybe"—she offered Fallon a pointed look—"He wanted to use all of this to bring together two old friends who needed each other."

"Don't—"

"Get my hopes up?" Her mom laughed as she poured one of the cans into the pot. "Oh, darlin', they're up as up can be. But even that I'm trusting to God."

This subject needed to change. "I think you're right about ordering the ornaments and I might need your help. How long do you think it would take to get them here?" Fallon lifted her phone and started searching for printing sites.

"Already ordered them this morning. They'll be here Friday morning."

"Mom!" Fallon lowered her phone. "How could you do that?"

"I knew you'd say yes eventually." She winked and returned to her task. "I just started to answer before you knew to ask for help."

She bit back a reply and headed to the door. She had an interview to prepare for. And this had become more than about the tree farm. It looked like the world was about to find out what Fallon James was up to.

She just hoped they weren't disappointed with what they saw.

Two days later as he waited for that interview, Cole questioned once again why he'd ever let Fallon talk him into this. He seriously felt like a show pony with the way the media was making a big deal over him. Cole tried to sit still as one woman held a light meter up to him while another brushed powder across his face.

If the guys on his team could see him now, they'd never let him live it down. He sighed. *Just think of it as camouflage.*

He glanced at the empty chair next to him. Where was Fallon anyway?

It was a nice day and they had set up the main tree lot with a good view of the barn in the background. If he guessed the angle of the camera correctly, the wooden letters that now fully spelled out James Tree Farm should arch right over them in the background.

Good thing he'd gotten all the letters fixed.

A woman with black hair and a polished look walked toward them with purpose in each step. "I'm Kaitlyn Andrews, and you must be the main attraction. And what an attraction you are." She eyed him up and down.

Yikes. But he didn't get the impression that she was hitting on him, just weighing his worth. But what worth? He extended his hand. "Cole Scott."

"Your name is Cole?" Her face lit up. "That is too perfect."

How was his name perfect?

She handed Cole a Santa hat. "They want it for the shot but that mug and those shoulders will boost the ratings all on their own."

He had never been a fan of social media, but today he might begin to loathe it. He'd get up and walk away right now if Fallon didn't need this publicity boost so desperately. She hurried away as he tugged the hat on and tried not to scowl.

Fallon stepped out of her house, taking in the whole crew on the lawn. He had seen a lot of sides of Fallon since she'd returned, but this boardroom-ready Fallon was new. And the more he got to know Fallon, the more he was convinced that there wasn't one side of her he didn't like. Her blonde hair fell around her shoulders in beach waves, while her white wool coat made her blue eyes pop.

Her lips were a bold red, and he couldn't keep from remembering how they tasted.

She held the framed painting of the farm. He still was amazed at how well it turned out. It was almost as if she envisioned the scene from this very point. The tree lot, the red barn, the lights. And unless he was mistaken, a recognizable figure in red flannel helping a family with a tree.

Fallon closed the distance and sat in the seat next to him. She leaned the painting against her stool and drew a deep breath. "You sure this is a good idea?"

"You'll be great."

She eyed his hat and bit her lip as if trying not to laugh. "Nice hat. You sure you don't want to be Santa?"

"Don't even think about it."

Kaitlyn Andrews returned and looked from Fallon to Cole then back to Fallon. "And you are?"

"My parents own the place."

"She's Fallon James." Cole sent her a look. She wasn't getting out of her part of the deal if he had to wear this hat.

The woman blinked at the name then did a double take at Fallon. "*The* Fallon James of the Tiny Angels ornaments?"

Fallon drew a deep breath, keeping a forced smile on her face. "That's me."

"Do you have anything new to show us?" The woman's eyes lit and she leaned forward. No doubt she was getting the story of the year—at least the story of the year for a small news station.

Fallon held up the painting.

Kaitlyn snapped her fingers and pointed to someone. "Move her to my other side. I want just me and Cole in the shot then we'll pan over to me and Fallon."

Fallon stood as someone rushed in to move the chair, then settled back into it.

"Quiet on set." A guy in a headset stepped back.

Kaitlyn straightened her shoulders and smoothed her sleek black hair.

The makeup woman reappeared, tapped his face one more time with a brush, then pulled away the tissue she'd tucked around his neck.

The reporter made a weird chirping noise as she rolled her head around and straightened her shoulders one more time before staring right into the lens of the camera and freezing with a smile on her face.

Was he supposed to do something? He glanced at Fallon, but she was just smiling at the camera too. He was about to ask when the guy behind the camera held up five fingers and then counted down with them.

"Thank you, Howard." Kaitlyn's voice came out loud and clear. "I'm here at James Tree Farm with Cole Scott, who has become quite the internet sensation overnight when he saved a young boy from a massive falling Christmas tree at the local tree farm."

She looked directly at him. "We have all seen the video, but tell us what happened in your own words, Cole."

What happened? He'd failed to stack the trees safely. He may have saved the kid, but he had also put the trees there. It was his job to see the threats before anyone else did. He'd failed and a kid nearly lost his life.

You aren't the villain, you're the hero. Fallon's words came back and he cleared his throat. "When I saw the trees moving, I acted out of instinct."

"Where did you learn to hone instincts like that?"

"Military." She seemed to be waiting for more, but she could wait all day as far as he was concerned. He may not be active but it didn't matter. No-information-to-the-public was drilled into him.

Her face grew a little tense. "Now you have to have seen all the posts asking for a date. Tell all our watchers what they really want to know. Are you single?"

What kind of interview was this? When he didn't answer, Kaitlyn laughed. "Is that a difficult question?"

"No. I mean yes, I'm single. And staying single." His gaze darted to Fallon but she was staring at Kaitlyn. "I'm focusing on my kids right now."

"Single dad? You just get better and better." Kaitlyn focused back on the camera. "What do you think, ladies, maybe getting 'Cole' in your stocking from Santa this year wouldn't be so bad."

Wait, *what*?

But before he could come up with a response, she angled toward Fallon. "But the story doesn't end there, folks. We have also discovered that one of the tree farm owners is Fallon James, the creator of the popular Tiny Angels ornaments. Tell us, Fallon, will there be any special edition Tiny Angels ornaments for sale here at the tree farm?"

Fallon's smile wavered just a hint before it was back in place. "This year I'm doing something different. We will be offering a limited-edition ornament depicting the tree farm with every tree purchased."

Kaitlyn stared into the camera. "I know where I'll be getting my tree this year and you can bet there will be other Fallon James ornaments here too." Fallon's face paled but Kaitlyn didn't seem to notice as she continued to stare into the camera. "If you haven't gotten your tree yet, come on down to James Tree Farm just off US 31 in Heritage. They have a lot of beautiful trees, limited edition ornaments, and one very hunky hero. Back to you, Harold."

She held her smile a moment then the guy with the headset yelled, "Clear!"

Just like that, everyone started to pack up all the stuff they had just unpacked. He glanced toward Fallon but she was already making her escape. He hurried after her up the steps of the farmhouse and inside. He caught up with her just before she disappeared down the hallway. "Hey, what's going on? I thought that went well."

"More Fallon James ornaments? I don't have more. One stretched me pretty far."

"Hey." He reached for her hand. "You can do this."

"Why do you think I can do this?"

He settled his other hand on her shoulder. "Because my Fallon can do anything she sets her mind to."

She took a quick step back. "I thought you were focusing on your kids."

Oh. He dropped his hands. "I just didn't know what to say. We haven't really said what we are. I thought we should talk before announcing it to the world."

"What do you want, Cole?" She stared at him, but what was he supposed to say? He wanted her, but if what Susie had said was right and she was only here for a few weeks, he needed to do a full reverse on those feelings.

Fallon nodded then disappeared down the hallway.

"If you love her, why do you have such a hard time telling her?" Fallon's dad's voice came from behind him.

He turned around. Tim sat in his recliner, stretched out. How had he not noticed him when he came in? He took a few steps toward him. "Love? Uh . . . I don't know."

"I'm sixty-five years old, boy. I know love when I see it."

"I just need to be careful. My kids—"

"Will be okay." Mr. James dropped the footrest of the recliner and sat up. "Do you know that God loves your kids more than you do? He has a plan for them. A better plan for them than you do. And they adore Fallon anyway, so that's a lousy excuse to begin with."

"I just want them to have stability. Their mom walked out on them—"

"Stability is a noble thing, but you can't protect them enough."

The older man pushed to a stand. "You can't love them enough. You can't give your kids a perfect life, but you can do the best that you can and leave the rest up to the One who loves them more than you. You told Fallon to take a risk with her art. When was the last time you really took a risk with this?" Tim pointed to his heart.

"But the kids—"

"Not the kids. Your heart." Tim patted Cole on the shoulder as he passed him on his way to the kitchen.

He wasn't about to disrupt her life or his kids' lives if this were only a passing crush. But nothing about this felt like something that was passing. In fact, for the first time in years, it felt like the only thing that seemed right. But was it love? Yeah, maybe it was. And if he was honest with himself, he'd loved her for a while now. And he'd never risked his heart. Maybe it was time for him to risk a little of himself too.

He walked down the hallway and found Fallon's door. At least he hoped it was the same one that had been hers in high school. He knocked gently. "Fallon?"

The door creaked open, her big blue eyes staring at him. "Yeah?"

He slid the door open farther and pulled her into his arms. "I want you." He leaned over and brushed a soft kiss to her lips. "I don't know if we can save the farm. And I don't know what the future has for us. But I want to try and figure that out together. I'll stand by you while you paint, and you stand by me while I try and figure out how to be a dad."

She nodded and rose on her toes and pressed her lips against his. "I like the sound of that."

So did he. Maybe he didn't have to have a strategy for everything. Maybe they could figure it out as they went together.

eleven

OW COULD TIFFANY HAVE WALKED AWAY from this? Fallon would give anything to be a mom. She smoothed the hair from Susie's eyes again as she sang out the final notes of "Baby Mine." When Susie's face relaxed and her breathing deepened, Fallon stood and switched off the small bedside light. She walked out the door, leaving it open a crack, then made her way down the hall to Zane's room.

His door was open, so she peeked in. He had his nose buried in a book. "Don't read too late. Monday mornings are never fun."

He glanced up. "I'm only going to read another chapter."

"Thanks for painting with us. Your tank flamethrowing the Christmas tree was . . . creative. Very festive."

A small smile tugged at his face. "Nothing says Christmas like Santa in a tank. It was fun."

It had been fun. Letting go. Painting for enjoyment rather than aiming for the perfect product. Cole had been right. Once she had broken through her emotional wall, the inspiration was returning.

"We'll hang them on the tree after school tomorrow so the tree will be decorated when your dad gets home tomorrow night."

His smile dimmed a little as he nodded then focused back on his book.

She shut the door partway and made her way down the narrow steps to the main living area. The remains of their painting still littered the table. Zane had offered to help clean up, but she had dismissed the help. She had more still inside her and there was just something about the muddy rinse water with the brushes sticking out and the table full of creations that made her feel like tonight had been the family moment she'd always longed for. And she wasn't quite ready to let that go.

Even if Cole wasn't here to enjoy it.

He'd left on Thursday, and for some reason, seeing him go had wrapped a cold hand around her heart, despite his words from earlier. *I'm an analyst. Who sometimes carries a gun.* She focused on what else he'd told her. *I told Walker I didn't want to test any more vests.* He seemed to specialize in indirect answers. But she could trust him, right?

She settled down into the chair and picked up a brush. There were few places where life felt right—calm. At the tree farm with her parents. When she had a paintbrush in hand. And after this weekend . . . she could add being with Cole or his kids to that list. And that idea terrified her.

She was possibly losing the farm, and she had lost so much with her painting. And now she was falling in love with these kids—with Cole . . .

Please, God. She couldn't lose him too. It wasn't much of a prayer, and no answer came, but a peace settled over her. How long had it been since she prayed? Too long.

She stared at the image she had started earlier. She had modeled it after a photo she'd seen on the fridge of Cole and the kids. Susie was an infant cradled in the crook of Cole's left arm, while he held Zane with his right arm as the boy reached out to place an ornament on the tree.

The moment she'd seen it, the image had pulled the air from her lungs in a swirl of energy that she hadn't felt in a long time. That energy had traveled through her down to her fingertips, screaming to get out.

It was far from being complete, but the image had begun to take shape. It was like painting her own Christmas fantasy. Fallon dipped her brush in the green paint and dragged the long stroke across the watercolor paper following the light sketch she had put there earlier, letting herself get lost in the image.

The perfect Christmas moment. She just wanted to hold on to it.

A sharp knock on the door broke the silence and Fallon glanced at the time. It was past ten—who could that be?

She stood and tried to peek through the curtain. It was a woman, but she was backlit by the porch light. There wasn't a lot of crime in Heritage and the woman looked like a strong wind could blow her over, so how dangerous could she be?

Fallon cracked the door. "Can I help you?"

The woman's eyes widened and blinked a few times. "You?"

It took Fallon a second longer to put the pieces together. Tiffany was older and her life choices hadn't been kind to her, but there was no denying it was the same girl who had tortured her from third grade all the way through high school. Same long light brown hair. Same overdone eyelashes. And if she wasn't mistaken, the same bright shade of pink lipstick.

Tiffany seemed to snap out of the shock before Fallon and pushed past Fallon into the house, the heels from her boots clicking across the floor. "I'm here for my kids."

Fallon shot a look toward the stairs and lowered her voice. "They're sleeping and Cole's not here right now, so I think it is best if you leave."

"Where's Cole? Is he seriously shacking up with you?"

Fallon's mouth fell open. "What? No! I'm here watching the kids."

"You're babysitting my kids?" She gave Fallon a once-over. "Still trying to take my husband?"

Seriously? "Last I checked, Cole wasn't your husband."

"On paper maybe. But I can't say he doesn't enjoy my little drop-bys." With that smirk, there was no doubt Tiffany was just trying to push her buttons. But it wouldn't work.

Then Cole's voice drifted back from a couple weeks back. *She resurfaces every once in a while to ask for money, but she has had no contact with the kids.* Was there more? She didn't want to believe it, but the memory of his bruise came back. He was a master at evading things he didn't want to tell her.

Tiffany seemed satisfied with how she'd rattled Fallon and walked over to the stairs, but Fallon blocked her path. "What do you think you're doing?"

"I'm going to get my kids."

Fallon crossed her arms in front of her and stood up straight. Not that she was intimidating, but she refused to cower to Tiffany. "I told you they're asleep, and they definitely aren't going anywhere with you."

"Those are my kids." She jabbed a bony finger up the steps. "Not yours."

"I know you don't have custody and he left them in my care. I cannot and will not let you near them. Cole will be back tomorrow. You can come back and take it up with him."

Tiffany's face hardened. "I'll bring the sheriff."

"Then bring the sheriff. Unless you can produce papers that verify that you have custody of these kids, I don't think he'll do a thing about it. If you try to take the kids, I'll make the call myself." Fallon pointed to the door and waited until Tiffany started walking that way.

Her heart pounded against her chest.

Finally, Tiffany walked out the door. But the moment she reached the top of the steps on the porch she turned back. "Why are you sticking your nose into this anyway? It's none of your concern."

Fallon stepped out on the porch and pulled the door mostly shut. "It may not be my concern and maybe those aren't my kids, but I care about them and I care about Cole."

Tiffany made it down one step when the door swung open.

"Mom?" It was Susie.

Tiffany's face lit up, all of the venom gone. "Hey, sweetheart." She crouched and held open her arms.

Susie ran out in her nightgown and wrapped her arms around her mom. "I knew you'd come. I just knew it."

Zane had also come down and stood a few feet behind Susie, staring at his mom with an unreadable expression.

"Are you staying here or taking us?" Susie looked up at her mom without letting go. "Do I need to get my shoes?"

"I *was* going to take you guys with me tonight." Tiffany cradled her daughter's face in her hands. "But Miss Fallon here said she won't let me. She even threatened to call the sheriff."

The words hit her like a sucker punch. Because they weren't wrong, and the betrayal on Susie's face nearly crushed Fallon.

The little girl's eyes narrowed. "She's my mom. Not you. You'll never be my mom."

Another punch.

"I told her that." Tiffany kissed the top of Susie's head. "Go in and get warm. You're shivering."

"Why can't I go with her?" Tears sprang to Susie's eyes.

"It's not that simple." Fallon reached for Susie but the little girl pulled back. "Your dad has custody, and I can't let you go with her unless he gives me permission."

Tears ran down Susie's face and she pushed past Fallon into the house. Then turned, her words spiking the air. "I hate you!"

Tiffany finally looked at Zane standing just inside the door. "My, my, aren't you getting big? Looking more and more like your father every day."

When he didn't respond, a bit of the innocent expression disappeared from her face. "And the look you're giving me means you're turning out like him too."

Zane didn't comment, he just walked away. He hadn't asked to go with his mom or even where she'd been.

Susie came running back with her stuffed rabbit under her arm, a half-zipped bag in hand, and her coat buttoned over her nightgown. "I'm coming, Mom."

Fallon tried to catch her, but she slapped at her, running out the door.

Tiffany caught her. "I'm sorry, sweetheart. I don't want Fallon to call the police."

"But, Mom—"

Tiffany's phone rang and she answered it, holding her finger up to her daughter, whose eyes brimmed with tears. "I'm leaving now. No, I'll have to come back."

Come back for the kids? Come back for money? Probably the second.

She hung up and slid the phone in her pocket.

"I have to go, sweetheart." Tiffany walked down the steps without even a final hug. "I'll call your dad tomorrow and we'll get it all sorted out. He won't let Fallon keep you from me."

Susie stood staring, weeping, as her mom slid into the car and pulled away. Fallon stepped up next to her, but the little girl whirled around. "Stay away from me!"

The bag dropped out of her grip, and the contents spilled down the steps. Susie ran back into the house, slamming the door, followed by a faint click locking Fallon out. At least now she knew where the key was.

Fallon squatted down and gathered a random collection of items Susie had packed. Her dolls, her favorite princess dress, and a pack of gum. She wedged her hand through the gap in the steps to a doll dress that had fallen through. Finally, after what seemed like forever, with frozen fingers she unlocked the door and went inside.

She was two steps into the house when cold liquid hit her in the chest. Muddy gray water dripped down her white sweater and blue pants. She looked up at Susie standing a few feet away. Tears raked down her face and she held one of the glasses they'd used to rinse the brushes.

"I want you to go home." The little girl hiccupped a sob then threw down the glass and ran up the stairs.

Zane looked ready to speak but stopped and followed her.

Fallon locked the door then leaned against it. Was that her bag by the door? Susie must have carried it down in an attempt to get her to leave. At least that made changing easier.

She stepped over and unzipped it but stopped. Puddled inside was the water from the other rinse cups. Everything she had was wet with dirty gray paint water.

She stood, her gaze traveling to the table. Not only were all the cups of dirty water missing but all the watercolor work from their evening had been torn to shreds and several of her paintbrushes had been snapped in two.

Fallon picked up her dripping bag and carried it to the laundry room just off the kitchen. She dumped everything in the washer and added soap as she bit back the tears. Clothes could be washed, paintings redone, and new brushes bought. But those kids just wanted their mom.

She needed to stop lying to herself. Their mom wasn't her and never would be her. There was no happy ending waiting for her at the end of this Christmas fantasy.

Cole had never been this anxious to get home and leave a job behind, even the one where he'd taken a bullet to his chest, and that was saying something. Because it wasn't the *what* of the job that was getting to him but the *where*. Or more specifically, the *who* he was working for—Charles Winterbourne. Fallon's former father-in-law. After everything she'd shared with him, it took his highly trained skills to stay on task and not go rogue with his own plan. What he wouldn't give to have five minutes with that guy. But powerful men like that were never home anyway.

So Cole had done his task and gotten out of there as soon as he could. Walker tried to talk him into waiting until morning before he took off, but just being around the whole operation had settled under his skin and he wanted—no, needed—to see Fallon. He was a protector—a fixer—and yet he could do nothing about this. It killed him. It was that feeling of helplessness that had solidified the fact he was pretty sure he was falling in love with her.

Cole flicked his blinker, exited off US 31, and turned right toward Heritage. The dark road stretched out before him, and he didn't expect to see another car before he arrived at his driveway five miles ahead. He shifted to high beams, but the snow that had started to drift down from the dark sky created a lightspeed effect and he dimmed them again. Heritage was pretty quiet after ten but by three in the morning, it was stone cold dead.

Life with Tiffany had been different. In the beginning, they'd been two kids trying to survive the consequences of their choices. And even by the end, love had little to do with it. But he'd been committed to making it work. She had not.

Over the past four days he *had* come to one conclusion. Mr. James had been right. God cared about his kids more than he did, and maybe it was time to start acting like he believed that. And just maybe he was ready to start again. Marriage—yeah, maybe that too.

Cole slowed as he approached his house and shut off the headlights before he turned into his driveway. He didn't want to chance waking the kids at three in the morning, and with the full moon, combined with the snow outlining the drive, he didn't need them. He cut the engine and slid out of the Blazer and grabbed his bag from the back.

He hurried up the steps and pulled out his key, but stopped. What was he thinking? If Fallon heard him, she'd think someone was breaking in.

He glanced back at his car, but it wasn't like he could sleep in his car with the temperatures below freezing. And the way the snow had begun to come down, driving thirty minutes to the nearest hotel wouldn't be smart. He definitely hadn't thought this through. Thinking things through was what he did. What was wrong with him?

He ran through possible scenarios in his head but only came up with one that might work. He had to be quiet and try and get comfortable on a couch half his size.

He slid the key into the lock and clicked it open. The light over the dining room table had been left on, so at least he wouldn't risk tripping over anything. He set his duffel by the front door and took a step toward the couch but froze. Fallon stood by the couch with her arms crossed over her chest and eyes wide. "Cole?"

"Sorry. Didn't mean to scare you."

She checked the time. "What are you doing here?"

"Decided to drive home tonight." Because it was a better option than hunting down a multi-millionaire and giving him a piece of his mind. *Because I needed to see you. Because everything in me wants to protect you.* But maybe he couldn't say all that quite yet. "Why don't you go up to bed? I'll take the couch."

She shook her head and stretched. "You'll never fit on that thing. I can grab my stuff and drive home. No, wait. We need to talk."

Cole took in her oversized T-shirt and sweatpants. "Are those my clothes?"

"Sorry. I was going to wash them." She blinked at him. Maybe she'd fallen asleep on the couch and he woke her. "Mine are all in the dryer. We had an . . . incident and my clothes all got . . . dirty."

"It's not a problem." Why was his voice so low and husky? Because there was something about seeing her there wrapped in his clothes that made her feel . . . his. His to care for. His to protect.

No matter where he went, no matter what he chose to do with his career, he wanted to come home to her. There would always be reasons not to love someone. Not to trust. But with Fallon, there were so many reasons to love her.

He took a step toward her, his finger toying with the sleeve of the shirt. "Looks good on you."

"Thanks, but—"

"It looks *really* good on you." He brushed his fingers along her shoulders, stopping at the base of her neck.

The shrill in the little girl's voice traveling down the stairs was like a bucket of ice water to the moment.

They both turned but Susie wasn't there.

"Daddy." It came again.

Cole dashed up the stairs to her room. He did a quick scan for threats but she was alone. Her eyes were open but she didn't seem fully awake. He sat on the edge of the bed and smoothed her hair back. "It's okay. I'm here."

She blinked a few times then sat up and gripped him in a viselike hug. "I couldn't find you and I couldn't find Mommy."

"I'm back. It's all okay now." He kissed the top of her head and she seemed to melt into him.

The little girl tucked her rabbit under her chin. "Is Fallon going home?"

He reached out his hand to Fallon, who stood in the doorway. She stepped forward and took it. Her hand was a little cool. Maybe he needed to turn up the heat. "Probably, but tomorrow we'll go over—"

"No." She spotted Fallon and her face contorted into a frown as she threw a stuffed turtle at her. "Go away."

Fallon dropped his hand, her footsteps retreating down the stairs.

Susie seemed to think she won and sank into his chest. "I never want to see her again."

He needed to ask more, but he wanted her back to sleep so he could go talk with Fallon.

He laid her back on her pillow and Susie seemed to drift back off immediately.

He stood and stared down at his daughter. Last he had heard, Fallon could do no wrong in Susie's eyes.

He drew a few slow breaths then hurried down the stairs. Fallon was pulling clothes from the dryer and shoving them into a duffel. "I was trying to tell you."

He leaned his shoulder in the doorway. "What happened?"

"Tiffany showed up tonight."

He bit back a few words. He should've expected that, especially if his ex-wife had caught the interview. He released a sigh and ran his hand over his head. "Let me guess, after their bedtime. That's always her MO."

"That might have been helpful information." She went back to her laundry, her movements hurried and jerky. She dropped a shirt but didn't grab it.

He bent over and lifted the shirt, but she snatched it from his hand. He returned to his position in the doorway.

Finally, she paused and looked at him, her eyes more uncertain. "She suggested she shows up late to spend time with you."

"No!" He stood up straight. "She shows up for money, that's all.

Honest, we haven't touched each other since before the divorce. And if you really want to know, it was long before that. Believe me. Since the divorce, she has shown up a few times. Every time she says she wants to see the kids and every time I give her a couple grand to leave."

"Why would you do that?" She stood and dropped the bag, her shoulders slumped. "Don't you care that Susie is desperate for her mother?"

"You think I don't care? Her mother is a master manipulator, and I don't want to put the kids through any more of that." His voice rose and he paused to draw a calming breath. He wasn't angry at Fallon. "The first time she showed up, I offered her the money as a joke, but she jumped on it. And I knew—she wasn't there for the kids."

He took a step closer and laid his hands gently on her arms. "She was there to use them to get more money out of me. And I decided that I would give up the money and more to keep her from using them like that."

"You need to be more honest with them. They can handle it."

"I don't want them to have to handle it." He tucked a stray blonde hair behind her ear. "Do I care that Susie is desperate for her mother? I care more about that little girl than I ever thought possible. And I don't want to destroy the only good memories she has left of her mom. My whole world has become about protecting them even when it hurts me." Cole started to back up, but she snagged his wrist.

"And who's protecting you?"

"I think I can handle it."

He started to turn but she didn't let go. "I'm serious, Cole. I know you can handle yourself here." Her free hand landed on his bicep and the warmth of it soaked through his shirt. "But what about here?" She moved it over his heart.

He didn't have an answer for that. It had been so long since anyone cared for his heart.

Fallon zipped up her bag, carried it to the front door, then walked to the table and started cleaning up the painting supplies. He gathered up the dirty paper towels and carried them to the trash. He pressed the lever with his foot, popping the top, but froze. It was full of paper that had been torn up. And a few broken paintbrushes.

He picked up the top piece. It was part of an awkward, blobby tree. He picked up another and turned it over in his hand. It had a young Zane's face on it. The likeness was uncanny, but the watercolor made it feel magical.

"This is amazing. Why did you tear it up?"

"I didn't. Susie did after I wouldn't let her go with Tiffany."

"Fallon, I'm sorry. She shouldn't have—"

"She was hurting."

He stared back at the paper. It wasn't complete but what was there captivated him. "I think it's better than even your Tiny Angels collection you're so famous for. God may have closed that door, but He isn't done with you. I can promise you that."

"Yeah. Maybe." She swallowed. "I think I need to leave."

He made no move to argue, hating himself.

"Thank you for standing up to Tiffany. I know that couldn't have been easy."

"I can handle Tiffany. It's Susie I'm worried about."

He reached up to her cheek, but she took a step back. "She needs to know about her mom."

"You're right." He massaged his temple. "I just don't want to drag them through the ugliness of divorce that I went through."

"I respect that, but until you're honest with them about Tiffany, then you're making me the bad guy in the situation. And no matter how much I want this"—she pointed between them—"I won't be that person in their lives." She sighed. And the look she gave him made him brace himself.

"I think probably you need to focus on your kids, Cole. Your children do come first and maybe we're moving too fast." She looked away, as if trying not to cry. "I'll text you a list of what needs done at the farm. Take care of Susie and Zane. They'll still be hurting when they wake up."

She closed the door behind her. Cole walked over to the table and gripped the back of one of his cheap wooden chairs. Would he ever have something good in his life that Tiffany wouldn't try and destroy? A crack filled the air as the wood under his hands cracked the length of the grain. Cole relaxed his grip and drew a calming breath before he shot off a text to Tiffany.

COLE
____

I'm back and heard about tonight. Are you just here for more money? You can't keep doing this.

He slipped his phone in his pocket and carried his bag to the laundry room. She might respond in the next five minutes or not for another six months. Tiffany was anything but predictable.

Dropping his bag on the floor, he unzipped it and started loading the clothes in the washer. He had no doubt he needed to talk to the kids, but Fallon didn't understand how complicated being a single parent was.

He reached over to shut the dryer door that Fallon had left open but stopped. A white sweater had been left, tucked in the back. He reached in and grabbed it. A large grayish-blue stain covered the front. The way it splattered up, not just down, looked less like a spill and more like it had been flung at the shirt.

We had an . . . incident and my clothes all got . . . dirty. Fallon's vague words floated back. Had Susie or Zane done this? *You're making me the bad guy in the situation.* Some protector he was.

He had let her go into a battle unprepared. He should have been more forthcoming with her. And he needed to talk to the kids. For Fallon's sake, but also theirs. If Tiffany was back in town, then keeping them in the dark wasn't protecting them either.

twelve

C OLE HAD NEVER BEEN QUITE SO THANKFUL to have the school call a snow day as he was today. He needed a heart-to-heart with the kids and there was no time like the present. Especially after waking up to that text from Tiffany. He pulled out his phone and scanned it again.

I want to see my kids. This isn't about money. I've changed and I have a right to **see them**.

Had she changed? Everything in him wanted to fight that idea and shelter them from her, but he couldn't. He might have custody, but she did have a right to see them. And they had a right to see her.

He pulled up the Amazon app on his phone and searched for a sweater that looked most similar to the one now stretched out on the coffee table before him. Minus the grayish-blue stain, of course. He added it to the cart and paid the extra fee to have it there by six tonight. He had just submitted the payment when heavy footsteps clambered down the steps. He had moved one of the dining room chairs by the coffee table opposite the couch. He shoved his phone back in his pocket and waited.

"Snow day!" Susie was the first to the bottom. "I knew you were back. I saw your truck and remembered that you tucked me in last night. Zane said it was a dream but I knowed. Can we build a snowman?"

She made a beeline for him but stopped as her gaze landed on Fallon's white sweater on the coffee table.

Zane was only a few steps behind her and seemed to notice the sweater before he even made eye contact with Cole. "What did she tell you?"

"I want to hear it from you." He pointed to the couch. "Sit."

The kids took a seat, the look of embarrassment clouding their features, but neither spoke.

"Would you like to tell me what happened?" He took a moment meeting Susie's gaze and then Zane's. "Last I talked to you on the phone things were going well."

The kids exchanged a look then Zane met his dad's gaze. "Mom came home last night."

The words, despite the fact he'd expected them, hit him like a punch to his gut. Not that it was new information, but describing Tiffany's reappearance as "coming home" meant they felt like she *belonged* here. And there it was, that touch of hope in their eyes. Hope that the chaos train they'd been on since she'd left was over. Cole wasn't so optimistic. Not to mention this would never be her home. If she had changed, he'd have to let her into the kids' lives, but there would be no going back for Tiffany and him.

But one thing at a time. "Fallon said she stopped by. But what happened to the sweater?"

Susie's expression shifted to one of deep anger. "Mom wanted to see us but Fallon wouldn't let her—said she'd call the cops if Mom didn't leave. Can you believe that?"

"Yes. She did the right thing."

Both of the kids' expressions went from shock to confusion to frustration in a flash. Susie was the first to speak. "How can you say that? It's *Mommy*."

He leaned forward with his elbows on his knees for a moment, then focused on Susie. "Do you remember when you went to a friend's house a few weeks ago and told me to keep your bunny safe while you were gone?"

Her brow pinched but she nodded.

"How would you have felt if while you were gone, I let Zane take your bunny to the park?"

"Why would I take her stupid bunny to the park?"

"It's an analogy." He glanced at Zane and back at Susie. "How would you have felt?"

"I don't think I would have liked that because he could have left it there or gotten it dirty."

"Right. You trusted me with something important to you and I was careful with it. Same with Fallon. I trusted Fallon with the two most precious things in my life. She promised to protect you and keep you with her until I was back. She wasn't being mean to your mom, she was doing what I asked her to do."

"But our mom wouldn't hurt us." Susie's eyes began to fill with tears.

"I understand how you feel, but Fallon did the right thing. If she had let your mom take you somewhere without talking to me, I would have been very upset." He pointed to the sweater. "So what happened here?"

Susie looked down, the tears now running down her cheeks. "I threw paint water at her and then poured paint water in her bag because I was mad."

Cole rubbed his hand over his hair and struggled to keep his expression neutral as the image of Fallon pulling her clothes from the dryer and shoving them in the bag last night surfaced in his mind—all the clothes she'd brought with her. Maybe he'd include a hefty gift card with the replaced sweater.

He met his daughter's gaze again. "Is that how we handle our feelings when we get mad?"

Susie shook her head as the tears began to form again. "Do you think Fallon hates me now?"

"No. But I do think you owe her an apology."

"I tore up her pictures too." Her voice was small, and he could see the remorse in her eyes.

"I know. And she will forgive you." He leaned forward and reached for her hand and pulled her toward him. "Now we need to have another talk about your mother."

Susie climbed up on his lap burying her head into his shoulder. "Is she coming home today? Are we going to be a family again?"

He closed his eyes at the burning in his chest. He hated to break her heart, but Fallon was right. She needed to know at least some of it. Hugging her closer, he kissed the top of her head. "This is not her home, sweetie. And your mom and I are not getting back together, ever."

"But why?" Her lip quivered.

He glanced at Zane, but the boy didn't give anything away.

With her wrapped in his arms, he met Zane's gaze. "I should have been more honest with you two after she left. I can see that now. When your mom left, she didn't just go on a trip. She moved to a town called Las Vegas."

"Why?" Zane's voice was void of emotion.

"She met a man and wanted to live with him there."

"But she was married to you." The innocent confusion in Susie's voice broke him.

"She was." He slid a comforting hand over her hair. "But she decided she didn't want to be married to me, so we divorced."

"But now she's back. Does she want to be with you again?"

"No." At least he hoped not. "She's back to see you because she still loves you."

"But she doesn't love you?"

After seeing the way Fallon was so concerned for him last night, he wasn't sure Tiffany ever loved him. "We don't love each other anymore. And she won't move in here."

"But we'll see her."

"I'll do my best to make that happen." And he would. He'd give anything for Tiffany to have a healthy relationship with the kids.

"I think I need to apologize to Fallon." Susie's eyes filled with tears one more time.

"Me too." Zane hung his head. "I didn't throw the paint or break the brushes, but I didn't try and stop Susie either."

"I think that would be a good idea. I ordered her a new sweater and it is supposed to be here tonight. Maybe we can take it over after dinner."

"Are we grounded?" Zane stared at him, still void of expression.

"You both made mistakes but so did I. I should've explained all this before. Why don't we all agree to learn from our mistakes instead? Besides, you two have a snow day. We three have snow to play in."

"You're going to play with us?" The confusion in Zane's eyes was almost Cole's undoing. He needed to take more time for them.

And that started today. "Absolutely. But first, breakfast."

Forty minutes later as they finished off the last of the toaster waffles, Zane stood and lifted his plate, the closest thing to a smile Cole had yet to see this morning on his face. "Are you really going to play with us in the snow?"

"Of course." Cole stood, gathering plates as he went. "Why don't you two start gearing up and I'll take care of this."

The two ran to the mudroom off the kitchen and Cole carried the rest of the breakfast plates to the sink. He had just made his second trip when Susie's voice drifted out of the mudroom. "I'm still hoping now that Mom is back they'll fall in love again."

Cole winced and took a step in that direction, but Zane jumped right in. "Why would you want that? Mom and Dad always fought. Don't you remember that?"

Something clinched around Cole's chest. He'd hoped Tiffany and he had hidden it better than that.

"I remember he would bring her flowers after he had to go on trips." Susie's words were accompanied by a stomping foot as if trying to get in her boot.

"Well, I remember the guys who would visit Mom when Dad was on those trips."

Cole gripped the edge of the counter. Zane hadn't missed much. In fact, his son probably knew way more than Cole did about that part of things.

"They were Mom's friends. Weren't they?"

"I don't know." There was uncertainty in Zane's voice. "But I remember one was from Las Vegas."

Susie let out a small gasp. "Do you think that was the same man?"

"I don't know. I just know that Mom made Dad sad a lot. I don't want her to come back and make him sad again."

A pressure squeezed Cole's throat. Here he'd been trying to protect his kids and Zane was trying to protect him.

"Let me help you with your gloves." Zane's tone changed to something softer. There was some shuffling of material. Then he added, "Have you noticed how happy Dad is with Fallon?"

"You think he'll marry Fallon?" Susie's voice didn't sound sad. Just curious.

"I don't know. I think—"

A loud clatter cut off his words and Cole darted into the room. The box of gloves and scarves had fallen off the shelf, scattering its contents all over the floor. Zane looked up. "Oops."

Everything in him wanted to scoop up Zane for all he'd endured in his young life. But he didn't want the kids to know he'd been eavesdropping. And no doubt Zane would tell him he was treating him like a baby. Instead, he pointed to the pile. "Grab an extra hat and scarf. It's snowman time."

Susie plucked the red one from the top of the pile. "Got it."

"Then let's go." He lifted his coat and gloves from the hook. He'd meant it when he told Zane that he'd do his best to make sure they saw their mom. But how did he protect them from more hurt at the same time? He wasn't sure if that was possible. Maybe that was where trusting them to the One who loved them more than he did came into action.

Please, God, don't let me down.

How come everything couldn't go right at the same time? Fallon dipped her brush into the deep blue and pulled the paint across the paper. It had been sixteen hours since she'd left Cole's and she hadn't slept nor heard from him. Although the lack of sleep wasn't due to him. Not completely.

As soon as she walked in the house last night, or rather, early this morning, she'd sat down to paint. An image had come to mind and she had to get it out. That one image had birthed another, then another, until she was now looking at five completed paintings and a sixth in process.

Fallon set down her brush and stretched her fingers as she stared out the large bay window of her parents' house. It had stopped snowing by ten that morning but the drifts it had left behind wouldn't be disappearing any time soon. Even the tree boughs hung low with the thick, heavy snow.

She focused back on the sketch in front of her again, then closed her eyes, letting the image come to life in her mind.

"I thought you weren't getting back until later tonight." Her dad shuffled into the room, his gray hair still at odd angles from his late afternoon nap.

"Cole got back in during the night, so I came home." With her favorite brush she pulled more blue paint onto the mixing palette and touched the brush lightly to the green.

He picked up one of her completed works and studied it. Her dad had been the one to put the brush in her hand and she was always anxious to get his reaction. Her gaze bounced from the painting to his face and back.

It held her signature abstract style, but instead of small angels, it was the painting of a man with two kids. They were how Fallon imagined Cole and his kids might have looked five years back. The father lifted the little girl toward the tree as she topped it with a star. The boy hung his ornament on the far side as he smiled up at his father. If her dad saw the connection, he didn't say.

He set it down without a comment or even a brow lift and picked up another. This one was also a Christmas scene, but instead of a young family, an older couple stood hand in hand facing a tree that didn't look too different from the one that stood a few feet away. "You could have taken a few pounds off my middle."

"You don't like it?" Why did that idea hurt so badly?

"Not like it? These are amazing." He set it down and took a seat, but his eyes didn't leave the page. "There is so much detail and emotion. And I think they're stronger than the series that made you famous."

She bit her lip to keep from tearing up. She dipped her brush again in the blue, tested the color on a scrap piece, and added a bit more green. "Last night I remembered a series I had pitched to Winterbourne about four years ago. The Tiny Angels series had become so popular and it was an easy sell, but I was growing tired of it. I thought something fresh would be fun. I'm not sure what happened to those paintings, but they were family focused like these."

Her dad pointed to the one of Cole and the kids and winked at her. "Probably not just like these." So he had noticed. "They turned them down?"

"I think they said no before I could finish the presentation. They wanted me to stay in my lane. But now I'm glad."

"About what?"

"That they turned them down. These are better than I imagined. And I did what you said. I used them as a way to draw close to God. Each one an act of worship, so to speak."

"Glad to hear you're talking to Him again."

"Me too."

"These are fresh. That's for sure." Her dad held up another, this one of a mother nursing her baby by the light of the Christmas tree. "It's like embodying the heart of this tree farm. Celebrating Christmas is always first about the birth of Jesus, of course. But I also saw the Christmas tree as a way to make everyone slow down with the family and remember together. Remember why we celebrate and remember who we want to celebrate with."

"That could be the name of the series." She lifted the one of Cole and the kids. "Christmas with You."

"Series?" He lowered the one in his hand and eyed her over his dark-rimmed glasses. "Are you selling these?"

"We sold half of the other ornaments this past weekend. So I need to order more. I thought I could order some of each of these at the same time. But it is quite an investment and if people don't buy—"

"But if they do . . ."

"There's no way I can compete with the high quality of the Winterbourne ornaments by using rushed print-on-demand companies."

"Do you still have any connections in the industry? Any old favors to call in?"

Fallon mulled that over for a moment. Her friend Sarah might help her. They had become friends somewhere along the line when she still had her hand in the Tiny Angles ornaments.

Right. She put her brush in water, grabbed her phone, and opened up a text to her.

FALLON

Any space for a last-minute order of full-color wrapped five-inch globes?

SARAH

Girl, it's been too long. Anything for you. Is this more for the Tiny Angels line?

FALLON

Nope. I am not with Winterbourne anymore.

She sent off a photo of one of the paintings.

Her phone rang almost immediately. "Sarah, it would be a rush order."

"Consider it done." Sarah's excitement came through the line. "But are you really not with Winterbourne anymore? How did they let you go?"

"Creative differences."

It wasn't exactly true, but she wasn't going to drag them through the mud.

"Come work for us."

"What? I just need the ornaments—"

"We will do those. But promise me you'll consider it. I'll talk to Stacey and have you an offer in an hour."

With that, she was gone.

Wait. What just happened? A job offer at Great Lakes Printing? An interview at Hallmark? She set the phone down as Cole's face came to mind. She'd prayed about what to do next in her life and now she was more confused than ever.

A solid knock at the door pulled her from her thoughts. She walked over and pulled it open.

Cole stood there with Zane and Susie. Susie held a roughly wrapped present and both kids' eyes were looking at the ground. "Can we have a moment?" Cole said. All three had clumps of snow on the sleeves of their coats and red noses. How long had they been out there?

It took every ounce of self-control not to scoop them up in a hug, let them off the hook, and give them cocoa. But from the stern look on Cole's face, there were words that needed to be spoken. She took a step back. "Come on in."

Her dad took in the scene and stood. "I've got something that needs to be done downstairs."

Fallon led the kids and Cole to the living room. As soon as they entered, Susie shoved the gift into Fallon's hands.

"I'm really sorry." Her voice wavered as tears began to fall.

"I know." Fallon sat, then set the gift aside, and wrapped the little girl in a giant hug. "I'm sorry I couldn't let you go with your mom."

"My dad explained. You had to be respond-able like he was with my bunny."

Fallon looked to Cole for interpretation, but he bit back a smile and nodded in a way that seemed to say *just go with it.*

Susie wiped her nose with her sleeve. "And my mom will come back. I know she will. She told me she would."

Fallon looked at Cole again and the smile was gone. So, she hadn't returned today. And the look in his eyes made it clear it could be tomorrow or it could be months, and this was why he'd never told them.

"When she does, I wanted her to stay with us, but Dad said no. I think it's because he likes you. Are you going to date my dad?" Susie looked up at her with wide, innocent blue eyes.

Fallon glanced at Cole, but he seemed slightly shocked by the question. Then he smiled and cocked his head, as if waiting for her answer too.

"Um." The job offer possibilities flashed in her mind, but that was all they were . . . possibilities.

She glanced from Susie to Zane then back. "What do you two think? Do you think I should date your dad?"

They both nodded with a smile.

That was it. Job or no job. Right now, she wanted to be a part of this family. The rest she'd have to figure out later. She looked at Cole. Raised an eyebrow, then smiled. "Me too."

Susie jumped up and clapped her hands then shoved the present back into her hands. "Open it."

She peeled back the paper to reveal a white sweater much like the one that got ruined. "Oh, Susie. It's so much nicer than my old one. Thank you." She looked at Cole as she embraced the little girl. Oh, the man fought unfairly. She'd call it an ambush.

But she didn't hate it.

"I think it is cocoa time." Cole stood and held up his hand. "You relax. I've been here enough I know where it is."

"I'll help." Susie followed him out.

When they were out of the room, she glanced at Zane and found him studying her. She folded the sweater and set it aside. "Are you sure you're okay with me dating your dad?"

He nodded then glanced toward the kitchen then back at her. "But promise me you won't leave."

"Won't leave?" Her heart sank.

"Susie is getting attached and so is my dad. I just don't want them hurt."

He was such a little protector, like his father. She drew a slow breath and nodded. She couldn't promise things would work out, but she wasn't walking away, not now.

And hopefully not ever.

Her phone buzzed and she picked it up. It was the offer from Stacey. Fallon's jaw dropped with the amount of the starting salary. But it was a position at the main office in Chicago. She glanced up at Zane. *But promise me you won't leave.* She longed for more than a big paycheck and recognition. She wanted this life.

She started to respond when another message appeared.

STACEY
Think about it and let me know
by Jan. 1.

Cole returned, carrying a tray of mugs. Set them down on the coffee table. Susie picked one up and handed it to her. "I filled it with marshmallows."

"Clearly. I can't see the chocolate." Fallon took a sip and came up with a marshmallow mustache. "Just the way I like it."

Susie giggled.

Zane grinned, nodding.

And Cole—he wore a look of relief.

Fallon took it all in. This was the next moment she'd paint. And for the first time in her life, a family felt within her reach.

thirteen

WHY WAS THE DOOR UNLOCKED? COLE checked the time on his smartwatch. The kids shouldn't get off the bus for another twenty minutes. He instinctively reached for his sidearm, but of course, he didn't carry it on him these days. He scanned the door for signs of forced entry when through the window he caught sight of familiar brown hair by the couch. Seriously?

Three days had to be a new record for Tiffany. He pushed in and shut the door without looking away from her. "Breaking and entering now?"

She stood, lifted a Coke she had no doubt taken from his fridge, and offered a salute. "It wasn't breaking. I used the key. I was married to you for more than ten years. I know where you would keep the hide-a-key for the kids."

"Still, this isn't your house, so it is illegal." He slipped off his coat and hung it on the hook.

"So is keeping my kids from me."

"So is *abandoning* your kids." He turned in her direction, a fire in his gut.

"I left them with my parents. They loved the kids and I knew they'd be fine." She made a dismissive wave then narrowed her eyes on him. "Besides, I knew you'd come home. They needed you and you refused to leave the SEALs. You would have stayed in another ten years if I hadn't done something drastic."

She wasn't wrong, but did that make abandoning them okay? Nope. He circled the couch and took a seat in the recliner. "You left the kids for their sake. That's rich."

She sat on the couch again but stayed on the edge. "It's true."

He leaned back into the chair and propped his ankle on his opposite knee as he laced his fingers across his stomach. "Do you believe the lies you say? Let me guess, you shacked up with the man in Vegas for them too?"

"Don't make this about us." She set her Coke to the side and leaned forward over her knees. "I want to see my kids."

Were those tears in her eyes? That was the thing with Tiffany. She could turn them on or off to suit her needs. How was he supposed to know if she was being sincere? "If you wanted to see them so bad, why did you wait another three days to come back?"

"What?"

"You were here on Sunday to see the kids. I know Fallon told you I would be back Monday because I woke up to a text from you. I told you we had to talk first, then crickets. Why did you wait?"

She studied him for a moment, nothing in her expression readable. "I had loose ends to tie up in Vegas. But now I'm back and at my parents' house. Permanently."

"Permanently? Do you even know what that means?"

"I'm sorry about Sunday night, okay? I'll admit I didn't handle it well." She stood and started pacing the room. "I thought you'd be here. And seeing Fallon here . . . Where were you anyway?"

"I had a trip."

"Are you back in the military?" She settled back on the couch. After more than ten years as a Navy wife she should know he couldn't just hop in and out as he felt like it. But she had never paid much attention to his life. Didn't matter, this was not a social call. "What do you really want, Tiff? Money?"

"Please, Cole." She leaned forward dropping her elbows on her knees. "I know I don't deserve a second chance with them, but they *are* my kids."

When Cole still didn't respond, she sat back again. "Don't villainize me, Cole. I was a good mom to them for eleven years. Eleven years I was there day in and day out while you went off to—well I don't know where you went because I don't have the clearance to find out."

"You left them. Abandoned them." *And had guy after guy in the house while I was gone.* No, he didn't want to open that conversation. She was right. This wasn't about their marriage.

"I left them with my parents. But I'm back. I want a do-over. Don't try and tell me you haven't made any mistakes."

And she had him because he had a list of mistakes a mile long. He *did* know what it was like to make a stupid-in-the-moment decision and then have to face the consequences for years.

"You said you had to tie up loose ends. Loose ends like severing all ties and moving here? Or loose ends like you're waiting for what's-his-face to show up and beg you back? Because if you're back, that is one thing, but they don't need you to disrupt their lives just to retreat again. So if you're still a flight risk—"

"I'm here to stay. I want another chance with my kids."

His gut told him not to trust her, but he wasn't sure if it was just the bitterness speaking. And he'd been honest with the kids. He did want them to have a healthy relationship with their mom. And the only way to get to that point was through this. "We can have dinner here tonight. But I'll be present for all the visits. You aren't taking them anywhere."

"Fine. I'll take that for now. I could even move in here if you'd prefer."

"No, I would not."

"Oh yes, wouldn't want to mess up what you have going on with Fallon. Seriously, Cole, *her* of all people?"

"Say one more word about Fallon and I'll take back my offer for dinner."

She held up her hands as her eyes narrowed. "Fine. I just hope you know what you're doing. I mean, you're worried about *me* being a flight risk—"

"What do you mean by that?"

"She always looked down on Heritage. Miss Most Likely to Succeed had always had bigger and better plans than Heritage could offer. Do you really think Fallon plans on staying here?"

Before he could answer, the door opened and both kids walked in and dropped their backpacks.

"Mommy!" Susie ran to her mom's side and wrapped her in a hug. "I knew you'd come back. Zane said you wouldn't, but I knew."

Tiffany's face changed to something sweet as she pulled the little girl on her lap. "I'm going to stay for dinner. And I moved back to Grandma and Grandpa's, so I'll be seeing you a lot more."

"Are we going to do the week switch?" Susie reached up and touched a strand of her mom's hair and it twisted something in Cole's chest. Susie missed Tiffany in a way he couldn't fill on his own. "My friend Jenny does that. One week with mom then one week with dad then one week with mom then—"

"I get the idea." Tiffany glanced at Cole, but he sent her a hard stare. That was not happening. At least not until she proved that she was here to stay. "Maybe eventually, but right now I'll just visit with you here."

She held out her free arm toward Zane. He hesitated a moment before settling on the couch and leaning in to her side.

Maybe this was a good thing. A healthy shared custody situation would be best for the kids. And Tiffany did seem to be here for them.

Do you really think Fallon plans on staying here? Tiffany's words tumbled over again in his mind. Of course she was staying. He knew she'd talked about leaving, but that was before everything had changed.

It was just another of Tiffany's lies, trying to tear his life apart again. Because he simply refused to believe that he might have just added another person into the kids' lives that had the power to break their hearts.

Fallon hadn't anticipated how nerve-racking it would be to put her art back out there again. She broke the tape of one of the boxes of ornaments and lifted it in the dim light of the Sugar Shack. These were her ornaments, her art. She peeled back the packing materials and lifted one by its gold string. They were all round white-pearl globes with one of her family watercolor paintings covering half. On the back, her well-known Fallon James signature was scrawled out in gold. And on the bottom the year was written in a deep red.

She hung it on the tree in the center of the Sugar Shack. It was the perfect addition to the white lights and gold bows.

"That's beautiful," her mom spoke from next to her.

She took her mom in, already decked out as Mrs. Santa with gray curls, a red cape, and silver spectacles.

"They turned out so much better than I had even hoped." Fallon picked up another and added it to the tree. "The print-on-demand ones we're giving away with each tree are nice, but these . . ."

Her mom removed several from the box as well. "Guess it paid to call in a favor."

A favor that had resulted in regular texts from Sarah pushing her to accept the job in Chicago. Maybe she was dumb for not jumping on it. After all, the top designer position had always been her dream, but that was before she'd fallen in love with the farm again. Before she'd fallen in love with the slow pace of Heritage again. Before . . . Cole.

Her mom started hanging them on the tree. "The Winterbourne family might have pushed you away, but many people still remember and love Fallon James the artist and businesswoman."

Fallon picked up as many ornaments as she could handle and carried them to the new rack that Cole had constructed on the wall and hung them on one of the metal hooks. "Do you think they'll sell?"

"I have no doubt. Our sales were up by fifty percent last weekend. And with all those silly internet videos you keep showing me, I expect more this weekend. Don't know how we'll keep up."

"I'm pretty sure most of them came to see Cole. Too bad he wasn't here." She stepped over and opened another box.

"But if word got out he'd be working this weekend, then our numbers could go up even further." Her mom sent her a wink.

"What did you do?"

"I know how to work Instagram too." She didn't clarify and Fallon decided it would be best for plausible deniability when she talked to Cole. "Is that why you hired a few high schoolers to help with parking and the cash register for this weekend?"

"Perhaps." Her mom lifted an ornament and studied it. "Is it my imagination or does that one bear a striking resemblance to a family we know with a little blonde girl, teenage boy, and military dad?"

"What can I say? I paint what I love." Fallon's hand halted. Had she really said that? She glanced at her mom.

Her mom gave her a quick side hug. "Don't worry, your secret is safe with me. But just so you know, we figured it out, so it isn't much of a secret."

"I'm not sure . . ." She didn't even really know how he felt. There had been that one vague conversation with the kids about them dating, but since then—nothing.

She didn't blame him. With Tiffany hanging around he hadn't wanted to leave the kids alone with her. But the idea of them hanging out as a perfect little family irked something in her. Did that mean love or just old rivalries coming to the surface?

Her mom laid a comforting hand on her shoulder. "One day at a time. You don't have to be sure today. Now I'll leave you to finish hanging these. I've got to make sure that Santa is in his big red suit."

"You sure Dad is still up to it? He was so worn out last weekend."

"I'm not sure I could talk him out of it even if he wasn't. But he agreed to put the bench next to the big red chair for the kids he can't lift or are shy."

Three hours later, she spotted Cole stopped by yet another group of girls over by the tree lot. He set down the tree he was moving and then gave them his charming but less-than-sincere smile. They all giggled. If they liked that, they should see his real only-you-exist-in-this-moment smile. They gathered around him, held out a phone, and all said something as the phone flashed. He picked up the tree, smiling as he left, and they all moved on but not without a few more glances and photos of him carrying the tree.

It had been happening all night. For hating the attention as much as he claimed, he sure seemed to be enjoying this.

She shouldn't complain, since every time one of those photos got posted, it drove up business. More business meant more tree sales and hopefully more ornament sales.

She glanced at the Sugar Shack. She needed to go check how the ornaments were selling, but the idea that they weren't selling cemented her in place. She just wasn't ready to face that.

Her phone vibrated and Fallon pulled it out. It was from Amy, the girl working the register.

Is there anyone to cover for me
so I can run to the **restroom?**

Fallon texted back that she'd be right there then slid the phone in her pocket. Guess it was time to find out how they were selling, ready or not.

Fallon walked to the single back door behind the register and waved Amy away. "I've got this."

She typed in her code to the new register and looked up at the next customer. "Do you have a tree tag?"

The woman passed a tag to her and then set five ornaments on the counter. "I had to get one of each. They're selling so fast I wasn't sure if they'd sell out."

Fallon glanced at the purchase and looked down the line. Everyone held at least one ornament, but most had multiple.

"I'm glad you like them." Her throat pinched with emotion, but she kept her voice steady. Maybe God did still have a plan for her art. She bagged up the ornaments and handed over the receipt.

The next woman stepped up. She wore her brown hair in beach waves over her shoulders. She laid five ornaments on the counter. "Aren't these gorgeous?"

"Thank you." Fallon reached for the first one and scanned the tag.

"I'm here with my fiancé. We just got engaged and we're going to have a huge tree."

"These will look perfect." She wrapped the ornament in paper and set it in a bag.

"The house has vaulted ceilings and large windows that overlook a lake." The woman ran her fingers over one of the delicate bulbs. "This one is my favorite."

Fallon reached for the next tag. "Thank you. I love th—"

Ice traveled through her veins. No. It couldn't be.

The woman was wearing Fallon's engagement ring. She would

recognize it anywhere. It was one of a kind, an heirloom from Robert's family. A princess cut vintage from the nineteen twenties. The ring Robert had presented her with on one knee. The ring she had accepted with hope of a family and life together.

She blinked hard and tried to focus back on the cash register.

What was it doing on another woman's finger? Yes, it was the family ring, and yes, she'd given it back to his mother shortly after the funeral. But she'd given it back because it was a family heirloom, not so it could be given to another person. Maybe giving it to someone else in the family made sense to her brain, but her heart didn't seem to want to catch up.

"I love that one," Fallon finally finished as she met the woman's gaze for the first time. "Do you have a tree tag?"

Bryce appeared next to the brunette. "Just the ornaments for us today."

He looked at her, clearly not surprised to see her, wearing the same sickening smile as when he told her there was no longer a place for her at the company. No longer a place for her at what had been her house for her future family. No longer a place for her with the Winterbournes.

It *had* been her ring. And that house with the vaulted ceilings had been her house. Fallon tried to control her breathing, but it was all too much. The ring, the house. All of it.

The room began to lighten to a strange yellow color as her vision became blurry just before a warm hand landed on her back. Cole's voice spoke next to her anchoring her back to the moment. "Did you guys find a tree okay?"

"We bought it earlier." The woman spoke up again. "We just stopped in to buy some of these ornaments. Aren't they lovely?"

"My girl is amazing." Cole's fingers affectionately ran over her arm and everything began to slowly come back into focus. "They're all from paintings she made."

Bryce's gaze landed on Cole's hand on her arm. She stepped

away from Cole, letting his hand drop. Why did she do that? It wasn't like she was doing anything wrong.

Bryce gave a disdaining look at the small building. "Good to see you doing so well for yourself, Fallon."

With that, he turned and left. The words were polite, but she knew Bryce. What he hadn't said was, *You've gone from being a Winterbourne to this?*

"Merry Christmas!" Cole yelled after them then lowered his voice to her ear. "Are you okay?"

Amy reappeared at her side before she could answer. "All set. You ready for me to take over?"

Fallon nodded and hurried out the back door.

Cole was only steps behind her. "Who was that?"

"She had my ring." Fallon leaned against the side of the building then bent over, gripping her knees. Deep breath.

"She stole your ring?"

Fallon shook her head as tears filled her eyes. "She has my ring, my house, the life I was supposed to have."

"You aren't making any sense." Cole pulled her into his arms and rested his forehead against hers. "Slow down and breathe. Can you start again?"

He brushed her hair back from her face.

"My engagement ring from Robert. It was his great-grandmother's. That was his brother Bryce." She wiped a hand under her eyes, hating her emotions. "It's not just the ring. She's living the life I was supposed to have. She is living in my house. My house with vaulted ceilings that overlooked the lake. It was magical."

He drew a slow breath then let it out as he wrapped his arms around her middle. "You don't talk about him much."

His presence seemed to soothe her. "There is nothing here in Heritage that reminds me of him."

"Nothing?" He leaned back, his eyes locked on her face.

"He never came to Heritage. He was too busy working or off

pursuing some adrenaline rush. I have no memories here with him. The whirlwind romance and marriage almost feel like a memory from a different lifetime."

"I don't want to overstep here, but it doesn't sound like a healthy marriage."

"It wasn't."

"But you still think it was the life you were supposed to have?"

"How do I answer that? Anything but yes sounds like I'm glad he died. I'm not."

"I'm not talking about Robert. I'm talking about a vaulted ceiling overlooking a lake . . . a ring that would rival a value of a house . . . a big city corporate job. Because I can tell you right now. That is not my future. And if you stay with me, that is not our future."

He pressed a kiss to her forehead. "It's just me."

"Of course I don't care about the house and the ring. It was just a shock."

"And the job?" When she didn't answer, he dropped his arms. "And the job?"

"I was offered a job at Great Lakes Printing, and Hallmark wants to interview me in January."

Cole's brows lifted as he stared at her then took a step back, seeming to control whatever was going on inside him. Breathing in slow.

He looked away. Shoved his hands in his pockets and looked back. His smile distant. "I would expect nothing less. You're extremely talented and I'm not the only one who sees it. Are you going to take one of them?"

"Wouldn't I be crazy not to? The farm is holding on by a thread, and even if I do save it, it's not mine. Maybe I'll inherit it one day, but it'll never make enough to support me."

"Okay." He nodded. A beat. "I get that you don't have it figured out right now, but what do you want?"

What did she want? Like that was a simple answer. She wanted her art back. She wanted a family, she wanted . . . him. But was it that simple? She needed work and Heritage had no work for her.

When she didn't answer he shifted his weight to the other foot. "I'll fight for this." He motioned between them. "But I need to know you want to fight *with* me for it."

"I do. I just . . . "

His eyes pleaded with her to lay it out there, to say it all didn't matter and that she wanted him. But she couldn't. She couldn't be that raw, that vulnerable until she was sure.

"I don't know."

He closed his eyes a beat and drew in a slow breath as he opened them. Stared into the dark woods and then back at her. "Someday you're going to have to fight for something you want."

With that, he walked away.

Everything in her wanted to run after him, to promise she'd stay. But she'd be a fool not to pursue these dreams. Everything was happening too fast. It was too much. And right now, she had nothing to give him.

fourteen

FALLON TOOK ONE END OF THE MEASURING tape from Sadie and walked across Kensington's private basket-ball court.

"Stop." Sadie's words echoed in the room as she made a note on the clipboard then tore off a piece of masking tape and marked the floor.

Laying out the floor plan for the reception wasn't how Fallon planned on spending her Monday morning, but with the wedding in just over two weeks, she had little doubt her friend was stressed.

What she wanted to do was find Cole. They still hadn't talked since just after she'd been faced with Bryce, and she wanted to talk. Smooth things over. But he seemed to be everywhere she wasn't.

Still holding her end of the measuring tape, Sadie stepped off several paces, her lips moving with every count. She stopped, made another note, then started on the tape again. "Things any better with Cole?"

"I think he's giving me space to figure out what I want." But she didn't want space. There were only nine days until Christmas, which meant the end of the season at the farm. Which meant not seeing him. The thought made her nauseated. "I know I hurt him, but he wants me to have it all figured out."

"Can you blame him?"

"What?" Fallon spun toward her friend. "You're supposed to be on my side."

"Are there sides?" Sadie made a final note on the clipboard. "Sorry, but he is a dad of two kids. He doesn't want to uproot his kids again and you said that you saw staying here in Heritage as a failure. And you wish you had your old life with Robert. You also mentioned two impressive job opportunities that he can't compete with. What did you want him to do?"

"That isn't what I said."

"I'm just saying that as a mom, I would have never agreed to that first date with David if he had said that. I refused all dates with him—even though I was falling for him—until he decided to stay. At least I'd thought he'd decided."

"But what if David decided to leave next year? Would you go with him?"

"Yes. But we would decide that together." Sadie took a step closer, her brown hair escaping the messy bun she had thrown it up in. "And we would make that decision based on the relationship we have developed over time. You're asking Cole to make that decision before you have even gone on a first official date. Besides, Cole didn't ask you to lay out the future. He asked you what you want. I think he needs to know that if he is going into the unknown with you that you really want him."

"He should know—"

"Should he? Have you ever told him how you feel? Not felt in the past. But feel right now. Does he know that you want him? Not someone to replace Robert. Not his family. Him."

Sadie's phone rang and she scanned it. "Shoot, I have to go.

I'm supposed to be meeting Romee at Heritage Flowers in five minutes."

Fallon followed her back out to their cars. Sadie tossed her clipboard on the passenger's seat, turned back, and hugged Fallon. "You're my oldest friend, and I'm always on your side. But realize that dating with kids is hard. He is making decisions not just for him but for his family. And I think you need to decide after the excitement of Christmas at the tree farm is over if same ol' Heritage will still be enough for you. Will Cole be enough?"

Sharing her feelings had always been the hardest thing for Fallon to do. That was why she'd started painting in the first place. The one place she could be fully honest. Maybe she'd been doing that again because there was a definite theme to her new paintings. So maybe it was time for some honesty with Cole.

Fallon walked over to her car and pulled out her phone and the texting thread for Cole.

FALLON

Can I stop by? I want to talk.

COLE

Kids are home on break. We'll never have privacy. I'll meet you at the gazebo across the street.

FALLON

About five minutes away.

With that she slid her phone in her purse and made her way toward Cole's. The large properties gave way to closer set Victorian houses. And as she approached the square, she was taken aback yet again by the picturesque scene before her. So much had changed since her high school days. Once rundown and sad, it was now like driving into a Christmas card. Lights strung over the street. The tree lit in the square. Even Otis had a Santa hat. She pulled up along the curb and climbed out.

Cole was already by the gazebo on one of the benches. He lifted his head as she approached. "Hey."

She sat on Otis's back a few feet away. "Hey."

Maybe the best way was to dive right in. "Bryce's girlfriend isn't living the life I was supposed to have. I should never have said that."

He leaned forward, propping his elbows on his knees, but kept his gaze on her. "Why did you?"

"I was caught off guard. I once heard grief described as a ball floating inside another ball and every time the ball on the inside bumps against the ball on the outside, it is sheer pain. When you first experience the grief, the inside ball is big, and they hit a lot. But as time passes, the inside ball shrinks and bumps it less often. Grief changes but never really goes away. And on occasion when something makes the small ball hit the side again, it is deep pain all over again. And sometimes that pain looks like anger. I'm sorry."

His eyes studied her, giving nothing away. "Do you miss him?"

"There is still grief, but like I said, it has changed over time."

"I'm sorry you lost him." He stared at the ground for a moment. "I am so sorry you had to go through that."

When he didn't continue, she tilted her head. "Aren't you supposed to tell me that it all will work out for good and that God still has a plan?"

"I'll never tell you that losing your husband was good. Do I think God still has a plan? Yes. But that plan isn't Him purposely putting suffering in our lives. That plan is that even when the ugliness of the world finds us, He has a good future for us."

"You believe that?" Fallon stood and walked over and took a seat next to him on the bench.

"I have to. I need to believe in a God who can lead my kids to a good future even though their parents have made some pretty bad choices." Cole reached over and lifted one of her hands. "I need to believe in a God who still has good things for *us* even though I made a mess of our past."

"I don't like you because I need a replacement for Robert." She let her thumb trail across his hand. "I don't need the house, the jewelry, the job. And as much as I have grown to adore your children, that isn't what this is about either. I like you, Cole. A lot. So much that it scares the Skittles out of me."

His face turned toward her, a smile playing at his eyes. "Skittles?"

Her face warmed. "My grandma always used to say that. She ate a lot of Skittles." She bit her lip then squeezed his hand. "I don't know what I want to do about the job. It all feels so overwhelming."

"I can help you with the overwhelming. I just have to know what's going on in there." He pointed at her heart.

"I know. I'm not good about saying how I feel. I never have been. But I think I—" She dropped his hand, stood, and paced to the gazebo steps but turned back. He had stood from the bench and faced her but didn't walk her direction. She could do this. She could tell him how she felt. "No, I *know* that I . . . " She met his eyes again. She could get lost in those blue eyes.

He finally took a step toward her. "You know that you . . . ?"

She swallowed. Another beat. "I'm in love with you."

His face lost all expression for a fraction of a second. Then his gaze turned a little hungry as he closed the distance and pulled her into his arms. And when his mouth came down on hers, everything seemed to explode inside her. She loved him and there was no doubt in her now. She slid her hands over his shoulders and behind his neck, pulling him closer.

Then as if a practiced move, his hands traveled down her back and closed on her waist just before he lifted her to the bottom step of the gazebo, putting them almost eye to eye. He trailed his mouth over her jaw then back to her lips. The first kiss had been an explosion of built-up hunger and longing. This time Cole seemed to be taking his time. Learning every inch of her lips, every curve of her face. Declaring his heart as he memorized her, and she was going to treasure every second of it.

After a moment he pulled back and drew a deep breath. "I love you too. I'm pretty sure I have always loved you."

"Always? I don't think so." She poked him in the chest.

His face sobered as he tucked a wisp of hair behind her ear.

"I fell in love with you at sixteen even if I was too young to know what to do with it. And when everything happened with Tiffany, I boxed up those feelings and refused to think about them. About you. I might have even convinced myself that they were gone. But the moment I saw you at your parents' house the day I came to collect my kids, it all rose to the surface. I didn't recognize it at the time. But your words wouldn't have bothered me that day if I hadn't already cared about you."

The anger that had surfaced in her at seeing him that day flashed in her mind. Maybe part of her had never stopped loving him as well because he was right, if she didn't still care about him, she wouldn't have been quite so angry fourteen years later.

He brushed another soft kiss across her lips. "Go on a date with me."

"When?" She dropped off the step but kept hold of his hand. "This weekend is—"

"Tonight."

"What about the kids?"

"Zane can be in charge. I'll make them pasta before I leave. Please. I've been putting this off too long and I'm tired of waiting."

"Okay."

"God still has good things for you, Fallon." He tugged her back to him. "I want to be a part of that. Do you trust that?"

"I do." She wrapped her arms around his middle and buried her face in his chest. She did trust him. And for the first time in a long time, she found herself wanting to trust God.

"Dad!" Susie stood on the sidewalk by the street. "Can Mom sleep over tonight too?"

Fallon stiffened, but Cole didn't let her go. "It isn't what you think. Her furnace went out in the night. She slept on the couch. I went over and fixed it today. Nothing happened. Nothing will ever happen."

Fallon nodded, but she must not have been convincing because his hands landed on her cheeks. "Please believe me. I need you to believe me."

"I do." She placed her hands over his. "But I need you to believe me that she's up to something. She has always had one goal, and that is to hurt me."

"She said that she's back for the kids."

"Maybe. Or maybe she's back because I'm in your life again. And that is enough to make her want you, manipulate you, and use you all over again."

"I'm not so easily manipulated anymore."

"I know. Just don't underestimate her."

"And I would ask the same of you. Don't underestimate me." He dropped a kiss on her nose. "Now go get ready for our date. I'm going to call for reservations."

"Fancy."

"Only the best for my girl."

Cole hadn't been on a first date since high school, but he didn't remember them being this hard. He was ready to call it off and it wasn't even supposed to start for another hour. He stood in front of the small mirror on his dresser in his bedroom and held up the blue tie, then the red, and then the blue again. He hated ties. Maybe pulling off an epic first date was a little much, considering he'd only asked her out a few hours ago.

Susie burst into the room. "What's for dinner?"

"Shoot, the noodles." Cole dropped both ties on his bed and raced down the stairs. He grabbed the colander and dumped in overcooked mushy noodles. He shook out the water then dumped them back in the pot and set it on the stove. Not the best, but edible. He grabbed a jar of sauce from the cupboard right when the doorbell rang. Who could that be?

"Mom!" Susie's voice carried from the other room.

Tiffany? He set the jar of sauce aside and walked to the living room. Sure enough, Tiffany stood by the tree with two big bags of gifts like she owned the place. "Who wants presents?"

"I told you tonight wasn't a good night." Cole spoke through the best smile he could force.

She shrugged. "I won't stay long."

"You should have called."

"Well, the best surprises are that—a surprise." Then she seemed to take him in from his white button-up shirt to his khakis to his hair still wet from the shower. "Do you have a date?"

"Dad is going out with Fallon." Susie did a twirl and landed sprawled out on the couch.

"Is he, now?" Tiffany eyed him up and down again, her gaze shifting to an interest he hadn't seen on her face in a very long time. Oh boy. Fallon's voice came back to him. *Maybe she's back because I'm in your life again. And that is enough to make her want you, manipulate you, and use you all over again.*

He wasn't worried about himself. There was nothing in him that was tempted by Tiffany. But any game she played now, the kids were liable to get caught up in the crossfire.

"Don't even think about it." He said the words low as he sent her a look of warning. He wanted to say a lot more, but he needed to keep it civil in front of the kids.

She pointed to the bags. "Well, then we better open these quick. Your dad has places to be."

What was she up to now?

"Don't we have to wait till Christmas?" Susie hopped off the couch and sat right next to a bag, trying to peek in.

Zane walked in and plopped on the couch. "What's going on?"

"These are for your birthdays that I missed. I'll bring the Christmas gifts later." One of the boxes began to whimper and Tiffany pulled the box from the bag and held it out to Susie. "Besides, I don't think you should wait on this one."

Susie took the box and lifted the lid. "A puppy!"

"A what?" Cole could feel the heat building inside him as Susie lifted a white fluffball from the box.

"He's a Maltipoo." Tiffany scratched the puppy on its head. "He looked just like the one in the photo you showed me."

It sure did and he'd looked up the cost of those dogs. They were around three grand. Seriously? How about just a new winter coat? The muscle in Cole's jaw ticked. "You can't get her a dog without talking to me."

"Come on, Cole. She has always begged for a puppy." As if that justified it.

"She asked for a horse the other day too. Are you wanting to buy her one?"

"The newest Xbox? Are you serious?" Zane started jumping around.

Cole's gaze drifted to the one he'd saved for and hunted all over the country for now wrapped and under the tree for Christmas morning.

Cole looked at Tiffany and pointed to the laundry room. "We need to talk." Then he looked at Zane. "Can you add the spaghetti sauce to the noodles?"

"I want to try my new game." The voice had way too much whine in it for a thirteen-year-old.

"That's okay." Susie jumped up and slapped her leg. "Polly and I will do it."

Cole looked around the room. "Polly?"

"My puppy. Princess Polly" She slapped her leg again. "Come on, Polly."

The dog followed after her, sniffing and jumping as he went.

He marched out of earshot of Zane and turned on Tiffany. "You can't buy her a dog. That is a big responsibility. I have a lot going on, I don't have time to train—"

"Relax. I'll keep it at my parents' house. If I have the kids half the time—"

"Half the time?" He pinched the bridge of his nose as he drew a slow, calming breath. "I said visits. Not shared custody. You need to be back for more than a week if you want me to consider—"

Susie's scream filled the house and Cole sprinted from the laundry room to the kitchen. Susie stood in the middle of the kitchen with sauce, well, everywhere. The jar lay upside down on the kitchen floor. "I dropped it."

He reached over and lifted the jar from the ground. At least it hadn't shattered. It wasn't even cracked. He set it in the sink and evaluated the scene. Ragu was on Susie, the floor, the cupboard, and even a bit of the ceiling. It was even on Polly, but she seemed more than content licking it off.

"I would love to stay and help with this"—Tiffany stood next to him—"but I have to get going. I'm meeting someone."

Of course she was.

If things couldn't get worse, Polly decided to offer a full body shake, sprinkling Cole's pants, shirt, and the kitchen with little red dots.

The front door opened and shut as the clock chimed six o'clock. He was going to miss his date.

He picked up his phone but wasn't quite sure what to text. Instead, he sent a photo of the kitchen with the words *Not sure this will work tonight.*

He pointed to Susie and the dog. "You two. Get cleaned up in the bathroom. Use the dark towels."

Just then the noodles on the stove began to smoke and Cole grabbed the pan and tossed it in the sink. He'd drained them but somehow switched the burner to low instead of off in the chaos of Tiffany's arrival.

He glanced over at Zane, already deep in his game. Awesome. He grabbed a rag and began the process of wiping the white cabinets, but ten minutes later all he'd managed to do was smear the little dots of red sauce so the cabinets all looked pinkish orange.

A knock at the door made Cole freeze. If Tiffany was back, he was making her help. Either that or she could go bathe Polly at her parents' house. He didn't even want to imagine what the bathroom would look like after this.

Cole walked over to the door and pulled it open. Fallon stood there with her hair pulled up in a bun and her coat over an old T-shirt and sweatpants. She held up a bucket and a few cleaners. "Need help?"

"I could kiss you right now." He opened the door wider and stepped back.

"I hope you don't greet all help that way."

"Just you."

"Then I'll take it." He took a step toward her, but she held up a finger. "Maybe after you get cleaned up."

She followed him into the kitchen and surveyed the damage. "This is all from one jar of spaghetti sauce?"

"And Polly."

"Polly?"

"Tiffany got Susie a dog."

She peeked at the glob of noodles in the sink and handed him the bottle of 409. "You wipe, I'll make a new dinner. How does fettuccine Alfredo sound?"

"Polly!" Susie's voice grew as her footsteps bounded down the stairs.

The door cracked open and a wet, very soapy Polly ran into the kitchen followed by Susie carrying a towel. "Naughty Polly."

But with the little girl's tone, he doubted the dog heard anything but *good dog*.

"Meet Polly." Cole scooped up the dog and carried her to the sink. "I wanted to give you the first date you deserve."

"And miss all this fun?" Fallon turned on the water and got it warm then handed him the sprayer. "It's nice to meet you, Polly."

"Princess Polly." Susie still held out the towel grinning from ear to ear.

"Forgive me, Your Highness." Fallon rinsed the last of the bubbles away. "*Princess* Polly."

"I'm serious." Cole set the pup in Susie's waiting arms then looked up at Fallon. "Go with me to the annual Christmas Adam dance."

"What is a Christmas Adam dance?" Susie cuddled Polly to her chest as the dog wiggled to get free of the towel.

Fallon bent down and helped towel dry the dog. "You've heard of Christmas Eve on December 24th, right?"

"And Adam came before Eve." Zane stood in the doorway shaking his head. "That is so dumb."

"But it is a tradition in the town on the twenty-third every year. So, Fallon," He pulled her to a stand. "Will you go with me?"

All three seemed to be waiting for her answer. "Yes."

Both the kids smiled. Maybe he was finally getting something right.

He ushered the kids and dog out, then leaned his back against the counter, wiping a bit of the sauce from his hands. "I did have a great night planned."

"This is better—real life."

Was this what marriage was supposed to be like? Tiffany and he had never been on the same side. Always on opposing teams. If he was home, she was taking off. If she was home, he was deployed. Most of their marriage had revolved around passing off the kids. They never dealt with problems together. Tackled the hard things together.

The moment in the square that Fallon had said she loved him, he'd known he loved her too. It hadn't been hard to say it. But right here in the midst of the messiness of life, love had never felt more tangible.

"I think I like real life with you." His voice had gone rough, and he cleared his throat. "I could get used to real life with you."

She stared at him for a long moment then started to reach for him but seemed to think better of it and pointed to his shirt still covered in sauce. "And real life is cleaning up before I hug or kiss you."

Cole laughed before tossing the rag aside and then shutting himself in the laundry room. He grabbed a pair of athletic shorts and a T-shirt from the dryer and made a quick change before tossing his formerly nicest outfit in the wash.

Real life it was, and real life was going to start with him claiming that kiss in the kitchen. He stepped out of the room as Fallon was hanging up her phone. He took a step toward her. Her face was tense and pinched. "Who was that?"

She moved back to the stove and added a box of noodles to the boiling water. "My dad tried to move a tree by himself and threw out his back again."

Cole reached for his keys. "Do we need to go?"

She shook her head. "It isn't as bad as it was the first time. They called the doctor and she said to rest. But he's supposed to stay in bed for a week."

"That means he'll be there until almost Christmas."

"And people are expecting Santa this weekend." She stared at the noodles, then looked up at him. "Unless—"

"No way. Remember, that was one of my first conditions to help at the tree farm. No Santa."

"Please."

Real life is tackling hard things together. His line of thoughts from a few minutes ago floated back. "Okay."

"Okay?"

He nodded and she wrapped her arms around him. He'd take it. Real life was looking better and better, even if it meant putting on an old red suit.

fifteen

FROM THE MOMENT HE'D DECIDED THAT HE loved Fallon, Cole knew he'd do his best to protect her from anything—even dressing up as Santa to keep away hordes of angry parents who wouldn't be pleased with no Santa. But Saturday's Santa's North Pole experience was supposed to open in five minutes, and he was about one minute from escaping out the back door. Because angry parents were one thing—this was something completely different.

Cole sat in Santa's big red chair with the suit on and beard in place, trying his best to look jolly as he eyed the long line of women that stretched the length of the Sugar Shack. Women waiting to sit on Santa's lap. They ranged from twenty to forty, with maybe only a kid or two among the whole lot.

"I didn't sign up for this." Cole leaned toward Fallon, his voice low. "I can handle the kids . . ."

"Even that kid yesterday who wet his pants while he waited in line?" Fallon adjusted a setting on the camera.

"Yes, everything about yesterday was better than this."

The line the first night had been pretty full, but they had all been kids under ten.

She tried and failed at smothering a smile. "Maybe they want to stand in line to ask Santa for 'Cole' this year."

Last night, Fallon had teased him about a TikTok post that had shown up. It showed him talking to some kid with the caption: *Is that sexy Santa? I'm totally asking Santa for "Cole" this year.*

He was so tired of social media he didn't want to see another smartphone as long as he lived.

Cole rubbed his sweaty forehead, dislodging his Santa hat. "If I thought that post would lead to this, I would've gone home. What am I supposed to do with all these desperate housewives?"

Fallon eyed the line of women then looked at him, a smirk tugging at her lips.

"It's not funny," he grumbled as he shifted in the suit. Man, this thing was scratchy. "This is not what I signed up for."

"So you said."

"Do you really want all those women sitting on my lap?"

Fallon instantly sobered. "No, this is not the kind of establishment we're running."

He was trying to go for jealousy rather than proper business practices, but he'd take anything that got him out of this.

She scanned the area, then pointed to the bench they had put next to his chair for kids who didn't want to sit on Santa's lap. Fallon grabbed a paper and black Sharpie and wrote in a flowy script *Anyone over ten must use the bench.* Then underlined "must" three times.

"How's that?" She taped it to the board at the front of the line.

Grumbles filled the room, but he didn't care. He had only agreed to help the farm and rescue Fallon from a difficult situation.

Zane came running up. "Sorry I'm late."

"Just in time." Fallon pointed to the camera. "It's all set."

Cole adjusted his beard as Fallon smiled at him and turned back to the checkout counter.

Zane eyed the row of ladies and looked at his dad. "This is so weird."

"Tell me about it."

The first two women came up together and looked like a mother-daughter pair. The daughter was in her twenties, the mom close to fifty. *Please don't let them hit on me or ask me for my number.*

"It is so good to finally meet you." The daughter spoke first, her cheeks pinking up slightly.

"It was quite a drive." The mother added, but there was no interest in her eyes. She seemed more focused on the daughter.

There was a slight almost Southern accent to their words. They squeezed on the bench and smiled at the camera, each holding up a piece of coal.

What in the world?

"On three." Zane counted and Cole smiled just before the flash went off. Then his son lowered the camera and handed them a piece of paper. "This explains how you can access the photo."

Cole looked at the women. "What is the coal for?"

"Hashtag: Cole for Christmas." The mother seemed to be holding back a smile.

His confusion must have shown because the daughter tapped at her phone for a moment and then turned it around. "It's a TikTok challenge. We drove up from Kentucky."

That explained the accent.

"Nice meeting you." The mother started to steer the daughter away. "We've been in line for over two hours, and we are going to go find some of those sugar cookies."

The daughter gave a final wave. "Thanks."

"Two hours?" Zane lifted one eyebrow at him. "Sorry, Dad, a photo with you isn't worth all that."

"Agreed." Cole glanced down the line. Almost every person

was holding a black chunk of coal. They weren't here to date him. They were here because he'd become a TikTok challenge. He wasn't sure if that was better or worse. If they were here to ask for dates, at least he could say no. But #ColeForChristmas had taken a life of its own and he was powerless to stop it.

He glanced to Fallon for help but she was talking to a man by the ornaments. Why was the guy looking at her like that? She shook her head and handed him another ornament. He leaned against the wall next to her and Fallon laughed. Actually *laughed*.

"Easy, Santa." Deb sat down on the bench next to him. "You're turning from sexy Santa into scary Santa."

"Sorry. It's just that Fallon—"

"Is helping a customer?"

"But he—"

"Is harmless. Fallon can handle herself. What's really bothering you?"

"I just don't like it."

"If you feel that strongly, then maybe you should consider asking her to stay?" Deb walked back to the counter.

Maybe he needed to do that tonight.

Three hours later as he shed the red coat back in the main house, he was ready to buy the place for Fallon just to avoid another night like that. His movements stilled as the idea settled in. Her parents had talked about selling the place, but what if he bought it? What if *they* bought it?

He shook his head and folded the red coat and pants and dropped them in the bin. He was getting ahead of himself. They hadn't even had a successful date yet. Maybe he should start there. His phone buzzed and he picked it up. Startled at the name on the screen. Rock? He hadn't heard from his old teammate in over a year.

"This is Cole."

"It's Dixon—he's in a bad way. Thought you'd want to know."

The words stabbed him in the chest. Dixon had just joined the team before Cole had gotten out. He was only a kid. Too young for this. "What happened?"

"Bad intel. We were blocked in without a way out. Backup eventually showed, but not before he took two shots to the leg. He lost a lot of blood."

Cole sank into a chair and buried his face with his free hand. Intel was what he'd been in charge of. If he'd been there, he could have prevented this. Maybe.

Still. He couldn't escape the idea he'd let his former team down.

"I've got to go." Rock's voice was distant. "I'll let you know if there's an update."

The line went dead and Cole swallowed the burning pressure in his chest. He'd given up protecting one family to protect another. His kids needed him but so did his SEAL brothers.

He walked out of the Jameses' house and almost directly into Tiffany and the kids walking up the drive from the Sugar Shack. Susie held her mom's hand and Zane walked a few feet behind.

"Dad." Susie dropped her mom's hand and ran up to him. "Can we stay at Mom's tonight?"

His gaze darted to his ex's. Their agreement had been only supervised visits, but the last few evenings he'd gotten slack on that, letting her walk around the tree farm with them as he worked. But overnight visits were another story.

"Please." Susie tugged at his hand. "I want to sleep with Polly."

Tiffany had been true to her word about taking the dog to her parents' place. She'd brought him with her for her daily visits, but she had handled the whole pet thing.

Imagine that.

Tiffany stepped forward, her perfectly arched brows pinching together. "You're going to have to trust me sometime."

She was right. And if ever he needed a night to clear his head, it was tonight.

"Fine. I'll pick them up for church in the morning at ten. And"—he eyed the kids—"your bedtime stands."

Susie cheered and Zane almost looked pleased. Maybe they could make this co-parenting work. Susie hugged his side. "Night. See you tomorrow."

Zane nodded at him and followed his mom to her car. Cole hurried to the Sugar Shack. He pushed through the double doors and found Fallon counting money at the register.

"You're good for business, sexy Santa." She set aside a stack of twenties, made a note on a piece of paper, then picked up the tens and flipped through them.

"Glad to help." His tone was dry as he leaned against the counter. "Just tell me I don't have to do that again."

She winced and pointed to the sign. *Santa will be here through Sunday, December 22nd*. She finally met his gaze. Frowned. "Everything okay?"

"Just got news a former SEAL buddy of mine is hurt. Critical."

She dropped the money, came around the counter, and wrapped him in a hug. "I'm so sorry. What can I do?"

"This." He buried his face in her neck, drawing in her deep vanilla scent. He could get used to doing life with her. "I can't help but feel like if I had still been active . . . if I had been with my team—"

"No." She leaned back, framing his face with her hands. "That *was* your team. Your kids now are your team and they need you. You did the right thing."

He pulled her into another hug. She was right. He couldn't protect everyone, and right now his team was his kids . . . and just maybe, her.

"Hello?"

He pulled back and looked at the man in the doorway. A man in a business suit holding a briefcase stood a few feet behind them.

Fallon took a step back. "Can I help you?"

"Sorry to arrive so late but I got turned around in the dark. Took me a bit to find this place."

"If you need a tree—"

He held up his hand. "My name is Timothy Cardwell. I'm a lawyer who represents Winterbourne Enterprises. I'm just here to give you this and I'll be on my way."

Fallon took it and the man walked back toward his car. The corner of the envelope said The Law Firm of Cardwell and Cardwell. She opened it up and flipped through the first few pages, her face going paler the further she read.

Cole took a step closer. "Fallon, talk to me. What's going on?"

Her voice emerged soft and shaky. "I'm being sued by Winterbourne."

Cole took the papers and scanned them over. This was bad. Winterbourne was taking Fallon to court for breach of contract. If she was on his team or not, he was pretty sure he couldn't protect her from this.

This was worse than she'd originally feared. Fallon stared at their lawyer across her parents' dining room table as he explained the paper she had received Saturday night. She'd spent all yesterday waffling between stressing out and believing it wasn't as bad as she feared. She'd been wrong—it was worse than that.

"So because they're not just suing Fallon but also the farm, we could lose it all?" her mom clarified.

"I'm afraid so." Gerald Donavan flipped the paper and pointed to the part that must have made that clear to him.

"I don't understand how they can do this. I *just* painted them." Fallon stood and paced the small space by the dining room table and then back. "They don't have rights to all my paintings for the rest of my life."

Mr. Donavan flipped a page, then another. "It says that you presented this idea to them four years ago."

"The idea, not these paintings. And it wasn't exactly this idea. Besides, they turned them down." She threw her hands into the air, but her pacing didn't stop. She had to calm down.

He followed the text with his finger, mumbling as he went. "They did. But according to this, they retained the right to pick them up for . . . " He followed the line a little farther. "Five years. They still had one more year to pick them up according to the contract you signed."

"But those were for different paintings." She dug her hands into the sides of her hair.

"They're arguing that you pitched the concept, not actual paintings, and these fall under the concept."

"But last year they told me they wouldn't be renewing any of my contracts."

"Did you get that in writing?" The lawyer looked hopeful for the first time.

"I didn't think I needed to." She dropped back into her spot at the table. "I didn't even know they held the right to concepts."

"That is a gray area. The fact that they are different paintings is a solid case, and you *could* win." He leaned back in his chair.

"Could?"

"I'll be honest." He pulled off his wire-rimmed glasses and tapped the earpiece against his lip. "The legal fees alone for this type of suit may be enough to bankrupt this place. And I'm not talking about me. Court fees are no joke."

"So what are you saying?" Her father set the paper he'd been reading down in front of him and stared at the lawyer. The wrinkles around his eyes were a little deeper than they had been.

"I'm saying it may be best to take the settlement they offered." The lawyer flipped through pages and made a note on his paper then slid it to them.

Her heart sank as she skimmed the paper. They wanted the paintings. All of them. They'd take everything just like they had done with the Tiny Angels collections and leave her with nothing. A few small royalty checks and steal her work again.

Fallon dropped her head in her hands. "But I didn't do anything wrong."

"Sorry to say that right and wrong don't always work out in the court system."

Her mother massaged her temples. "If we sell the place then we could afford to fight them on—"

"Sell?" The air left Fallon's lungs. All they had done and now they would walk away with less than if she hadn't come and gotten involved in the first place.

"I'm not sure there is another way." Her father gave a resigned shrug.

There was another way. She tapped the paper with her finger. "I will agree to this."

"Fallon." Pain laced her mother's voice. "You can't."

"I have to. After all we've done, I'm not going to let you lose the farm now." She reached for a pen. "Now where do I sign?"

sixteen

COLE HADN'T BEEN TO A CHRISTMAS ADAM dance since he was eighteen, but he'd felt just as out of place then as he did now. His gaze darted to the entrance of the community center as the door opened yet again. Not Fallon. He adjusted the tie at his neck and checked his cufflinks.

"Stop freaking out, Dad. You look great." Susie spun around him in her shimmery pink dress, making it flare out. Then she looked up at the white lights draped along the ceiling creating a starry effect. "Everything is so pretty. It's like a dream. Why can't we come here every day?"

He lifted her hand and helped her spin again. "Because the community center doesn't look like this every day. They just put all these decorations up to make it feel special for the dance."

"It is very special." She gave another turn as the band on the small stage on the far side of the room broke into a modern version of "Winter Wonderland." "I can't wait until Fallon gets here."

"Me too." He should've picked Fallon up, but Deb had called him to tell him that the meeting with the lawyer had gone long and she'd meet him here. But when? Most of the town had already arrived. He'd call her to check on her, but she had left her phone at his house last night when she'd come over for a movie with him and the kids.

She'd been so distracted by the summons all evening he wasn't surprised when he found it wedged in the couch cushions this morning. He'd offered to bring it over, but she said she'd just get it here. Cole was praying that with this meeting over, she could put it all behind her and enjoy the dance—enjoy Christmas.

He pulled her phone from his pocket as if it would offer some clue as to when she'd arrive. Of course it didn't. Although he did appreciate that she'd made her locked screen a photo of them.

"Don't you clean up nice?" Tiffany appeared in front of him. Her red dress was a size tighter than what looked comfortable and had a fair amount of cleavage spilling out. She hadn't gone light on the perfume, that was for sure. She moved her body to the rhythm of the music, a teasing glint in her eye. "Want to dance?"

"I'm good." He slipped Fallon's phone back in his pocket. The door opened and his gaze flicked that way. Just the Taylors. Zane saw them too and hurried off to hang out with their oldest, Jimmy. Cole turned away from Tiffany and stepped over to the refreshments. He gulped down a cup of lemonade, letting the sour taste linger. Maybe he should go to Fallon's house. If the meeting hadn't gone well, maybe she needed him.

"Come on, Cole." Tiffany had evidently followed him. "For old times' sake. We were good together once." She stepped up and laid her hand on his chest. "Remember?"

"No. I don't remember it ever being good." He took a step back. "I remember you manipulating me. Maybe that was how you liked it, but I don't think of that as good."

She looked ready to argue, but her face softened. "Okay. But we do need to talk about Christmas and the kids. Do you want to step outside where it's quieter?"

His phone buzzed and he checked it. Deb.

He pocketed his phone and glanced at Susie, who was dancing in the corner with friends from school. He looked back at Tiffany. "You have five minutes."

He led the way to the main door and stepped out into the crisp air. He scanned the parking lot. Still no sign of Fallon. He shoved his hands in his pockets. "They can go over to your parents' house with you Christmas afternoon, but they're spending Christmas Eve and Christmas morning with me."

"*I* want to be with them on Christmas Eve. You've had the last two Christmases with them."

Was she serious? "That was your choice."

She stared at him a moment. Then, "Can I at least come over to your house and join you for part of Christmas Eve?"

Last night he and Fallon had talked about her joining them when she'd been at his house. Nothing was set in stone, but Fallon and Tiffany there at the same time? "Not this year."

And suddenly all her pretense seemed to fade as she stared at him with a sad smile. "Fine. But next year. And I'm holding you to it."

If she were still around next year, he wouldn't have a problem granting it.

"Thank you for letting me back in their lives. I mean it. I know I don't deserve it, but I do love them." She reached up for a hug and after a moment's hesitation he obliged, aiming for what he hoped would come across as the least affectionate embrace in history.

"We'll figure it out. And I'm glad you're back—for their sake."

He relaxed the hug and attempted to step back but Tiffany didn't let go. She pulled him tighter and pressed a kiss to his neck.

"Oh, Cole, I'm glad I'm back too. I've missed you so much. I've missed us."

"What are you doing?" He pushed her shoulders firmly back until she finally stepped away. "Let's get one thing straight. I'll let you back in the kids' lives, but we are *not* getting back together. Ever. Understand?"

Her eyes narrowed as crossed her arms in front of her. "You may think you see a future with Fallon, but I wouldn't buy a ring yet—"

"This isn't about Fallon. I don't know if I see a future with Fallon." Where had that come from? He wanted Fallon more than life itself. Did he still have a crushing fear that in the end she'd walk away from him like everyone else did? Yeah, maybe. But Tiffany was the last person he would discuss any of this with. "But whether I buy a ring for her or not, you and I are done. Through. Over. Never again. Do I make myself clear?"

"So you *haven't* bought a ring?" One eyebrow lifted.

Ugh, this woman had a knack for prying things out of him that he didn't want to give. Did she practice that, or was she naturally gifted at emotional treachery? "Tiffany, I swear . . . "

She looked at the ground then up at him. Wells of tears in her eyes. The woman was all over the place emotionally. "I have made so many mistakes. I just really love the kids. I want them to be happy. And I know they want us to be a family again."

Boy, did he understand that. Regrets, pain, even the willingness to do almost anything to make his kids happy. Getting back together with Tiffany would make the kids happy, at least temporarily, but it wasn't the answer. He didn't love her, and he didn't think Tiffany even knew what love was. Creating healthy boundaries was the best way for him to love his kids right now. Even if they didn't fully understand that.

"I know you love them. So do I. If you're really back to stay, we can make this work. Not a romantic relationship, but a workable, cordial shared custody." *And no hugging.* He stared off for a second.

He couldn't stop his mind from settling on memories of Susie in her Christmas pj's, sitting in her mother's lap opening presents, her ear-to-ear grin filling up the room.

Susie is desperate for her mother. Fallon's words came back to him. He sighed. "If you really want to be with them on Christmas Eve, you can come over and stay until they go to bed."

Fallon would understand. The kids hadn't spent the past two Christmases with their mom, and he had no doubt Susie wanted that.

"I'd like that." Tiffany stared at him for a half second before nodding and retreating inside. He didn't follow her. Fallon should be here soon, and the silent parking lot seemed better than stepping back into the chaos alone.

His phone buzzed and he pulled it out and stared at the screen. But it wasn't his phone. Right, he had Fallon's too. He lowered it to return it to his pocket but the partial message on the screen snagged his gaze.

JAN
I know you are interviewing with
Hallmark too. But

That was all it showed. The phone needed to be unlocked to read the whole message. He shoved it back in his pocket. He shouldn't have even read that much. But who was Jan and what did she mean interviewing at Hallmark too? Was Fallon still planning on leaving?

Doors slammed and Cole's head jerked up. He met Fallon's gaze as she and her parents walked toward him.

The woman was walking elegance. The shimmery navy dress wasn't tight but moved over her curves in a way that sent fire through him. Her blonde hair was pinned up with wispy curls falling around her face. All he wanted to do was pull her into his arms and recreate that kiss he'd been thinking about every moment she wasn't with him.

He took a step toward her. "You look . . ."

Great, she'd reduced him to a tongue-tied thirteen-year-old kid who was practically drooling all over himself.

Her lips tipped up into a flirty smile. "So do you."

He blinked and looked at her parents. "Evening."

They nodded and offered smiles. Tim looked ready to say something, but Deb's hand landed on his arm. "We'll see you two inside."

As soon as they were gone, Cole tugged her toward him then slid his other hand around her waist, pulling her close.

Her free hand slid up his chest, but she dropped a single finger on his mouth. "You can't mess up my lipstick." His disappointment must have shown because she dropped her hand and added, "Not until after the dance."

He rested his forehead against hers, his voice low. "I'll hold you to that."

"I hope you do." Her minty breath fanned across his face. Man, was she testing his self-control. Lipstick had to be the worse invention ever.

He pulled back but didn't release her hand. "Dance with me?"

She nodded and he led her inside and out onto the floor. The way she curved into him ignited every cell in his body and set him at ease at the same time. He could spend hours like this and never feel the time pass. And in that moment, he knew what he'd said to Tiffany wasn't true. He could see a future with Fallon. He could see dancing with her for the next fifty years here on this dance floor. He could see raising Susie and Zane together . . . maybe even another. He could see it all so clearly it nearly overwhelmed him. Because he could see forever with her. And suddenly, he wanted forever to start right now.

How could everything be coming together and falling apart at the same time? Fallon tucked herself against Cole's shoulder, letting the soothing music wash over her. Here in his strong arms, there weren't lawyers to face, futures to plan, dreams to lose. Here she was safe, protected. Hidden.

He wasn't one for cologne and she'd always loved that about him. But tonight, he wore a fragrance that was smooth and, if she had to admit, a touch feminine. She'd have to find a way to tell him she preferred his natural musky scent. His natural scent just smelled like home.

He brushed a piece of hair over her shoulder. "I got a call about my buddy Dixon. He's in the clear. It will be quite the recovery, but he'll live."

"That's great." She closed her eyes and relaxed into him. "What time should I come over Christmas Eve?"

His dancing stilled for a fraction of a second. "How about we do Christmas morning instead."

"Okay." She'd looked forward to Christmas Eve with him, but maybe spending it with her parents would be better. Especially if it were the last one they'd be spending in the house.

He pulled her a little closer. "How did the meeting with the lawyer go?"

She shook her head then tucked herself back into his shoulder.

"Fallon?" He stopped their movement and lifted her chin.

She finally met his gaze. "I have to sign away my rights to the new series."

His whole body seemed to freeze. "What are you talking about?"

"They aren't just suing me. They're suing the farm. Their offer was they would drop the lawsuit if I signed over the rights to the new series."

"That's crazy." Gone was the soft gentle Cole. This was the Cole who walked across enemy lines to go toe to toe with the world's most wanted. "We'll fight them."

She had no doubt that he would too.

She shook her head and led them toward the refreshments. "It's done. I already signed the papers."

"Why would you do that?" He kept his voice low, but the intensity remained. "You can't let them win."

"I'm not letting them win." She lifted a cup of lemonade and took a gulp of the tart liquid. "I'm surviving. It's what I do."

His jaw ticked and he glanced at Susie. "Wait here."

He walked over and leaned down to whisper in Susie's ear.

"Men are such fickle creatures." Tiffany appeared next to her, her eyes on Cole. The woman looked stunning, if not a touch desperate. And she wore enough perfume for the entire room. An alarm went off in Fallon's brain, but she couldn't place why. "Dancing all sweet one moment, arguing the next."

"Honestly, I'm not in the mood for your—"

"Having a *moment* with me wrapped in his arms as we plan Christmas Eve together, then turning around dancing with you next."

In his arms? Fat chance. But Christmas Eve? Was that why he said they couldn't spend Christmas Eve together?

She shook the thought away, refusing to let Tiffany get to her. "You honestly think I would believe anything you said?"

"Probably not. But facts are facts. Take a good look at his collar." Tiffany started to walk past Fallon but stopped when their shoulders were even. Her gaze still straight ahead. "He'll always choose me when I'm an option. He did before. And now that I'm back, he will again. He told me he wasn't sure if he saw a future with you. He volunteered that tidbit." The triumphant smile was almost more than Fallon could bear.

"Look him straight in the eye and ask him," Tiffany added before Fallon could respond.

She wandered away just as Cole left Susie and walked straight for her.

"I told Susie where she could find me." He slipped his hand into hers. "Let's talk outside."

He led them out through a side door. Pulling off his suit coat, he slipped it over her shoulders, its warmth instantly erasing the chill in the air. He paced a few feet away and then back, just as his phone rang. He reached in his pocket and silenced the call. "Okay, I was thinking. I have a friend who's a lawyer and—"

"Stop. This isn't your problem to fix. You can't fix everything. Sometimes you have to accept life for what it is."

"No, you need to fight for what you want." He stopped right in front of her and locked eyes with her. "You need to fight for your paintings. Fight for what should be yours after Robert died. You should've fought for your dreams when Robert was alive—like having kids."

"Are you saying I didn't fight for kids? I fought for them." Why was he so mad? This wasn't his life. "We agreed to wait."

"You agreed or you let him win? Because I don't think that's what you wanted."

"What do you know about what I want?"

"I've seen you with the kids. I know you desperately want kids. I'm just saying you should have fought harder. Robert won like you're letting Winterbourne win now. You need to—"

"I don't need to do anything. I made my decision. I'm not one more thing for you to fix." Cole's eyes hardened but suddenly it all made sense. He showed up to help her fix the farm, then he had to help her fix the fact she couldn't paint. And now he had to fix this. What would happen when she didn't have anything left for him to fix? "Will I ever be enough for you just the way I am?"

"What?" His face twisted in confusion. "Of course you're enough for me, I just—"

His phone rang again but he sent it to voicemail again without looking.

Her eyes focused on his collar. Red. Matching the exact shade of Tiffany's lipstick. "What are you doing for Christmas Eve?"

"What? Where did that come from?"

A cold chill that had nothing to do with the weather traveled through her veins. "Answer the question."

He shoved his hand in his pockets and shrugged. "Tiffany is coming over to be with the kids. I thought Susie would want—"

"She wasn't lying." The whole world seemed to tip. Fallon leaned against the brick wall at her back.

"Who?" Cole reached for her, concern filling his face. "What's wrong?"

She blinked hard and looked at his collar again. And just like that, she pinpointed the strange cologne on his coat. It matched Tiffany's perfume. All of a sudden, it became hard to breathe. Tiffany had been telling the truth about both of those as well. "There's lipstick on your collar."

"What?" He reached up right to where marks were. Was that guilt in his expression?

"And this smells like her." She tugged his jacket off and held it out. The cold night air now bit at her shoulders. At least it wasn't as cold as it had been lately.

"Nothing happened." He didn't take the coat. "You either trust me or you don't." When she didn't respond he met her gaze as his voice dropped into crisis management mode. "She was crying—"

"And you had to fix it?" She whipped the coat at him and he caught it. Draped it over his arm.

"No." He took a step closer. "She threw herself at me."

"And you caught her."

His phone rang for a third time, but he ignored it again. "I told her we were not getting back together."

"Before or after she kissed your neck?"

He took a slow breath, a cloud of fog filling the night. Gently he laid his hands on her arms. "She was crying about the kids and she hugged me. I let her do that. But when she tried to kiss me, I pushed her off and told her that it would never happen. Told her that in four different ways. That is all."

"Was this before or after you made plans with her for Christmas Eve?"

When he didn't immediately answer, it was enough. He may have told Tiffany no, but he'd turned around and agreed to an evening with her. "Right."

He dropped his hands. "Is this how it will always be? You're going to have to trust me sometime, Fallon. Like it or not, she will never be out of my life. We have kids together. But I don't love her. I love you. And you may not trust her—I sure don't—but you do have to trust me. You can't go doubting me every time she says something to get under your skin."

"*Do* you love me?"

His hands were back on her arms again. "Of course I do."

"Because in there you just listed all the things wrong with me. How I don't measure up."

"What are you talking about? I never said that."

"No, you said I don't fight for things, that I let people walk all over me, that I needed to change."

"I don't think you need to change. I think you need—"

His phone rang for a fourth time. Fallon held up her hand. "Just take it."

He pulled it out. Walker. "I'll send him a text. We aren't done with this conversation."

He tapped at his phone as Fallon tried to find a place for all this to land in her mind. Tiffany's words on a loop. *He'll always choose me when I'm an option. He did before. And now that I'm back, he will again.*

She didn't want to believe it, but he was choosing her on Christmas Eve. And after he'd laid out all the things wrong with her a few minutes ago, she was beginning to doubt if he was choosing her now. Maybe he was just choosing the idea of her. Much like Robert had done. Robert had tried to mold her into who he wanted, and she had let him. She couldn't do that again.

It couldn't be true. Could it? *Look him straight in the eye and ask him.*

Her body seemed twice its normal weight. Everything in her fought against the question, but as much as she wanted to trust Cole, she couldn't shake the dread. She opened her mouth, but her throat refused to speak. She knew it was a lie. But Tiffany hadn't been lying about anything else. And the image of that infuriating smile burned in her mind. The sudden flood of anger at that memory forced the words out before she even realized she was talking.

"Did you tell her you weren't sure you saw a future for us?"

Caught off guard, mid text, Cole's unprepared reaction confirmed the truth she had refused to believe.

"No. Well, Fallon—" Where was the straightforward, confident man she had grown used to? "I . . . wait . . . "

She took a hesitant step toward the door. Then another. "I think I need space to think."

"About what?"

"Us . . . the future . . . whether this should continue."

"Is this about Tiffany?" His hands raked through his hair, leaving it at odd angles. "Or is this because you still have those interviews scheduled and this is a convenient excuse to exit?"

"What? Where did that come from?" Fallon shook her head, trying to catch up.

He pulled her phone from his pocket and passed it back. "Jan texted. It flashed on the screen earlier."

"You're reading my texts now?" She took it but didn't open it. "Sounds like you trust me."

"You're one to talk. A known compulsive liar says something

to you and you believe her over me?" Something hard settled into his gaze.

His phone rang yet again.

"Just take the call." She was practically shouting. Some latecomers in the parking lot looked their way.

Cole's jaw twitched before he answered his phone. "This better be important." He paced a few feet away.

The side door opened again. Tiffany walked out, smirk in place.

Perfect. Fallon closed her eyes, taking a second to erase any emotion from her face. Last thing she needed was to give Tiffany any more ammunition. She lifted her head and used the calmest voice she could muster. "We just need a moment."

"I know we have had our differences, Fallon." Tiffany gave what seemed like a genuine, soft smile. "But Cole thrives on solving problems, helping the helpless, so if you want to keep him, you need to make sure he knows you *need* him."

Only Tiffany would suggest manipulation as a tactic to save a relationship.

When she didn't respond, Tiffany tilted her head. "He told me he hadn't bought a ring yet, but I didn't think you two were this close to ending it."

The thing with Tiffany was she rarely dealt in full-on lies. She specialized in half-truths and twisted truths but rarely blatant lies. Which meant no matter what he'd actually said, he probably had talked to Tiffany about a ring. She understood Tiffany would always be in their lives, but Fallon couldn't handle her being between them. She wasn't going to fight a battle she'd already lost.

seventeen

COLE GRIPPED THE PHONE SO TIGHT IT'S A wonder it didn't crack. How could she not trust him?

"I need you to be on your way to Detroit in the next twenty minutes," Walker growled. "So I'd say that's important."

He shoved his hand in his pocket. "I can't. Christmas Eve is tomorrow."

"It isn't a request." Walker's voice was tight. "The team needs you. Besides, it's just in Detroit. I'll have you back tomorrow in plenty of time for Santa."

Walker rattled off a payment that had him catching his breath.

"You can't be serious." He glanced back to where Fallon and Tiffany were talking. That couldn't be good.

"It's a past job we did and there was a breach earlier today, and it spooked them. We must have missed something. Which means it makes us look bad."

Winterbourne? What were the chances? Then again, everything seemed to go back to him. Cole resisted the urge to throw his phone against the brick wall in front of him.

"I need you to help me fix this." Walker's voice shifted from authoritarian to a desperate friend asking for help.

How could he say no? His team had always had his back and he had theirs. "You promise I'll be back tomorrow?"

"By dinner at the latest."

He glanced back at Fallon and Tiffany. There was a new tension in Fallon's shoulders. Awesome. He walked that way. Maybe Tiffany would back off if she knew he could overhear.

"I'll leave within the hour." He met Fallon's eyes. Was that disappointment? He ended the call and slid the phone in his pocket.

Fallon took a step toward him. "Don't leave, not tonight."

"My team needs me."

She flinched at his words. "Your kids are your team."

His kids. Not her. The words were like a punch to the stomach. *I think I need space to think.* Maybe he had messed up by agreeing to let Tiffany come over on Christmas Eve, but was that really worth throwing what they had away? One mistake and she was done. Just like she'd done in high school. He'd always be the person who failed her. Just like he'd always been a disappointment to his dad.

Cole stared at Fallon. "I think you were right about us both needing space."

She recoiled as if she hadn't been the one to suggest it.

"Don't worry. I'll watch the kids." Tiffany slid her arm into his. He shook it away but not before that flicker of suspicion filled Fallon's eyes again. "I was planning to spend Christmas Eve with you guys anyway."

Fallon nodded, resigned, and took a step back.

He guessed that answered if she trusted him. If she wanted him. If she'd even try and fight for him. He reached in his pocket for his keys.

The door opened and Zane came out with Susie trailing behind. "What's going on?"

Tiffany tugged Zane close, whispering something to him.

Fallon stepped forward and a spark of hope rose in him. Maybe she would fight for him.

She lowered her voice. "I know you're mad at me, but don't leave the kids with her."

Was she serious? Maybe that was all she cared about. He knew she wanted to be a mom, but he'd thought that would be a wonderful by-product of their relationship, not the reason for it. He shook his head. "They'll be fine. She is *their mom* after all."

She flinched at the words as Zane marched toward his dad, fire in his eyes as he stared at Cole. "You're leaving again?"

Cole closed his eyes a moment and drew a slow breath. He looked at Zane and laid a hand on Zane's and Susie's shoulders. "It's a job. I'll be back—"

"It's always a job." Zane shrugged his hand off. "First the military, then your job at JJ's. Now you're always flying off to some job you won't even tell us about. Why do you like working better than you like us?"

"Zane, I don't—"

"Whatever." He shook his head. "I'm glad you're leaving. I'll spend Christmas with Mom. She may have been gone for two years but you've always been gone."

Fallon made eye contact with Susie then Zane. "If you guys need anything, I'm only a phone call away."

"We don't need you." There was a venom in Zane's eyes Cole had never seen before. "We don't need either of you."

"Zane—" Cole's voice grew louder.

"They'll be fine." Tiffany stepped between Fallon and the kids.

"I'm so done with this. I'm going home." Zane ran in the direction of the house.

Tiffany looked at Zane's retreating form. Was that real concern in her eyes?

"I'll make sure he got home before I take off." Cole handed

Tiffany his house keys. "You can plan on staying at the house with the kids tonight. I'll be back tomorrow."

Cole knelt and kissed Susie on the head and then stood and turned toward Fallon but only caught the tail end of her dress as she walked back into the dance. Walking away from him like everyone eventually did.

Cole hurried to his car, trying to wrap his mind around what had just happened. Thirty minutes ago, he would have been on one knee if he'd had the forethought to buy a ring. And now? Now he couldn't see a future for them at all. He couldn't be with someone who didn't trust him. And he couldn't be with someone who cast him aside the first time he disappointed her. His mind flashed to the half text. And could he be with someone who was living with her foot out the door waiting for something better?

He parked in front of the house and hurried up the front steps. Every light was on, so Zane must have beaten him there. No doubt he'd cut through a few yards. His to-go bag was waiting at the door. Guess Zane was ready for him to be on his way.

He knocked on the door.

"Just leave already." Zane's words muffled through the door.

His hand hovered over the doorknob just as his phone buzzed with an incoming text.

WALKER

On the road yet?

Maybe this conversation would be better when they were both cooled down a bit. At least he could confirm that Zane was here.

He made a quick change out of his suit and scooped up his to-go bag as he headed out to the Blazer. An address was waiting in his texts.

He plugged it in his GPS and sent a text to Walker.

COLE

ETA: 3.5 h

But it only took three. Cole stopped at the address and eyed the gate in front of him. The ornate W on the gate confirmed his suspicion. Of course the previous assignment would be Winterbourne. He gave the guy his name and he let Cole through. He parked his Blazer next to Walker's truck, hopped out, and hurried down the hall of the security building to the office where they had set up their command post last time.

When Cole stepped into the room, Walker was standing over a map displayed on a computer, mid-conversation with Hanson, the top guy of Winterbourne's security.

Hanson walked away and raised his voice to the room. "Run it again, have Emmerson do it this time."

Cole stood next to Walker. "Catch me up."

"There was an intruder yesterday who got all the way here"—Walker dropped a finger on the map—"before they apprehended him. No one is quite sure how and the guy isn't talking. We have guys trying to replicate it so we can find the weak point, but so far no one has been able to get through. And we need to get this done." Cole didn't need to look away from the screen to know that Walker's jaw was rigid and tense. "Winterbourne has the clout to kill our reputation, and he's spiteful enough to do it thoroughly."

He had no doubt about that.

Cole put everything out of his mind and dove into the job. Walker was right. All the chips were on the table for this one. But twelve hours later they weren't any closer to a solution. He eyed the clock. He'd have to leave in the next hour to be home for dinner like he promised.

He turned toward Walker but Hanson walked in and slammed his hand on the table. "We have to be missing something. Winterbourne wants it all wrapped up before Christmas. Him being cooped up in there on Christmas Eve isn't making any of us look good."

"Mr. Winterbourne is in the house?" Cole's head jerked toward him.

"This is his private estate. But don't worry, he's safe. He is over here." Walker motioned to the map then moved his finger to another room on the map. "There's no getting in there."

"Is that so?" Cole studied the plans over. It wasn't close to their operation but close enough. "Put me in the rotation to try and infiltrate." He powered down his phone and dropped it in a bin on the desk in front of Walker, followed by his wallet, keys, and radio.

Walker shook his head. "We need your eyes out here."

"We're missing something, and I need to see it for myself." It was a flimsy excuse at best, but Cole wasn't going to budge. Nothing had gone how he wanted tonight. He'd fought with Zane, lost Fallon, and his truck started making some expensive-sounding grinding noises just before he pulled in. And to top it off, the chances of him making it home by dinner were disappearing. If ever he needed a win, it was now. If nothing else, he was going to face off with a bully. And this time Winterbourne was not going to come out on top.

Today had not been the Christmas Eve she'd always dreamed of. Fallon wrapped her blanket around her a little tighter as she stared into the glittering-colored lights of the tree reflected off a menagerie of unique ornaments, each one bringing back a different memory. When she was a kid, she and her parents would light candles, read the Christmas story, and drink cocoa. Then they would share about all the good things God had done over the year.

Not this year. It was only eight o'clock, but her parents had gone to bed an hour ago. No cocoa. No story. Not even one lit candle. Maybe because there wasn't a lot to celebrate. Maybe they were just worn out from everything.

Maybe she should go to bed as well but just the idea seemed to suffocate her. Not the idea of sleep. But the idea of waking up to the last Christmas in this house. The last Christmas in Heritage. But not the last Christmas alone.

She really had believed things would be different this time. But here she was alone again.

Her dad wandered out his red plaid pajama pants. His footsteps paused when he spotted her by the tree. "Can't sleep either?"

She shook her head then focused back on the tree.

He settled in the recliner next to her and extended the footrest. "Spending a week on bed rest has my clock all messed up. What's your excuse?"

She kept her focus on the colored lights of the tree. "I'm . . . fine. Just not tired. It is only eight o'clock."

"Is it really?" His brow wrinkled as he stared at the clock on the mantel. Then shook his head. "Like I said, my internal clock is all messed up. Spill it."

When she looked at him, he angled his head. "You may be over thirty, but you're still my little girl and I can tell when you're holding something back. You keep so much close to your chest—"

"And whose fault is that?" The words burst from her and she ducked her head again. "Sorry."

"No, continue." When she hesitated, he leaned forward and squeezed her hand. "Please."

"When everything happened with Tiffany in elementary school, you made it clear that my job was to put on a polite face and not fight back. What can I say? I've been trying to do it ever since."

Her dad removed his glasses and rubbed the bridge of his nose. "Parenting is a tricky thing. You try and do your best in the moment. But words are powerful and can have a rippling effect you never intended." He slipped on his glasses and met her gaze. "We never meant for you to ever feel you couldn't be fully honest. And we never meant for you to believe it was okay to let the bully win.

But there is a time when we need to seek peace and times we need to stand for truth. Your mom and I thought we were taking the better road on that issue. Maybe we didn't. I'm sorry."

"As an adult I can see why you did what you did. Unfortunately, it seemed to create habits and patterns difficult to let go of."

"The only way to break a habit or unhealthy pattern is to practice." He folded his fingers across his stomach. "So, what has you up this late on Christmas Eve?"

Fallon stared at the tree. Was it that easy? No, opening up might feel completely unnatural, but she knew he was right. The only way to the other side was through it. She drew a deep breath and met his gaze. "I thought with Cole and the kids that maybe it would be different this time."

"Different?"

"Every good thing God puts in my life He takes away." Now that she'd started, it was all coming out. "It's like He's playing a game with me."

"God doesn't play games, sweetheart."

"Really? What about the fact He gave me Robert then took him away? Gave me my paintings back only to take them away *again*. And Cole? Gone too." Her voice rose as the frustration that had been building for years seemed to flow out with every word.

Her dad didn't seem shaken by her outburst, though. "What happened with Cole? I thought things were going well."

"We had a fight." She rubbed at her eyes. "I fear Tiffany will always be between us."

"Did something happen with them?"

"He was adamant that nothing did. And I believe him. Mostly. But he smelled like her perfume, and her lipstick was on his collar. And she says stuff that I shouldn't believe but . . . Like I said, I think she will always be between us. And I'm not sure I can live like that."

Her dad stared at the Christmas tree for a moment then back to her. "Would you say that the tree is between your chair and mine?"

She looked at the tree to her left then forward to her father again. Since the furniture made a circle then . . . "Yeah, I suppose I would."

"Now come stand in front of the tree." She did as he said then he pointed to where she'd been sitting. "Now look at your seat and look at my seat. Is the tree between us?"

"No." The tree was behind her so she couldn't even see it.

"If you think Tiffany is between you, then maybe you're looking at it from the wrong perspective. Before your focus was on the tree, and you could only see how it stood between us. But once you put the tree behind you, everything changed."

"You're saying that Tiffany can only stand between us if I let her." She sighed and sank back into her recliner. "But what if Cole lets her? Her lipstick was on his collar. He agreed to do Christmas Eve with her. He even chose her to stay with the kids at his house last night when he left."

"It's almost as if he is trying to give those children a good relationship with their mom."

"But she is so manipulative. With the kids. With him."

"Either you can trust him or you can't. Your mom is beautiful now, but when we got engaged, she could stop traffic. She couldn't even go over to the beach without getting hit on by other men. At first, it drove me crazy. I was terrified that she would meet someone she liked better and leave me. But I had to come to the conclusion that I either trusted that she loved me like she said she did, or I didn't. And if I couldn't trust her, I shouldn't marry her."

"And you trusted her."

"Yes. Because regardless of others' actions, she was always faithful to me. And I think if you look at Cole and Tiffany, he is faithful to you. I see the way he looks at you. He's in love."

"He was. But he was so mad when he left. I have never seen him that mad. Maybe it's too late."

"One fight doesn't destroy love, my dear. It doesn't destroy the love between a man and a woman, and it could never destroy God's love for you."

"What do you mean by that?"

"You say that this is about Cole. That you aren't sure you can trust Cole. But everything else you say backs up the fact you can trust him. Watching you two together the past six weeks has told me that you do, in fact, trust him. Who I think you don't trust is God."

"It's not—"

"There is a time for peace and there is a time for honesty. And with God, He always wants your honesty. God can handle your honesty. In fact, He can't work in our hearts until we are fully honest. He doesn't want obedient robots. He wants His broken children to come to Him with every hurt, every fear, every bit of anger. He wants to hold us as we cry and give us hope of a good future."

"A good future like losing my husband? A good future like losing my paintings—twice? That is not a good future."

Her father stood and walked to where one of her unfinished paintings lay. He lifted it from the table and carried it over to her. "I'm not sure what you're complaining about. This isn't your best work. It feels flat. Where's the depth? Where's the detail? I don't see your heart in it at all."

What? That was a bit out of nowhere and very unfair. "I'm not finished with that one." She took it from his hands. "I'm going to add shadows and details. You can't judge what it *will* look like by what you see now."

"Exactly." He gently took it back and put it on the mantel. "God has a plan. A good plan for you. A good plan for Cole. A good plan for your art. Don't judge His intentions by what it all looks like now. Know God is for you. And just like Cole, you either trust Him, or you don't."

She stared at the half-finished painting again. Maybe her story wasn't a failure. Maybe her story was just unfinished.

Her father pulled one of her new ornaments from the tree and handed it to her. "When you painted those, you told me that you felt like it was an act of worship. That they were a gift to God. Is that still true?"

"Yeah."

"Then don't take it back. Trust Him with it. If they belong to God, then they aren't yours to lose. Trust Him with your career. Trust Him with Cole. Trust Him with your desire to be a mom."

Her gaze darted to his.

"You think we don't notice how you look at those kids?" He sat back in his spot but didn't sink back. "I don't claim to know how He will fulfill your desires, but I know if you trust Him with all of it, He will fill your heart."

She tucked her head. Her parents really didn't miss anything.

Her dad stood and placed a kiss on her head. "Off to try and sleep again. See you in the morning."

He disappeared down the hall, followed by the soft click of his bedroom door.

Trusting was so hard for her. And maybe that was her real problem. Either she could trust God or she couldn't, and there was no point in believing in a God she couldn't trust. She stared at the tree again, the ornaments coming into focus. Life had given her a lot of hard moments. But God had given her many beautiful ones as well.

She had lost Tiffany as a childhood friend, but God had given her Sadie. Sadie who was still a source of strength and wisdom to her today. She had lost Robert, but God had brought back Cole into her life. She had lost her house with vaulted ceilings that overlooked the lake, but He had used it to bring her home. That until yesterday, this was the best Christmas season she'd ever had.

He had taken her paintings, and they were still gone, but who knew what the future held? Her story wasn't done.

Okay, God. I will choose to trust You. With my art, with Cole, with my dreams.

It wasn't the fanciest prayer she'd ever prayed, but it just might be the most sincere.

Her phone rang and she glanced at the display. Zane? What could he want? Cole should have gotten home a few hours ago.

"Zane, everything okay?"

"No." There were definitely tears in his voice, accompanied by crying in the background. "Mom left, Dad isn't home, and Susie cut her head."

Her cocoa sloshed on the end table as she set it down and stood. "How big is the cut?"

"I can't tell. But there's a lot of blood."

Head wounds were bleeders, but she couldn't chance that was all it was. And if it *was* more, they had a limited time. "Hang up. Call 911. I'm on my way."

"I'm scared." There was a tremor in his voice.

"I know." Fallon slipped on one boot then another. "I'm coming. I promise. Now call 911. Can you do that?"

"Okay." The call ended and Fallon grabbed her coat.

Lord, please, we need Your help.

Nothing like putting her new trust to the test. What if this went poorly? What if—? She couldn't even think it. She had to believe that no matter what she'd face, God would be there to walk with her through it all.

eighteen

M AYBE HE HADN'T THOUGHT THIS THROUGH. Cole stood in Winterbourne's private office with his hands in the air as three of Winterbourne's rent-a-cops had their guns trained on him. He'd done it. Made it through, found the loopholes of the system. It had taken him a few hours to find the hole but once he did it made him feel worse about missing it on the original job. But he hadn't stopped there, he'd taken it a step further. Maybe a step too far by the look on Winterbourne's face.

"Just what do you think you're doing?" The man's demeanor was undeniably fierce. No doubt using his powers of intimidation had been a large part of how he'd acquired his wealth.

But Cole wasn't easily cowed. "I wanted a private word."

"What makes you think—"

"Fallon James."

The older man froze for a second before his face reddened. "Get him out of here."

They secured his hands behind his back and escorted him out of the office, out of the main area of the house, and back to the security building. He could've no doubt broken free, but he was already in enough hot water. And by the look on Walker's face when they walked them both in an empty room with no windows, the guy was about to let him have it.

As soon as the door clicked shut, Walker turned on him. "What were you thinking?"

"I wanted a word with Winterbourne."

"You wanted a word? A word? You work for me. You do what I say. This is my company's name on the line here. Honestly, I'm not even sure I can get you out of this. They could prosecute you, and from what I've heard, the Winterbourne lawyers are not to be messed with."

Cole was too acquainted with the Winterbourne lawyers.

"There was just something I needed to try and fix—"

"Have you considered it wasn't your problem to fix?"

Fallon's words echoed in his head. *This isn't your problem to fix.*

"Did you even think about your kids? What will they do if you go to jail?"

Jail. The word bounced around in his head as ice flowed through his veins. What had he done? He hadn't thought. Just like when he'd gotten shot. He rushed in, sure he could fix it. Only to put him and his family both at risk. He reached for his phone to check the time, but he didn't have it on him. But it had to be well after six which meant he definitely wouldn't be making it home for dinner.

"At least that seemed to shake that cocky grin off your face. I'm going out there to see if I can find out what's going on. But if you have any hope to get out of this without being prosecuted, you'd better pray to a higher power to save you because I honestly don't think I can." His boss walked out and slammed the door in his wake.

Everything in Cole shook. He rushed in to fix things. And now, not only might he not make it home for Christmas, but what would happen if he had to serve jail time? Walker would get him out of this, wouldn't he?

You'd better pray to a higher power to save you because I honestly don't think I can. He knew Walker didn't believe in God, but that was probably the best advice he could have given. Because Cole knew he didn't need to pray to *a* higher power but *the only* Higher Power.

But where did he even begin? A verse came back to him from his days in the Navy.

The Lord will fight for you; you need only to be still.

He was a fighter. He was trained to go in so others didn't have to. Everything in him resisted sitting still and letting someone else go before him. But there was nothing more he could do. And he had to trust God.

You either trust me or you don't. His own words to Fallon came back to him. Maybe she wasn't the only one with trust issues. Because if he really trusted God then maybe he should have listened to his gut and not taken this job, listened to his gut and not charged in headfirst. Because just maybe, it wasn't his gut. Just maybe, God was telling him to slow down and trust Him.

He'd messed up. Instead of seeing what God wanted to do, he had run in with his own plans. His own agenda. The verse echoed in his mind again and he almost laughed. Now there was nothing to do but wait and be still and trust that God could still use him.

All right, God. I give up. It's all You.

It was well over an hour before the door opened again. Walker walked in and shut it behind him. He passed him a Coke and leaned against the wall. "They won't tell me anything. Want to tell me why you did it?"

Cole cracked the can open and drew a long gulp. "That's Fallon's former father-in-law."

Cole's brows rose. Yup, he had his friend's attention now.

"When her husband died, they gave her nothing and now are

determined to take her art too. I wanted to make it right. But maybe you're right. Maybe it isn't mine to fix."

"Wow, so you really love this girl."

Did he? Yeah, he supposed he did, because as mad as he'd been earlier, he still ran to defend her, protect her the first chance he got regardless of the potential cost. "Doesn't matter. She asked for space."

"Ouch."

"Yup."

"What did you do?"

"Tiffany—"

"Do not let that woman get her hooks into you again."

"I didn't. I haven't. But Tiffany does things—says things. But Fallon should trust me."

"Even after you pulled this stupid stunt,"—Walker motioned to the room—"I would still trust you with my life. But that didn't come overnight. I trust you because you showed up over and over. When I needed you, you had my back over and over. You have to build that trust with Fallon."

"What if it's too late?"

"If it were too late, you wouldn't have just faced off with a billionaire trying to defend her honor like some knight fighting a dragon."

"Maybe you're right."

"Of course I'm right. I'm brilliant." Walker stepped to the door. "Now I'm going to try again to find out if that dragon is going to eat you."

Cole stared at the door as it shut. He needed to get out of here. He needed to see Fallon. He needed to let her know that he would show up again and again for her because he wanted to be someone she could fully trust.

Another hour passed before the door opened once more but this time it was Winterbourne. The deep lines of displeasure on his face were still cemented in place. Awesome. He stepped in the room alone and secured the door. "What did she tell you?"

Cole sat up a bit straighter. He hadn't expected this. Then again, when you let God fight for you, big things happen. Cole reclined back in his chair. "Enough that if someone went to the papers it would look very bad for the Winterbourne image."

He offered a cocky shrug. "It's her word against ours."

Cole propped one foot on the opposite knee and laced his fingers across his stomach. "Funny thing about the public. I don't think they would need more proof than that she had been married to your son and now she is penniless. That says enough right there, doesn't it?"

"She wouldn't—"

"You're right, she wouldn't. But much to my displeasure, I have developed quite a social media following. It would only take one post by me to—"

"You wouldn't." The way the older man's eyes narrowed, Cole knew he had his attention now. "That's slander."

"It's only slander if it isn't true." Cole dropped his knee and stood. The man was several inches shorter than Cole. "And I definitely would."

"What do you want?"

"Drop the lawsuit. *All* her rights returned to her. And a reasonable inheritance from her marriage to Robert."

"This is blackmail."

"No, this is you doing what is right. And letting you know that if you don't do what is right, then the public needs to know about it."

Mr. Winterbourne's gaze bored into him for a long moment. No doubt he'd gotten lesser men to back down that way. But Cole wasn't a lesser man, and he wasn't fighting for himself. He was fighting for the woman he loved. Because whether she loved him or not, trusted him or not, wanted him or not, he was all hers. And as soon as he got out of this room, he was going after her to tell her as much. He stared back without so much as a flinch.

The controlled fury on Winterbourne's face made Cole think the man would be willing to pay any price rather than give in. But in the end, his ruthless business sense proved to be even greater than his substantial ego.

The older man finally nodded. "I'll call my lawyers."

"Now." Cole pointed at the phone by the door.

"It's after nine on Christmas Eve."

"I have a feeling they'll take your call."

Winterbourne glared at him but did as he suggested. Cole was fairly confident the man wasn't used to being told what to do.

Twenty minutes later, after pointing out the weak points in the security system to Hanson, Cole retrieved his phone and powered it up. His heart sank. Ten missed calls. Four voicemails, and twenty new texts.

He scanned the texts first.

ZANE
____

Mom left.

ZANE
____

When are you getting home?

ZANE
____

Susie is hurt and I don't know
what to do.

ZANE
____

Dad!

ZANE
____

There is so much blood.

ZANE
____

I need your help!

He halted, the words on the phone blurring as the ground seemed to drop out beneath him. With trembling hands, he dialed his son's number. Straight to voicemail. Panic clawed at him as he tried again, only to be met with the same recording.

He dialed Tiffany's number. Each unanswered ring ratcheted his pulse higher and higher. But there was no response, no reassuring voice on the other end.

His chest tightened with a suffocating weight as a thousand scenarios raced through his mind, each more terrifying than the last.

"I've got to go." Cole sprinted to his Blazer. He climbed in, turned the key. The engine turned, making that awful grinding again, but it didn't fire up. He tried again. "No!" He slammed his hand into the steering wheel.

This couldn't be happening. He grabbed his phone, but his battery had gone dead. This was not his day.

There was a knock at his passenger window. Walker was breathing hard. The guy must have run after him. "What's going on?"

"I need your car. There's an emergency at home. I don't know the details. I can't get ahold of them. All I know is there was a lot of blood and this thing won't start." Cole slammed his hand into the steering wheel again.

"Breathe." Walker had his phone out. "I'm calling in a favor. A UH-1 will meet you on Winterbourne's landing pad in twenty. It's around back. You'll be in Heritage in less than an hour and a half. I'll call the local hospitals and let you know if you need rerouted there."

Cole nodded, grabbed his bag, and headed that way. It was beyond him how Walker had gotten the old Vietnam-era helicopter there on the spur of the moment. The man knew how to get things done, that was for sure, but every minute still felt like an eternity. Even after thirty minutes in the air the panic hadn't left him.

The Lord will fight for you; you need only to be still.

That was easier when his life was on the line, not his child's.

He'd never known fear like this. He closed his eyes, resisting the urge to be sick, knowing it had nothing to do with the breakneck pace the copter was setting. The thump-thump-thump of the rotors pounded inside his head, but it wasn't enough to drown out the thought of Susie covered in blood. Of Zane alone. His hands began to shake. It was him and his sister all over again. The panic he'd felt when she'd fallen out of the tree house and he'd been alone. Helpless. Only, his sister had turned out okay. What if Susie wasn't? Another verse that he'd memorized during his deployment resurfaced in his mind.

I will never leave you nor forsake you.

Following God didn't mean that everything would turn out okay. But it did mean that no matter what dark times Cole had to walk through, God would be there to walk through it with him. His mom had left him, his dad had left him, Fallon had even left him for a season and could very well leave him again. God was the only one who would never leave him. Would never forsake him.

The grizzled vet in the pilot's seat motioned to him and he pulled on the headphones.

"Walker radioed in. There isn't a Susie Scott listed at any of the surrounding hospitals but there was an ambulance dispatched to 247 Richard in Heritage about an hour ago."

Cole's hand shook. "That's my house."

"Do you know if there's a place to land nearby?"

Cole shook his head. "Do you have a drop line?"

"What do you think I am, a commercial tour? I was dropping grunts in this bird before you were born, kid. Compartment under the bench in the rear. Gloves behind your seat."

"Then get me close and I'll fast rope it to the ground."

He checked the time. They'd get to Heritage about eleven thirty. Nothing like a little noise in the center of town on Christmas Eve. But right now, he didn't care. He needed to get to his kids.

Not going to the hospital was good. Deep breath.

I trust it all to you, God. Fallon, the kids, our money. I'm done trying to figure this out on my own. To fix it on my own. Whatever I'll face, I'll face it with You.

A peace settled over him. And he had no doubt that no matter what the future held, God wouldn't abandon him. He only prayed that Susie was all right. And Zane too.

Fallon had never known fear like the moment she turned onto Richard Street to find the flashing lights of the ambulance sitting outside the Scott house. She pulled along the curb, threw the car into the park, and rushed up the steps. "Zane?"

She opened the front door to find Luke Taylor and Thomas Thornton standing in the living room. They each wore a navy jacket with the letters HFD on the back and a smile on their faces. That had to be a good sign. She scanned the room. Susie sat on the dining room table with a butterfly bandage on her forehead. Zane sat on a chair next to her, still slightly pale. He lifted his head as she walked in. His eyes widened. "You came."

Fallon walked over to him, rested her hand on his shoulder, trying to project more calm than she felt. "Always." She looked at Susie. "How are you feeling?"

Susie slid off the table and hugged Fallon's side, tears filling her eyes again. "I almost died."

Fallon looked from her to Luke and Thomas. Thomas bit his lip, but the corner of his mouth couldn't completely suppress the grin. Luke did a little better. He shook his head. "Head wounds bleed a lot. But she'll be all right."

Thomas squatted down to look Susie in the eye. "How about a sucker for being such a good patient."

When Susie nodded, Thomas stood and led her a few feet away.

Luke angled his shoulders so his back was to the kids. "She

doesn't need stitches, but you need to watch her for a concussion. She's not showing any signs, so I'm comfortable with her staying here tonight. But this is a list of some things you need to watch for."

He handed her a paper and then walked back to the kids. "And you"—Luke gave Zane a fist bump—"did a great job calling 911. Way to take care of things."

Zane smiled up at him and nodded, his color slowly returning.

As soon as the guys packed up the first aid kit and left the house, Fallon studied Susie, from the blood in her hair to the blood stains on her pj's. "What happened?"

"I was chasing Polly and I slipped. I hit my head on the corner of the table." She pointed to her footed pj's.

She checked her watch. It was just after nine. "We better get you cleaned up if Santa is going to be here."

"I'll start a bath." Susie walked carefully up the stairs.

Fallon turned to Zane, who was just staring at her. "Do you need to clean up too?"

"She left us." His voice was hollow as he seemed to look right through her. "She left, again."

"What time did she leave?" Fallon didn't need to ask who.

"About four o'clock. She got a text then said she had to go. Said that my dad should be home to feed us dinner. Then she just left. But Dad didn't come. And I can't get ahold of him. And Ms. Margret is gone to visit her nephew."

She walked over and slid into the chair next to his. "I'm so sorry."

"I kept thinking what if my dad was shot again? What if he's dead? What if we're really alone now? And then I thought I hope he *is* dead because if he isn't, then he just doesn't care, and that's worse. Then thought about the fight and what I said to him . . . I don't want him dead I just . . ."

Oh, Zane. She placed her hands on his shoulders. "I don't know why he isn't answering but I know he cares about you and Susie more than anything. We all said things we regret. He'll understand."

He nodded but didn't go on.

She stood and took a step toward the stairs, but he wasn't done. "I was afraid you wouldn't come."

She turned back. "What?"

He stood and wiped away a tear. "After what happened at the dance and how I said I wanted to be with my mom, I thought . . . I was afraid you wouldn't come. I was so afraid."

"Listen to me." She placed her hands on the sides of his face. "No matter what happens with your dad and me, you can always call me. I'll always show up if you need me."

"But I said—"

"I can handle your anger. And so can your dad. There is nothing you can do to make him not love you."

"Promise?" He took a step back and wiped his face with the back of his hand.

"Promise." And just like that, she could see it. There was nothing she could do—nothing she could say—to make her Heavenly Father stop loving her. And just like Zane, she didn't always understand why He didn't respond the way she expected, but His love was never changing. But unlike an imperfect earthly father who didn't answer for who knew why, God's wisdom was beyond what she could understand, and she had to trust He had a plan even when He didn't answer.

Zane wrapped her in a hug and buried his face in her shoulder as sobs racked his body. The boy was broken. His sister had been hurt, and both of the people he was supposed to be able to count on didn't come through.

"I'll always come if I can. But you're never alone. God was with you. He helped you make wise decisions, and He is with your dad right now, wherever he may be." She eyed the blood stains on his shirt. "You look like you could use a little cleanup too. Why don't you get changed and then we can have cocoa and I'll read the Christmas story to you and Susie by the tree."

"You're staying?" A weight seemed to lift from his shoulders.

She ruffled his hair. "As long as you need me."

"Forever?" His brows rose, but she couldn't promise that.

"How about until your dad gets back?"

"Okay." He took a few steps toward the stairs then turned back. "I'm not sure what you guys fought about, but I know he loves you."

Sometimes love isn't enough. She would give it all she had, but if he walked away, she couldn't stop him. But she wasn't letting him walk away without a fight. He wanted her to fight for something. He was about to get it full force.

Zane nodded as the whine of a dog filled the air, accompanied by some scratching.

Fallon looked toward the laundry room. "Is that Polly?"

"I locked her in there. She wouldn't leave Susie alone and kept getting into the mess." He pointed to where Susie must have fallen. "She was yipping at first but she must have fallen asleep for a while."

Fallon sighed and reached for a rag on the table. "I'll clean that up and let her out."

He nodded and hurried up the stairs and Fallon pulled out her phone and tapped Cole's number. It went straight to voicemail. She hung up and typed out a text.

FALLON
____
Where are you?

FALLON
____
The kids need you.

The text went from a blue iMessage to green. His phone was off. If he was only in Detroit, why would he have his phone off? That was, unless he hadn't been honest about that. No, she had to decide to trust him sometime, and that would start now. She didn't know why she didn't hear from him, but she had to trust he'd been honest with her.

She slid the phone back into her pocket and went in search of hot cocoa.

Thirty minutes later, the kids were clean, in fresh jammies, and sipping cocoa. She had lit a handful of candles and read the Christmas story out of Luke.

"Now what?" Susie took another sip of her cocoa, depositing a dollop of whipped topping on her nose. Polly, who had claimed the spot next to her, stretched up and licked it off.

"Now we go around and say what was good about the year. Like getting a dog." Fallon ran her hand across the furry white back.

"I love doggie kisses." Susie laughed and started wiggling away from Polly. "Sometimes. And I love ballet."

"That's a good one." Fallon squeezed her close.

Zane took another sip of cocoa, leaving a trace of mustache behind. "I started working out at The Arena."

"That's awesome too."

"What about you?" Susie looked up at her with wide blue eyes.

"I . . ." The only things running through her mind were all the bad things. Losing the house, the lawsuit, losing the farm. No, that was only part of the story. Many good things had happened too. She swallowed and set her cocoa aside. "I met you two and I can honestly say it has been the best part."

"That's one of my favorite parts too." Susie smiled.

Zane nodded and looked at his cocoa as if embarrassed. "Me too."

And suddenly she didn't have to push all the hard parts of the year away. They faded in the light of what God had given her. And the hope He still had so much for her future. Her story wasn't over. And even if things didn't work out for her and Cole, God had given her this moment. Snuggled up in front of a Christmas tree with the two most amazing kids in the world. Even if this was her only Christmas with them, she would remember this moment always.

"All right, you two. It's time for bed. Santa can't come if you don't sleep."

As if on cue, a low thumping sound started, soft at first, but building quickly until it was rattling the windows.

"Is that Santa's sleigh?" Susie sat up straighter.

"That's a helicopter!" Zane jumped off the couch and hurried to the door.

Susie was right behind him. "Santa is coming by helicopter?"

Fallon hurried to catch up and opened the front door, only to be blasted by a rush of air and noise. They covered their heads and stepped out on the porch. A helicopter hovered over the square. What was happening? A rope dropped, followed a moment later by the silhouette of a man sliding down the rope to the ground, narrowly missing Otis.

"I totally think that might be Santa!" Susie yelled over the noise.

The man detached himself from the rope and sprinted toward them.

Cole?

The helicopter faded in the distance, still trailing the rope, as Cole ran toward the porch. He bounded to the top in three strides and scooped up Susie in his arms, burying her in his chest. "I'm so sorry."

Susie shivered and Cole led them inside. He set Susie down and put a hand on each of their shoulders. His eyes were rimmed red with emotion. "I'm so sorry I'm late. I'm so sorry I wasn't here when you needed me. You guys are my team. You'll always come first. Do you hear me?"

Both kids wrapped their arms around him and he pulled them into a giant hug.

A lump formed in Fallon's throat. The deep love of a father. She stepped over to the door and lifted her coat from the hook without a sound. As much as she wanted to stay, this was their moment. She walked out and closed the door.

She drew a deep breath of the crisp night air and slid one arm in her coat, then the other. This would definitely be a memory she'd treasure for a long time.

She had only made it down two steps when the door opened again.

"Fallon?" Cole hurried outside after her.

"I thought you three might want a moment. They were worried about you."

He met her on the steps then took another step down so they were closer to eye level. "Only them?"

"No, I was worried too. I'm sorry for what I said. I do trust you. Fully. I believed that if I didn't let myself fully trust you, then it would hurt less when you left."

"When I left?"

"If you left."

He reached up and snagged her fingers with his. "Both of us have been burned pretty badly. But what I said in there is true. I didn't just mean I want the kids and me to be a team. That 'we' included you. That is, if you want—"

Fallon gripped the front of his shirt and pressed her lips to his. His lips were cool from the night air but warmed and softened against hers. His arms slid around her waist and traveled up her back into her hair. The whole moment whispered of forgiveness for each other and trust in each other.

His hands found her waist again, pulling her closer, as if trying to keep her anchored to the moment. But he didn't need to worry. She wasn't going anywhere. This was exactly where she wanted to be. Where she wanted to be every day for the rest of her life.

She released a contented sigh and wanted so much more. But all in good time. Cole's hand traveled over her back again, as if he too was ready for their future to start today. But then he seemed to intentionally slow the kiss.

He leaned back slightly, resting his forehead against hers and releasing a ragged breath. "I love you so much, and you can trust me. And I'll prove that to you as long as you'll let me."

"I trust you. I do. Fully. A hundred percent. I think it was God I didn't trust. Not you. But I know I can trust Him. I'll daily choose to trust Him."

Cole leaned back and brushed her hair from her face. "Sounds like He had work to do on both of us."

His fingers toyed at the skin at her waist where her sweatshirt and jacket had slid up. His touch left a trail of fire in its wake, sending shivers cascading down her spine.

"We better get you inside before you freeze." He brushed another brief kiss across her lips but didn't move.

"We should go inside." She moved her lips along his again. "The kids are probably wondering what happened to us."

"They can wait." He pressed another kiss to her lips. "I'm serious about you being a part of the team. If you think I should quit, then—"

"No. You're good at your job." Her finger landed on his lips. "God made you for this. And there is no way you want to go back to bagging groceries. But I would like us to consider each job opportunity and make decisions that affect the family, as a family. As a team."

"You're so wise." His hands came up and captured her face. "Never think you aren't enough for me, Fallon. *You* are my first choice."

First choice.

He loved her and she loved him and she was his first choice.

A car door slammed nearby and they turned to see Tiffany approaching across the street.

Cole's body tensed under Fallon's fingers. "What do you want?"

"Is she okay?" Her voice shook. She might just be a good actress, but the woman looked panicked. "I got a panicked message from Zane and I drove here as fast as I could."

Cole slid an arm around Fallon's waist and pulled her to his side. "No thanks to you."

"I want to see her." Her voice was still small but with a touch of strength in it now. And as she drew close, it was obvious she'd been crying.

"If you think—"

Fallon laid her hand on his chest. "I think you should let her."

Cole stared at her.

"I think deep down Susie would like to see her mom right now. I think Zane would like to be honest with his mom right now. You don't need to fix this for them, Cole. You said in there that you're a team. Empower them. Help them make choices that will benefit the team. Because as you reminded me before, she will always be their mother. Decide as a team what that will look like."

"What about you?"

"I'll go home." When a touch of disappointment filled his eyes, she leaned her forehead against his once more, lowering her voice. "Because we both know that after that kiss, it is probably not the best idea for me to be here after the kids go to bed anyway."

His gaze shifted to something full of hunger and longing, but he nodded and backed up. "Right. Can the kids and I come over in the morning?"

"As early as you want."

Cole looked at Tiffany then motioned her toward the house and she stepped past them. Fallon took another step down the stairs, but Cole snagged her hand. "Are you sure you're okay with this?"

"I trust you, Cole. I trust you a hundred percent. And I look forward to seeing you tomorrow, because our story is just beginning."

nineteen

IT TOOK EVERY OUNCE OF SELF-CONTROL COLE could muster to follow Tiffany inside rather than Fallon out to her car, but Fallon was right. Susie needed to see her mom and the kids both needed to express their feelings.

He stepped in behind Tiffany and secured the door. Both kids stared at her wide-eyed. Finally Zane's gaze darkened. "Why are *you* here?"

Tiffany looked at Cole, but he was done making excuses for her. She turned back to the kids. "When I got your message, I was in the security line at the airport and missed the call."

"You were going back to that man, weren't you?" Zane again.

"Your father should have been here. I didn't think that—"

"Don't blame Dad." Zane took a step toward his mom. "Dad already apologized for not being here. This isn't about him right now. It's about you, and all I've heard you do is make excuses. You were supposed to spend Christmas Eve with us and you already had a plane ticket to leave us again."

Cole wasn't surprised that Zane had put that together, but the way Susie's face dropped at the words, his heart broke for her. Cole squatted down and pulled the little girl into his arms. She buried her face in his neck and sobbed.

Tiffany's defensive stance seemed to crumble in front of him. No doubt she always snuck off because she knew she couldn't handle seeing their faces as she broke their hearts. She stepped closer. "Susie?"

Susie let go of Cole and took a step back from her mom, her face scrunching up as her eyes filled again. "Go away. I wish you had never come back."

With that she ran upstairs. Zane stared at his mom. She took a step toward him, but he shook his head and followed Susie.

Tiffany looked at Cole. And for the first time, Cole could see deep regret in her eyes. "Do you think they'll forgive me?"

Cole sighed and shrugged. "Does it matter? If you're going back to Vegas and they won't see you for another two years, why do you care?"

"I panicked, okay?" She paced to the Christmas tree and back. "We were enjoying Christmas Eve together and Susie said something about next Christmas and the Christmas after that, and I was trapped all over again. Trapped in a life I had never planned on. I'd planned to travel and see the world, and when we were married I barely saw anything but naval bases."

"I wouldn't call Vegas seeing the world."

"You wouldn't understand. You always get what you want—"

"Are you kidding me? I wanted to go to U of M. When that didn't work out, I wanted to be a SEAL. You took that from me too."

"Fine, blame me for everything. I'll always be the bad guy to you . . . to them."

"Only if you choose to be. They want a relationship with you. But a relationship starts with honesty. A relationship is built out of consistency. You let them down, and right now they don't trust you. You destroyed that. Don't you see it?"

"Of course I see it. I just don't know how to fix it."

"Start with admitting what you did was wrong. They may be kids, but they respect that. Then you need to decide what kind of relationship you want with them. The kind that visits once every couple years from Vegas or the kind that's a part of their lives. And if you want to be a part of their lives here, then you show up. Again and again. And eventually you rebuild that trust. But that won't happen tonight."

"But I—"

"No. You need to decide what kind of mom you want to be before you see them again. You can't jerk them around like this. And I also want to talk to them. Give them a voice in all this."

"Then why even invite me in if you weren't going to let me see them?"

"I did let you see them. But instead of apologies, you blamed me for your actions. They're old enough to see through that. Go home. The kids and I will call you on the twenty-sixth. If you're still in town, we can talk."

Tiffany stared at him for a long moment, then walked out the door. He locked it behind her, shut off the lights, and hurried up the stairs. Both kids were on his bed on top of the covers. Zane was leaning against the headboard and Susie was holding one of the pillows.

Zane crossed his arms across his chest. "Are you mad at us?"

Cole lay across the end of the bed, propping himself up on his elbow. "Of course not. I said we are a team and I mean it. We'll figure this out together. But it's late and Santa needs to come. Why don't we talk more about this tomorrow."

Zane stared at his hands a moment then looked at Cole. "I have to tell you something."

"Oh yeah?" Nothing like a loaded statement.

"Wait here." Zane hurried down the hall toward his room and came back a moment later. He walked in with a recognizable worn brown box with the words Stan Scott written on the side. The tape on the top had been broken but the box was folded shut. He set it on the bed and opened the top. "I got this out of your closet when you left. I'm sorry for disobeying. But I think you should look at it. There's a letter from your dad in there." Zane pulled it out and held it out to him. "I know what it's like to say things you don't mean to your dad, and if it were from you, I would want to read it."

Cole took it then stepped over to Zane and wrapped him in a hug. "I'm sorry too."

"You aren't mad?" Zane still watched him with wide eyes.

Cole glanced at his closet then back at the kids. "Just because I'm an adult doesn't mean I get everything right. I think it's time for me to unpack all those boxes. I've been so caught up in giving you guys a good future I forgot to make this place a home now."

Cole pulled them both into a hug that ended with Polly trying to join in. Susie giggled and pulled the puppy into her arms.

Zane walked to the door but waited for his sister. "Let's get to bed so Santa can come."

When had his boy become a young man?

Susie followed but spun back to face him. "Are we going to see Fallon tomorrow?"

"She invited us to come over in the morning." Fallon's words from earlier came back to him about making decisions as a team. "What do you two think? Should we?"

They both smiled and nodded then disappeared out the door.

Cole sat on the edge of the bed and turned the letter over and over. It was a business envelope with his name in blocky bold script on the outside. Closed but not sealed. Finally, he opened it and pulled out a folded piece of yellow legal paper.

> Cole,
> There are many things I regret in my life but there is nothing I regret more than our last conversation. The truth is, I'm not disappointed in you. I am so proud of who you are. I flew out to see you in San Diego, to tell you that. You were at the park with your kids. I didn't see Tiffany. The way you laughed with the kids and chased them around, I had no doubt you're a good father. I know I should have gone to you in that moment, but I chickened out. What can I say? You're a much better father than I ever was.

A day at the park? Cole blinked through his memories but couldn't really narrow it down. That was often how he spent Saturday with the kids when he wasn't deployed.

Cole lowered the paper. He had been so hard on himself for never being there enough for the kids when they were young—and he no doubt could have done better—but he *had* tried. He had been intentional. It was like his dad's words broke free all the lies he'd let Tiffany wrap around him. He was a good dad when they were little, and he was a good dad now. And he would always strive to be better every day.

He lifted the letter and continued reading.

> There are a few things in this box I wanted you to have from the family. One was your grandmother's wedding ring. I don't know if there will ever be the right occasion for you to use it, but I wanted you to have it. She was a praying woman who was a champion for their sixty-year marriage. Marriage is work. After

your mother and I went our separate ways,
I gave up on love. Don't let that happen to
you. May the ring be a reminder to fight for
love. Always.

I'm sorry I never told you all this in person,
but I'm so proud of you.

I love you.
Dad

His dad wasn't disappointed with him.

His dad loved him.

His dad was proud of him.

He blinked back the emotion that clogged his throat.

The Lord will fight for you; you need only to be still.

God had repaired this relationship before Cole knew how to ask for it. Maybe it wasn't how he imagined, but it was enough.

Cole dug back into the box. He moved a few things around until he spotted the small black box. Cole took it and flipped the lid open. A beautiful antique ring sat inside. Cole had seen it once as a child but had forgotten about it. He pulled it out and pulled it close as studied the diamond. It wasn't the fanciest ring, but the half-carat oval solitaire had a timeless quality. An inscription on the inside band read *Patrick and Lisa 9-10-1950*. His grandparents. They had been married sixty years. Life hadn't always been easy for them, but they fought the battles together. They had been a team.

May the ring be a reminder to fight for love.

It looked like he had a gift for Fallon after all, because it was time to fight for love.

Why was it so bright in her room? Fallon blinked her eyes open then blinked again. The morning sun was up but it was more than that. She climbed out of bed and pulled back the curtains. White. The world had a fresh layer of white making it look clean and new. She rubbed her eyes against the brightness, taking in the beauty. A new day with no mistakes in it.

She thought back to Cole. Had all that really happened?

Her phone vibrated next to her and she picked it up. Elise Winterbourne? What did Robert's mother want? That made no sense. She accepted the call.

"Hello?"

"Fallon? I'm sorry to bother you on Christmas morning, but I had to talk to you." Were there tears in her voice?

"Is everything okay?" Fallon sat on the edge of her bed.

"No. I just had a long talk with my husband, and I had no idea about everything that had transpired. I'm so upset. Robert would be heartbroken."

"I'm sorry. I'm having a hard time following. What are you trying to say?"

"All of it is a mistake and we'll fix it. The lawsuit. The inheritance. The house. Your job. We'll fix it all. Please forgive us."

"Fix it?"

Another voice came on the phone. "Fallon, this is Charles. My wife is a little emotional. Let me help. It has been brought to my attention that perhaps we could have handled things between us better. I contacted our lawyers last night. The suit is being dropped, all your rights will be returned to you, and we are writing up details of what you should have received from Robert. However, when I discussed it today with Elise, she is adamant that you deserved more. Including a phone call of apology, so we are calling to apologize."

Mrs. Winterbourne's apology seemed a lot more heartfelt than his, but his desire to avoid his wife's wrath seemed heartfelt at least. But Fallon would take anything at this point. "I don't know what to say."

Mrs. Winterbourne took over again. "Don't say anything. Go enjoy Christmas with your family. We just didn't want the lawsuit to darken your Christmas. We'll contact you soon."

With that the call ended and Fallon stood, grabbed a hair tie from her dresser, and pulled her blonde hair into a messy bun on top of her head. Slipped on some clothes and hurried out to her parents. This changed everything.

She stepped into the living room. It was abustle with Christmas music but no one in sight.

Just then her mom walked in from the kitchen with a platter of bacon in her hand. "Oh good. You're up. Your dad should be back any moment with Cole and the kids. I guess his Blazer is in Detroit or something."

As if on cue, the front door opened and in walked her dad, brushing snow from his head. He kicked off his boots in the mudroom and walked in, followed by Cole dressed in a red-and-black flannel, jeans, and a big red Christmas hat. Behind him, Susie wore a Christmas dress, and carried a roughly wrapped present that was almost half her size. Zane was last, and he brushed the snow from his head. Had he even showered?

Cole's eyes locked with hers. And any fear that last night had been a dream fled. That look was enough to remind her of that kiss and hope they'd find more time today to revisit it.

Before Cole said anything, Susie rushed over and shoved the present into her hands. "Open it."

Fallon glanced at her mom, who smiled and nodded. Maybe breaking the order of things was okay sometimes. She sat and pulled it onto her lap. "Is this from all of you?"

"Nope, just Zane and me."

Fallon peeled off the paper from the back of the gift. Her heart sank a little. This was the painting she had left for them under their tree. Had they not wanted it? She pulled away the rest of the paper and flipped it around.

Oh my.

It was the same painting, but Susie had taken her own paints and added a rough but very love-filled version of Fallon with yellow hair and bright blue eyes in the gap between Cole and Zane. They were a family. She glanced up at Cole, a touch of apprehension in his gaze. Then she looked at Susie and Zane. "It's perfect."

She hugged Zane then Susie. The little girl whispered in her ear, "My dad has his present for you now."

She turned toward Cole and froze. He'd dropped to one knee with a ring box open. The oval solitaire glistened and reflected the light. The box was old, but the style was so classic that it could be from any era.

All this had happened so fast. Sadie's words from the day she arrived in town came back to her. *When you know, you know.* Her friend was right, and there had never been anything she'd been more certain of.

"Fallon," Cole started, his voice rough. "I love you and—"

"And we love you too!" Susie yelled, but Zane tucked her under his arm and shushed her.

"Change will be hard," Cole continued. "But even if you take the job at Hallmark or—"

"No."

"No?" Cole's face paled.

"No! I'm not saying no to that"—she pointed at the ring—"but I'm not going anywhere. I just got a call from Winterbourne. He's canceling the lawsuit, giving me my rights back, and enough inheritance from Robert I can buy this place and paint from here."

"It's a Christmas miracle!" Her mom's hands flew to her face as her dad walked over and gave her a giant hug.

"I know, can you believe it?" Fallon let go of her dad and focused back on Cole.

"Amazing." There was something behind his smile, but how could he have had anything to do with it? Then he motioned to the box. "Did you say yes to this?"

She tilted her head, holding back a smile. "I'm sorry. Did you ask me a question?"

"You *do* have to be difficult, don't you?"

She stopped holding back as a small laugh escaped. "You wouldn't recognize me if I weren't."

"Fallon James, will you marry me?"

"Well . . . how do you feel about Santa suits?"

Cole stood, lifted her in his arms, and pressed a firm kiss on her lips. "You're going to be the death of me, woman."

"Did she say yes?" This was from Susie. "Is she going to be Fallon Scott?"

Cole set Fallon down and stared at her with one brow raised. "You can still keep James if you want to."

"I don't know, Fallon Scott is really growing on me."

"Is that a yes?"

"Yes," she finally said, then sighed as he lifted her again for another kiss. When he set her down again, she wrapped her arms around his neck. "I want every Christmas to be like this."

"Getting expensive jewelry?"

"No, I don't care what you get me or if you get me anything. I just want Christmas with you."

"You want Cole for Christmas? That I can do."

Epilogue

New Year's Eve

WEDDINGS WERE SUPPOSED TO BE PERFECT, but Fallon didn't think she could promise Sadie that. All she could promise was a space to say "I do" that didn't have a hole in the roof. Which was more than the church could now promise after the two feet of snow that had blown in last night, collapsing the roof right over the altar. But perfect or not, Fallon would do what she could to make the Sugar Shack look as nice as she could for her friend. And right now, that meant attaching soggy bows to the aisle chairs.

The decorations had looked so magical last night at the rehearsal. This morning? Fallon shook the dampness off yet another bow. Today they looked like exactly what they were: soggy ribbons salvaged from a debris filled snow-globe of a sanctuary.

Fallon eyed Cole out the window. He'd gotten the snowplow attached to the tractor and had managed to clear the drive and had moved on to the parking lot.

Sadie burst though the double doors of the Sugar Shack in sweatpants, a heavy coat, and her hair up in hot curlers that were in no way hot anymore. She glanced around the room and clapped her hands. "Thank you! This is perfect."

Perfect?

Instead of the wood pews they had old folding chairs. Instead of an aisle runner they had a scuffed floor. And instead of the altar, they still had Santa's big red chair. Cole would have to help her move that.

She sent Sadie a questioning look.

"Okay, nearly perfect." She pointed a freshly manicured fingernail toward Santa's chair. "Maybe not Santa."

"You sure? We could have Pastor Nate wear the big red suit." Sadie stared at her, but Fallon couldn't hide her smile. "Cole said he'd help me as soon as he clears the parking lot."

"You seem to have it under control, so I'm off to finish getting ready." Sadie walked over and wrapped Fallon in a hug. "The wedding is in two hours and we have pictures starting soon, so I need to get in my dress. I think we're going to do a few in the trees and by the barn. Assuming my shivering doesn't make the photos blurry."

An image of Sadie and David in their wedding finery by the trees flashed in Fallon's mind and just like that knew she would paint that scene next for her Christmas with You series.

Sadie hurried toward the door then turned back. Her face softened as her eyes filled with tears. "Thank you. For everything." Then she made a small squeal as she dashed back to the door. "I'm getting married today."

With that she rushed out the door, passing Cole as he walked in. He brushed snow from the sleeves of his coat and banged his boots by the door. "She seems happy for someone who had to change her venue four hours before the wedding."

"Maybe she's in denial." Fallon stared after her friend as she hurried toward the house.

"What do you mean?"

"She called this perfect." Fallon motioned to the room. "I saw her wedding plans. This is not what she wanted."

"I disagree." Cole shed his coat and hung it by the door then stepped closer. His thermal Henley hugged his shoulders in just the right way. "Today she is marrying the person she loves. What else matters?"

Fallon reached in one of the bins and pulled out a pillar candle that had been smashed on one side. "She went to twenty stores to find the perfect unity candle and it was smashed by the cave-in."

Cole pulled the candle from her hands and set it aside. "Life is full of surprises. You plan the best you can, but in the end, you have to take the curveballs life throws at you. If they're legally married by the end of the day, that is all that matters."

"Maybe you're right."

"I know I'm right." Cole took her hands in his, pulled her closer, then reached up and framed her face. "I would marry you in a truck stop today if I could."

Fallon blinked at him. "In a—"

"I'm not suggesting it." He held up his hand. "I know you have big summer wedding plans and I want to give you the wedding you want. But I'm just saying, Sadie is happy to be marrying the man she loves today. Everything else is details."

When you know, you know.

Sadie's words from the day she arrived floated back to her. Fallon nodded and glanced around with new eyes. It wasn't the wedding that was important, it was the marriage. And suddenly Fallon was ready for hers to start much sooner than this summer.

She leaned closer to Cole and leaned her forehead against his. "Maybe we should plan a spring wedding instead."

A smile tugged at the corner of Cole's mouth. "I like the way you think, Miss James."

He pressed his lips to hers as he wrapped his arms around her. The kiss was soft and lingering as if he were treasuring today but promising tomorrow. She leaned back and stared into his dark gaze. "Make that an *early* spring wedding."

She was finally ready to give up the last name James. Because when you know, you know.

P.S. Goodbye

What if a woman who's all about the goals and plans falls in love with man who no longer believes his life has a purpose?

A novice life coach needs to cement her reputation with one great success story. When a wounded ex-Army officer walks in looking for a job, she decides to work with him—a win-win for them both.

If Caroline Williams had her way, she'd help everyone in town find their purpose in life—unfortunately, no one seems to want her help. But she refuses to give up, and her new status as a certified life coach should provide her with some badly needed credibility. All she needs is her first client. When Grant Quinn walks in looking for a job, Caroline knows he needs more than that—he needs a new plan for his life. But when Grant refuses to be honest about his dreams and his struggles, Caroline's business might come crashing down before it starts.

Wounded former Special Forces operator Grant Quinn understood the cost when he enlisted and served his country with pride. The scars on his face are reminders of what he lost, but he is moving on—now if he could just convince his family that he's fine. When Caroline steps back into his life and offers to help find him a job in exchange for being her Guinea pig in her new life coaching business, he agrees. After all, what better way to show his family he's okay than with a new, stable job? But when the anxiety he's been running from ruins his one interview, his plans come crashing down. Can he trust Caroline enough to be honest about everything?

Get your free copy today!

Want more Heritage now?

Come see what has one Goodreads reviewer saying "I love this small town of Heritage, MI . . . where gossip blooms like wildflowers but also where love, acceptance, and mercy flow like a wild river." (MJSH, Goodreads)

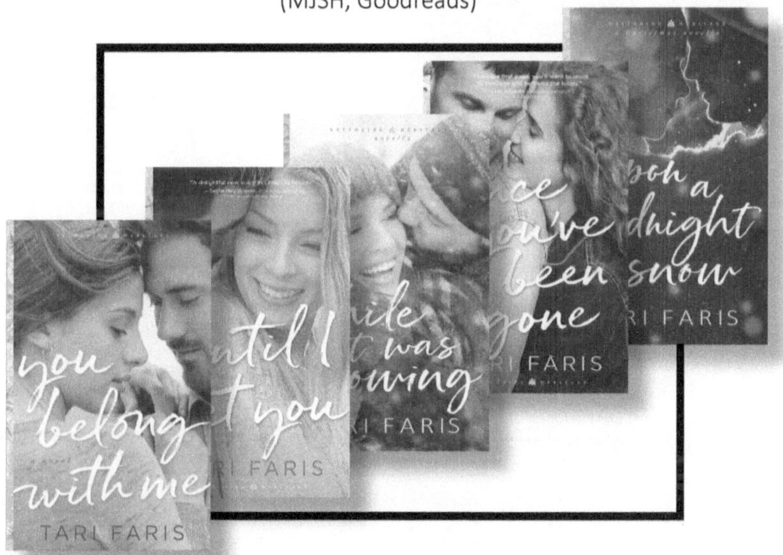

Six books, nine couples, and one mysterious hippo!

Start where it all began with Tari Faris' FREE prequel novella *P.S. Goodbye.*

Scan for a free download or go to: www.tarifaris.com/my-free-novella

Note to Reader

Thank you so much for reading Cole and Fallon's story. It was such a joy to bring them to the page. Some books I have written just flowed out of me while others really stretched me, and this one definitely stretched me.

In some ways, Fallon's struggle with her art mirrored my own. During the three years between the release of *Since You've Been Gone* and the release of *You're the Reason*, I did a lot of questioning. I never questioned God's existence or His goodness, but I did question if I had heard Him right when He called me to this writing journey. I had given it my all and yet every door was closing and book sales were dismal. Was it because all my books released around COVID lockdown? Was it because people just didn't connect with my stories? I had no answers but a lot of questions.

Then, my dear friend and mentor Susie May reached out and asked if I wanted to return to Heritage and continue this series with Sunrise. Maybe that is why the series title was so fitting. I, too, was going Home to Heritage. And through the process I felt God say, "I'm not done with you yet."

Not only did Susie give me the opportunity to write again, but she used her fabulous editing skills and pushed me to go deeper and make the characters stronger. (I even managed to write a scene with a gun.) I cannot thank her enough.

I also want to thank my friends who pushed me to keep going when it was hard and took phone calls when I was stuck:

Lisa Jordan, Mandy Boerma, and Andrea Nell. I couldn't have done it without you.

Thank you to my WiWee girls, MBT friends, Sunrise community, and my Arizona writer friends. Writing in community is really a blessing.

I also have to thank my family who put up with so much when I am on deadline, especially my amazing husband who takes over the cooking and keeps the family running.

Also, thank you to my coffee girls, especially Rikki, who answered endless questions about balancing new relationships and children. You are amazing.

And thank you, readers. I appreciate every review, every note, and every social media post regarding my story. You remind me that my writing journey is worth it, especially on those difficult days.

Tari Faris

<u>More Heritage Novels</u>

Home to Heritage

You're the Reason
Here With Me
Christmas With You

With three more arriving in 2025

Restoring Heritage

P.S. Goodbye (prequel novella)
You Belong With Me
Until I Met You
While It Was Snowing (novella)
Since You've Been Gone
Upon a Midnight Snow (Christmas novella)

About the Author

TARI FARIS lives in the Southwest with her amazing husband the three coolest kids on the planet. She loves writing in Heritage, because although she lives in the suburban desert now, a part of her heart will always be in the small Michigan town where she grew up. In her free time, she love coffee dates, traveling adventures, and time with family. She loves to hear from readers.

Connect with her at tarifaris.com.

More Sweet Sunrise Romance

Faith. Forgiveness. A future they never imagined.
It's time for a fresh start for the Fox Family.

Return to Susan May Warren's beloved town of Deep Haven now!
Find out more at sunrisepublishing.com.

Connect With Sunrise

Thank you again for reading *Christmas with You*. We hope you enjoyed the story. If you did, would you be willing to do us a favor and leave a review? It doesn't have to be long—just a few words to help other readers know what they're getting. (But no spoilers! We don't want to wreck the fun!) Thank you again for reading!

We'd love to hear from you—not only about this story, but about any characters or stories you'd like to read in the future. Contact us at www.sunrisepublishing.com/contact.

We also have a monthly update that contains sneak peeks, reviews, upcoming releases, and fun stuff for our reader friends. Sign up at www.sunrisepublishing.com or scan our QR code.